Murder of an Open Book

Center Point
Large Print

Also by Denise Swanson and available from
Center Point Large Print:

Scumble River Mysteries
  Murder of a Needled Knitter
  Murder of a Stacked Librarian

Devereaux's Dime Store Mysteries
  Dying for a Cupcake
  Dead Between the Lines
  Nickeled-and-Dimed to Death

**This Large Print Book carries the
Seal of Approval of N.A.V.H.**

Murder of an Open Book

A Scumble River Mystery

Denise Swanson

CENTER POINT LARGE PRINT
THORNDIKE, MAINE

This Center Point Large Print edition
is published in the year 2016 by arrangement with
New American Library, an imprint of Penguin Publishing
Group, a division of Penguin Random House LLC.

The text of this Large Print edition is unabridged.
In other aspects, this book may vary
from the original edition.
Printed in the United States of America
on permanent paper.
Set in 16-point Times New Roman type.

ISBN: 978-1-62899-973-0

Library of Congress Cataloging-in-Publication Data

Names: Swanson, Denise, author.
Title: Murder of an open book : a Scumble River mystery / Denise
Swanson.
Description: Center Point Large Print edition. | Thorndike, Maine :
Center Point Large Print, 2016. | ©2015
Identifiers: LCCN 2016008259 | ISBN 9781628999730
   (hardcover : alk. paper)
Subjects: LCSH: Denison, Skye (Fictitious character)—Fiction. |
Murder—Fiction. | Large type books. | GSAFD: Mystery fiction.
Classification: LCC PS3619.W36 M895 2016 | DDC 813/.6—dc23
LC record available at http://lccn.loc.gov/2016008259

Welcome to my new great-niece,
Emma Graham

Acknowledgments

Once again, I have to thank my amazing street team, the Swanson Sleuths. And a huge hats off to my new personal assistant, Mr. S.

CHAPTER 1

LOL—Laugh out Loud

Skye Denison-Boyd adjusted the straps of her bathing suit, then kicked off from the edge of the swimming pool. Her goal was to make it to the other end without losing her breakfast. Not that a couple of soda crackers and a cup of tea was much of a meal, but that was all she'd been able to tolerate in the mornings for the past month. And some days, even the saltines didn't stay down.

Refusing to think about tossing her cookies—or to be more specific, crackers—Skye concentrated on improving her butterfly stroke. Seven years ago, when she first returned to her hometown and started working as a psychologist for the Scumble River school district, she had swum most weekday mornings and often on Saturdays and Sundays as well. In the summer, she used the local recreational club, a lake formed from a reclaimed coal mine. And when it was cold, she did laps in the high school's highly debated pool.

Due to the source of its financing, the swimming pool was a hot topic among the Scumble River citizens. A while back, the district had received some extra tax money from the construction

9

of a nearby nuclear power plant, but instead of buying more up-to-date textbooks or employing additional teachers, the school board had spent the funds on athletic equipment and a pool.

The board members had been hoodwinked by a fast-talking salesman and a group of parents with their own agendas. It was the one time in anyone's memory that the board president, Skye's godfather, Charlie Patukas, had lost a vote. Because of that, she'd always felt a little guilty when she used the facility.

Those ambivalent feelings had helped her make excuses to skip her daily swims until eventually she rarely, if ever, swam at all. But a couple of months ago, after returning from her honeymoon, Skye had vowed to get back to her previous exercise routine. And a little bit of nausea was not going to stop her. Besides, the doctor had said that swimming might actually help the morning sickness.

Which reminded her, when she wiggled into her bathing suit at home, she'd noticed a definite baby bump. Up until now, because of her already generous curves, there hadn't been much danger that anyone would notice the three or four extra pounds she was carrying. Evidently, that anonymity was about to end.

She and her husband, Wally, would have to make some kind of announcement soon, or speculation would sweep the town. Scumble River's main drag wasn't known as Blabbermouth Basin Street for nothing.

Skye and Wally's motives for keeping mum about the blessed event were due in part to Wally's concerns about revealing the pregnancy prior to the completion of the first trimester. Furthermore, they hadn't wanted to take the spotlight away from Skye's brother and sister-in-law's baby shower, which was scheduled for Saturday.

However, the most compelling reason for them to keep quiet as long as possible was Skye's mother. May had a tendency to be a bit overbearing—okay, a lot overbearing. And as soon as she found out her daughter was pregnant, she would try to take over her life. Compared to May, D. B. Cooper was an amateur skyjacker.

May had waited a long time for grandchildren. Both Skye and her brother, Vince, had married relatively late—Skye had been thirty-six and Vince nearly forty—which meant May had been ready to be a grandmother for close to twenty years. And although Skye hoped her mother would be distracted by Vince's baby, she was pretty darn sure May would find the time to drive her daughter crazy as well. As an equal-opportunity meddler, May would make sure neither of her children felt neglected. She wouldn't want either of them to think the other was her favorite.

Wincing at the thought of her mother's reaction

to her pregnancy, Skye reached the opposite end of the pool. Performing a perfect flip turn, she started back, happy that she felt less queasy and determined to put May out of her mind.

Willing herself to relax and enjoy the sensation of the water sliding over her skin, Skye focused on her dolphin kick. Because the butterfly was one of the most exhausting strokes and she hadn't yet rebuilt the strength to swim more than a few lengths of the pool before having to rest, she wanted to put the time she had to the best use.

March in Illinois had been chillier than usual, but in the heated pool, Skye could pretend that she was back on her honeymoon. Even though the cruise had been full of surprises—including a dead body—she and Wally had both been able to unwind from their demanding lives and have an unforgettable trip.

Wally, as the chief of the Scumble River Police Department, had been badly in need of a break. Although the town's population was just a shade over three thousand, between the devious mayor and several murders, the community in no way resembled Mayberry. Which meant that Wally's work was no Andy Griffith kind of job.

Skye's position as the sole mental-health professional for the entire school district kept her stress level in the head-about-to-explode range as well. Add planning a wedding during the frantic Christmas holidays and her psych-consultant contract with the PD, and she, too, had been more than ready for a vacation.

Their honeymoon had been wonderful, but now that they'd been back for two and a half months, Skye had a feeling that their downtime was about to end. This was the final week before spring break, which in Skye's world meant frazzled teachers and students with cabin fever.

For Wally, kids out of school required preparing his officers for hordes of unoccupied teens with way too much time on their hands. Not many Scumble River families could afford to take off from their jobs and jet off to Florida or the Caribbean. So while they were busy making a living, their offspring were often left unsupervised and looking for something to do.

Skye finished her fifth lap, and as she rested against the side of the pool, she checked the clock on the far wall. It was only six thirty. Staff was required to be on duty at seven twenty, while students started their school day at ten to eight. Allowing half an hour to style her hair, slap on some makeup, and put on her clothes, she had fifteen minutes before she had to get out of the water and start to dress.

Because of her nausea, Skye had been up an hour before her normal time, and she'd gotten to the pool much earlier than usual. When she'd turned in to the school's driveway, there hadn't been a single car in the parking lot. Even the custodian's old red Silverado pickup wasn't in its usual spot by the Dumpster yet.

She'd used her key to enter through the back door of the empty building and made her way to the gym. The pool area's only entrance, except for an alarmed emergency exit, was through the student locker rooms. As she'd passed through the girls' side, she'd stripped off her sweat suit and placed it and her bag on one of the benches. The locked duffel held what she would need to get ready for the school day, as well as her purse and the leather tote full of files she'd brought home on Friday to work on over the weekend.

Most mornings there were other staff members using the pool, but because she'd arrived so early, the place had been deserted. At the time, even though Skye knew she shouldn't swim without a buddy, she'd been happy to have the water to herself. It was nice not to have to worry about colliding with another swimmer or slowing someone else down. However, now it felt as if she was no longer alone. Had someone else arrived to take a pre-workday dip?

Skye glanced from side to side. Almost the entire wall of the pool enclosure was made up of frosted blue safety glass. She squinted. Was that someone peering through the partition? She called out a greeting, but no one answered. That was odd. Her imagination must be getting the best of her.

She shoved her swim goggles up on her head and looked around for a second time. With the exception of a couple of safety rings and a pole with a hook on the end leaning against the wall, the area was empty. Taking a deep breath, she tried to calm her racing heart, but the scent of chlorine overpowered her. *Uh-oh!* Now she felt queasy again.

Swimming over to the ladder, Skye had just begun to climb out of the water when she thought she heard retreating footsteps. A chill ran up her spine. Had someone been watching her? *No!* That was silly. Why would anyone spy on her? Was pregnancy making her paranoid?

Skye shook her head at her own foolishness and heaved herself out of the pool. She hurried into the locker room and peeled off her swim cap. Catching a glimpse of herself in a mirror, she sighed. While the cap kept her hair dry, it also left it a snarled mess. Bending over, she ran her fingers through her long chestnut curls in an attempt to fluff out the strands.

She was busy trying to work out a particularly stubborn tangle when a hand descended on her shoulder and someone snapped, "You need to leave immediately."

With a scream, Skye straightened. Clutching her chest, she said, "Blair! You scared me to death. What are you doing here?"

Blair Hucksford taught junior and senior level

science and coached girls' volleyball. Although she'd been teaching at Scumble River High for nearly four years, Skye didn't know her very well. Blair hadn't sought out Skye's help with any of her students, and she rarely attended pupil personnel services conferences. PPS meetings, a multidisciplinary forum intended to assist students identified as exhibiting academic, social, or physical needs through supportive and preventative strategies and services, was Skye's main contact with most of the school's staff.

Blair's expression hardened. "More to the point, what are you doing here?" She crossed her arms. "I booked the whole pool area for my team."

"I don't see anyone." Skye looked around. She and Blair appeared to be alone. "Anyway, I'm going to get dressed right now, so I'll be out of the way by the time they show up." She smiled, sure Blair didn't mean to be as nasty as she sounded.

"You can't use the girls' locker room." Blair narrowed her jade green eyes. "As I just said, I've reserved it and the pool from six thirty until seven thirty."

"Well, I don't think the school board would approve of me using the boys' side," Skye joked. "Just let me take a quick shower, and I'll finish getting ready in the teachers' restroom."

"No." Blair tossed her coppery red curls and said, "The space is rightfully mine. You'll just have to figure out something else." She turned and marched away.

"Wait!" Skye ran after her. "This is silly. I just need five minutes." The thought of trying to wash the chlorine off her skin without the benefit of a shower made her willing to beg. "I—"

"Not even one minute." Blair stopped Skye. "You should have read the schedule. Your oversight is not my problem." She put her hands on her slim hips. "The rules state that once a teacher signs up for a space, that faculty member has sole possession for the allotted time."

"But . . ." Skye stuttered. Why was Blair being so mean? "Look, I—"

"It's really rude of you to talk while I'm interrupting."

"It's a mistake on my part to be here. You're absolutely right about that." Skye gritted her teeth and forced herself to sound conciliatory. She really needed to use that darn shower. "And I'm sorry."

"Of course you are." Blair let out an exaggerated sigh. "But sustaining ignorance is hard work, and I'm not that industrious."

"Are you always this sarcastic?" Skye was tired of apologizing.

"No," Blair sneered. "Sometimes I'm asleep."

"Seriously?" Skye crossed her arms. "You need to get over yourself."

"I tried once, but no luck." Blair smirked. "I'm

just too awesome." She turned her back, then said over her shoulder, "And you still have to leave right now."

Skye put her hand on the younger woman's shoulder. Trying one last time to make Blair see reason, she said, "Please. Two minutes in the shower. I promise to be out of the locker room before your girls get here."

"Too late." Blair moved out of reach, scooped up Skye's duffel bag, put the strap over Skye's shoulder, and thrust her discarded sweat suit at her. Grabbing both of Skye's arms, Blair said, "I just heard the team arrive."

"Take your paws off of me." Skye tried to wiggle free of the fingers clamped around her biceps. For a skinny little thing, Blair was surprisingly strong.

Ignoring Skye's outraged cries, Blair frog-marched her out of the room. As she shoved Skye into the hallway, she said, "Guess you'll have to make do with a sponge bath in the faculty restroom. Maybe next time you won't think that you're above the rules."

Skye stared at her, speechless at the teacher's utter rudeness.

Blair smiled meanly and said, "I just adore the sound you make when you finally shut the hell up."

CHAPTER 2

Sup—What's Up?

Skye absentmindedly reached down and scratched her calf. White flakes fell on the dingy gray carpet and she frowned. It had been impossible to wash off all the chlorine without a shower. She wished she could have driven home and gotten dressed there. Unfortunately, that hadn't been an option. The trip would have made her late for work, and then she would have had to face the wrath of Homer.

Homer Knapik, the high school principal, didn't tolerate tardiness from his staff. He could b late for everything from parent conferences to faculty meetings. But if any of his faculty checked in even a second past seven twenty, the public haranguing was enough to make them reconsider their choice of careers.

And Homer had a special way of intimidating Skye for any infractions—either real or imagined. He threatened to give her office to one of the other itinerant personnel. Since there literally was no other space in the school, she was always fearful of losing such valuable real estate. She had only wrested it away from the boys' PE teacher/ guidance counselor a few years ago, after pointing out that he already had an office in the gym complex. Up until then, she'd had to beg, borrow, or steal space to evaluate or counsel students.

Glancing around, Skye silently *tsk*ed. Who would have thought that she'd have to do battle for a ten-by-ten room with no windows? It was painted an ugly shade of greenish yellow that was made worse by the overhead light fixture. The fluorescent bulbs cast a sickly tinge over the beat-up desk, battered trapezoidal table, two folding chairs, and wooden file cabinet. All the furniture occupying the meager space were castoffs. Her old leather chair and the metal bookshelves that held her test kits had been discarded by someone with a budget to upgrade to nicer things, but Skye was grateful to have them. Even second-hand, the stuff was better than anything she had at either the grade school or the junior high.

After another bout of itching, Skye hurriedly checked her appointment book. She was scheduled to stay at the high school until noon, then go to the elementary school for the rest of the day. Maybe she could drive home during her half-hour lunch. If she didn't hit any traffic—and with only one stoplight in town, that was a pretty safe bet—it would take her only five minutes each way. As long as she didn't get her face or hair wet, twenty minutes was plenty of time for a quick shower and to make herself a sandwich.

Of course, that plan hinged on a smooth

morning. If there were any student, staff, or parent crises, all bets were off. In that case, her lunch would consist of another round of crackers, which would be a shame since her nausea usually passed by ten or eleven, and having eaten little or no breakfast, she was usually ravenous by noon.

Then again, there was that bag of cookies hidden in her desk drawer. She'd been saving the Archway Cashew Nougats for an emergency, and starvation certainly qualified.

Pushing aside her food and hygiene issues, Skye took out the stack of folders from her tote bag. She selected a bright blue one from the pile and flipped it open. In her quest to organize the humongous amount of paperwork her job entailed, she'd instituted a new system. Red for priority, green for new referrals, yellow for counseling cases, and blue for reevaluations.

Before Skye could do more than glance inside the file at the previous test protocols, there was a perfunctory knock; then her door slammed open and Trixie Frayne rushed inside. Trixie was the high school librarian and Skye's best friend. She also cosponsored the school newspaper with Skye, coached the cheerleading squad, and had recently started a community service club to promote volunteerism among the teenagers. Anyone else would be exhausted by all the extracurricular duties, but Trixie thrived on the constant whirlwind of activity.

"I found the perfect fund-raiser for GIVE." Trixie darted across the room and plopped onto one of the visitors' chairs.

"Give?"

"Get Involved, Value Everyone." Trixie bounced on her seat. "It's the service club's new name. Paige Vitale thought of it at Friday's meeting."

"She's a smart girl." Skye smiled, thinking of the dynamic junior. Like her idol, Trixie, Paige seemed to be involved in everything and she appeared to enjoy the hectic pace. "She's doing a great job with the newspaper." When Frannie Ryan and her boyfriend, Justin Boward, had gone off to college, Skye had wondered if they'd ever find an editor as good as they had been. "Paige is a great writer and extremely helpful in improving the other students' skills."

"Definitely." Trixie nodded, her pixielike face alight with pleasure. "She's really been kind to some of the kids from our special education program. I was pleased that several of the students with more challenging issues joined GIVE."

"That's great to hear." Skye had recommended that the special ed teacher encourage her students to join Trixie's club, thinking it would be a good place for them to make friends. "I hope Ashley Northrup is one of them."

"She is." Trixie beamed. "And her mom has been really helpful."

"You mentioned a fund-raiser." Skye peeked at

her watch. She'd been planning to spend the half hour before school writing a report, but her friend looked as if she was settled in for a good long visit. Closing the folder and resolving to finish the work at home, she gave Trixie her full attention. "What is it?"

"A rubber duck race down the Scumble River." Trixie's brown eyes sparkled. "The kids sell the ducks—well, actually, they'll sell the numbers on the ducks—for ten bucks apiece. We'll release them at the boat-launch area in the park, and the first fowl into the channel that we'll build under the railroad bridge west of town is the overall winner."

"Channel?"

"We'll string several swimming pool noodles together between poles, using water-ski ropes, to create a V-shaped passage." Trixie used her hands to demonstrate. "It will narrow down to a small opening that only allows one duck through at a time."

"Clever." Skye smiled at her friend's ingenuity. "Which charity gets the money?"

"The county's no-kill animal shelter."

"What does the owner of the winning duck get?"

"There will be several prizes." Trixie's voice was a little less confident. "At least, I hope there will be. The kids are going to have to persuade area businesses to contribute merchandise and gift cards for us to give away."

"That could be tough." Skye furrowed her brow. "Those folks are always being hit up for donations. You'd better see how that goes before the club members start selling the ducks. Otherwise, you might end up using all the money you collect on the sales to buy prizes."

"I'm not worried about that. I'm sure the business owners will be generous, especially since we'll be listing the contributors on the Scumble River High website and in the school paper. And since that particular issue will go out to all the parents, it will be glaringly apparent who was stingy." Trixie ran her fingers through her short brown hair and made a face. "But there are just a couple of tricky parts. That's why I wanted to talk to you before we both got busy this morning."

"Oh." Visions of the various potential problems conga danced through Skye's head. Possibilities included everything from kids going over the dam in the river to counterfeit duckies. "What do you need me to do?"

"It turns out we have to get a permit from the city council to have the race, and their monthly meeting was last week." Trixie peered at Skye from between her lashes. "I thought maybe you could ask your uncle Dante to grant us a mayoral waiver."

"No."

"Why not?"

"As you know, Uncle Dante isn't one of my

biggest fans." Skye crossed her arms. "Believe me—I'm the last person in town he'd do a favor for. No. Wait. Wally is the last person. I'm the second to the last."

Dante Leofanti, Scumble River's mayor and Skye's maternal uncle, resembled a cantankerous bowling pin. He was always in a bad mood, but even more so when one of his schemes was thwarted. He had recently hatched a conspiracy to outsource the town's law-enforcement services to the county sheriff's department. He'd planned to use the police-department budget for a hare-brained idea that involved building a mega incinerator on the edge of town.

When Skye had found out about Dante's shady arrangement, she'd exposed his plot to the community, and he blamed her for his recent approval-rating drop. The polls showed him lagging behind both of his future opponents— and one of them was a sock puppet named Napoleon.

"He's still mad at you two for pulling the plug on his get-rich-quick scheme?" Trixie's eyebrows rose. "When he came to your wedding, I figured he must have forgiven you."

"He arrived straight from his hospital bed." Skye's voice dropped. "And even though he passed all the tests and the doctor told him that all he'd had was a panic attack, Dante claims we gave him a coronary." She shook her head. "Just when I think things can't get any worse in city hall, there's an election."

Trixie snickered. "Okay. Maybe you aren't the best one for that job." She scratched her chin. "I'll find someone else to sweet-talk the mayor."

"Good luck with that." Skye screwed up her face, trying to picture her uncle being charmed into granting someone a favor. "You'd be better off looking for someone who has some dirt on His Honor. Or if you don't want to resort to blackmail, just wait for the next city council meeting."

"Well, that brings me to the second problem." Trixie studied the toes of her high-tops. "We can't wait because we want to have the race this Sunday. Sort of a spring break kickoff."

Skye's mouth dropped open, and she stared at her friend. "You intend to put this together in less than a week? Have you lost your marbles?"

"Not all of them." Trixie grinned. "But there's probably a rip in the bag."

"More like a hole the size of a meteor crater." Skye pressed her lips together. "Six days isn't long enough to pull off something as complicated as this event."

"That's where you come in." Trixie transferred her scrutiny to the KushandWizdom poster behind Skye's desk that read, MILLIONS OF PEOPLE CAN BELIEVE IN YOU, AND YET NONE OF IT MATTERS IF YOU DON'T BELIEVE IN YOURSELF.

"How's that?" Skye pushed her chair back, prepared to run if need be.

"We only have twenty-five kids in the community service club. I'm going to get my cheerleaders to help—one of the squad requirements is thirty hours of volunteering." Trixie examined the blue polish on her fingernails. "But we need more worker bees if we're going to get the race organized in time." She finally met Skye's gaze. "I need you to supervise the school newspaper kids we get to volunteer."

"No." Skye spoke rapidly before Trixie could continue. "You are welcome to recruit the paper's staff, but leave me out of it." As well as getting back to a regular swimming routine, another of Skye's post-marriage vows had been to learn to say no when friends and family tried to manipulate her.

"But—"

"I'll do what I can," Skye interrupted Trixie. "But I'm not going to be in charge of anything. I just can't take on too much right now."

"It won't be that much work." Trixie leaned forward and pasted a piteous expression on her face. "Nothing can stop Skyxie."

"Skyxie?"

"Skye plus Trixie." Trixie grinned. "Like Brangelina." Trixie wrinkled her brow. "Speaking of those two . . . I think they're trying to collect one kid in every color."

27

"Maybe so." Skye hid a grin. "But I bet they don't have a blue one yet."

"Yeah. An available Smurf has got to be hard to find." Trixie giggled hysterically, then sobered and said, "Anyway, Skyxie is a super team."

"Is it too late to change sides?"

"Please. I can't do this without you."

"Then maybe you shouldn't do it." Skye looked away from her friend's pleading eyes and hardened her heart. "Or at least not do it in less than a week. The weather will be better in May."

"The no-kill shelter needs the money by April second or they're going to lose their lease." Trixie grabbed Skye's hand. "If that happens, all the doggies and kitties will have to go to the county animal control, and it's a good bet most of them will be put down."

"Crap!" Skye yanked her fingers out of Trixie's grasp and admitted defeat. There was no way she could look Bingo in the eye if she allowed that to happen. Her cat might never be aware that she'd let his comrades-in-fur down, but she would know. "What do you want me to do?"

CHAPTER 3

Kk—Okay

Skye shuddered as she watched her friend fish a list from her pocket and unfold it, then unfold it again and again. Where had Trixie gotten a piece of paper that long? And more important, how many of the items on the page had Skye's name next to them?

"I need you to find a thousand cheap ducks." Trixie took a pen from behind her ear and made a check mark. "Once you get them, have the newspaper kids number each of them in indelible marker."

"Where in heaven's name do I get a thousand rubber duckies?"

"Look online."

"All right." Much to her credit card's detriment and despite her best efforts to remain a technophobe, Skye had become somewhat adept at ordering from the computer. "How do I pay for these critters?"

"Uh." Trixie scrunched her face. "I was sort of hoping you could charge them to your Visa and we could reimburse you after the event." She arched a brow. "Or that could be your contribution . . ."

"Fine." Skye rubbed her temples. She had just finished paying off the mind-boggling balance from her wedding, and she had hoped to keep the amount owed at zero for a few months. So much for that dream.

"Find a vendor that sells in bulk." Trixie smoothed her black-and-white-striped circle skirt. "You should be able to get them for around three hundred and fifty dollars, including expedited shipping."

"Got it."

"One more thing." Trixie fingered the ruffle of her cropped denim jacket.

"No." Skye put up her hands in the universal stop-right-now gesture. "If you are trying to drive me out of my mind, I warn you it might take a while because the exits aren't clearly marked."

"Really, Skye." Trixie snickered. "This won't even take you thirty minutes—three-quarters of an hour tops." She reached for the candy jar on Skye's desk and selected a watermelon Jolly Rancher. "You're friendly with Kathy Steele—"

"I wouldn't say that," Skye broke in before Trixie could finish, hoping to halt whatever request was coming. "We're more cordial than friendly. I'm not sure she's exactly friendly with anyone around here."

Kathryn Steele owned and edited the *Scumble River Star*. She'd appeared in town a little more than four years ago, purchased the local paper, and changed its content from mostly advertisements and local sports statistics to actual news—not a popular move with all of her subscribers.

She lived above the *Star*'s offices, and she was known for being on the job nearly twenty-four/seven. Which didn't leave much time for socializing. Skye had always wondered about the newspaperwoman's background and apparent wealth, but Kathryn was the type of person who held her cards close to the vest while managing to get everyone else to lay their losing hands down on the table.

"Okay, so you two aren't pals." Trixie twisted off the candy wrapper. "But you told me she's a member of Wally's gun club and that she was helpful the last time you went with him to shoot."

"Helpful in that she offered me a hand up when I fell on my butt after Emmy Jones had me shoot with her Smith & Wesson Centennial 642CT," Skye corrected. "And I haven't been out to the club in a month or so." Pregnancy had put a temporary stop to her quest to bond with her new husband over his love of weaponry.

"That's more of a relationship with Kathy than I have, so you're elected." Trixie took another piece of paper from her pocket. "You just need to persuade her to put this announcement about the rubber duck race on the front page of the *Star*." Trixie shoved the article toward Skye. "It has to be in by noon today so it will make Wednesday's paper, and we can't afford to pay anything."

"Wait a cotton-picking minute." Skye refused to take the sheet Trixie was thrusting in her direction. "How am I going to accomplish this before twelve o'clock?"

"Call Kathy on the phone. Convince her it's for a good cause. Then e-mail her the notice." Trixie popped the hard candy into her mouth. "Easy-peasy."

"Right." Skye's voice dripped sarcasm. "I'll schedule that in between the parent meeting at eight, the observation at ten, and the counseling session at eleven."

Trixie ignored Skye's sarcastic tone, crossed another line off of her inventory, and stuffed it in her pocket. "Great. I knew that I could count on you."

"You know, last time you tried to rush an event, it turned out to be a disaster," Skye said, attempting once more to get her friend to slow down and think through the consequences of ramrodding the fund-raiser. "You ended up with a garage full of junk and no buyers for your white-elephant sale."

"I eventually sold all that stuff." Trixie grinned, then shrugged. "Besides, some mistakes are too much fun to make only once."

"You peddled them mostly to your friends," Skye retorted. "The ones who had donated the items in the first place."

"Your point?" Trixie sniggered, then asked, "So what did you end up buying for Vince and Loretta's long-awaited baby shower?"

The baby had been born nearly three months ago, but the birth had been a difficult one, and Loretta had requested that the celebration be delayed until she had fully recovered. Skye suspected that her gorgeous sister-in-law also wanted to get her figure back before the party, but she had wisely kept that notion to herself. Loretta was a brilliant woman, and Skye didn't want her sister-in-law turning that mega-intellect against her.

"The Kate Spade Coney Island Stevie diaper bag." Skye was happy to divert Trixie's attention from adding her name to any more items on the ducky-do list, so she quickly added, "Vince told me that Loretta was finding it a teensy bit hard to transform from city lawyer to country mommy, so I thought a hip baby bag might help. It's her favorite shade of pink, and it has an awesome gold buckle, as well as a changing pad and stroller straps."

Skye and her sister-in-law, Loretta Steiner Denison, were sorority sisters—both alumnae of Alpha Sigma Alpha. Loretta was a hotshot defense attorney with a huge law firm in Chicago, and seven years ago Skye had reached out to her to defend Vince on a murder charge.

Loretta had surprised Skye when, despite the

high-powered lawyer's often-declared aversion to small towns and their citizens, she had fallen in love with Skye's brother, a humble hairstylist. That Loretta had ended up married to Vince and living in Scumble River was beyond amazing.

It helped that she was able to do so much of her job at home, having to make the ninety-minute commute into the city only for meetings and trials, but it had still been a tremendous sacrifice for her to live in her husband's hometown rather than remain in Chicago. And now that she was taking six months' maternity leave to stay home with their newborn, Loretta was having some difficulty adjusting to her much-less-glamorous life.

"That bag had to cost you a pretty penny." Trixie grinned. "Owen and I got them a starter library. A dozen classic children's books that the new mommy and daddy can read to baby. I included my favorites—*Goodnight Moon*, *Curious George*, and at Owen's insistence, *The Rusty, Trusty Tractor*."

"That's a great present." Skye smiled to herself. Trust a librarian to get the newborn started on the right foot with a gift of books. And trust her farming husband to include a volume on rural life.

"How's Loretta handling your mother?" Trixie asked, playing with her wedding ring.

"Probably better than how she's handling her own mom." Skye stole a glance at the wall clock behind Trixie. Ten minutes until the bell rang. Yep. She'd definitely have to write the report at home to make up for the work time she and her friend had wasted chatting. "Our mother nearly drove Loretta insane when she and Vince were building their house. Then, when Mom found out about the baby, Loretta threatened to get an unlisted number and a guard dog to keep her away. But she's a pussycat in comparison to June Steiner."

"Hard to believe that anyone could outdo May in the smothering department."

"So far, Mrs. S has hired a live-in au pair." Skye laughed at the memory of Vince's frantic phone call. "One day this woman just showed up on Loretta and Vince's doorstep."

"Did they keep the nanny? I mean, who wouldn't want their own Mary Poppins?" Trixie frowned. "Except for the dancing on the rooftops part."

"No. They sent the poor lady packing." Skye shook her head. "And shortly after that, Loretta's mom arranged for the baptism without telling them."

"Did they go through with the ceremony?"

"Uh-oh. And now Mom and Mrs. S are at war as to whether it will take place here at St. Francis or at the church the Steiners attend in the city." Skye scratched her forearm, scowling at how itchy she felt.

"You need to use some moisturizer." Trixie pointed to the white flecks on Skye's arm. "How come your skin is suddenly so dry?"

"It's all Blair Hucksford's fault." Skye glared. "She's impossible."

"What happened?"

"She kicked me out of the pool this morning," Skye said, then described her encounter with the teacher. After telling Trixie all about Blair's imperious attitude, Skye ended with, "And no matter how much I apologized or how nicely I asked, she refused to let me take a shower. Then she actually hauled me out of the locker room."

"She physically dragged you?"

"Yes." Skye slid open her top drawer. "It was just plain uncool."

"Uncool!" Trixie's voice rose. "Heck. That's assault. You should report her to Homer."

"Probably, but I don't want to start a war with that woman. She sort of scares me." Skye wrinkled her brow. "You know what I don't understand? I thought the girls' volleyball season was in the fall. Why is Blair working with her team now? And why are they swimming instead of on the court?"

"From what I hear, Blair has mandatory sessions with her girls all year long. And my guess is she uses the pool for strength training." Trixie pursed her lips. "You know, I'm not really surprised that Blair was rude to you."

"Why?" Skye dug through pencils, pens, and legal pads until she found a sample bottle of Kiehl's Creme de Corps. "Have you had run-ins with her, too?"

"Sort of." Trixie's lips thinned. "A couple of my cheerleaders tried out for the volleyball team, and even though the schedules don't conflict, she made them choose between the two activities."

"Did she give any reason?" Skye unscrewed the tiny lid and squeezed a dollop of lotion into her palm. "Besides being a controlling witch?"

"Bonding." Trixie bent to retie the laces of her black-and-white high-tops. "Blair claimed that the girls wouldn't bond with the rest of the volleyball team if their allegiance was diluted by their loyalty to the cheerleading squad."

"Seriously?"

"That was what she said."

"Wow." Skye smoothed the yellow cream on her arms, feeling an instant relief from the itchiness that had been driving her mad. Why hadn't she thought of moisturizer sooner? Were the baby hormones already sucking IQ points from her brain? "That seems pretty intense for high school sports."

"Yeah." Trixie straightened. "My girls decided they'd rather stick with my squad than play volleyball and put up with Blair. They even came up with a cheer about her."

"Oh?"

"Yep. I saw them doing it before practice one day." Trixie giggled. "It goes:

> 'She's stuck-up.
> We're fed up.
> And she needs to shut up.' "

"How apropos." Skye chuckled.

"Yes, it is." Trixie chortled. "I had to pretend I didn't catch them doing the cheer or I would have had to punish them."

"Of course."

"I've heard that parents have had problems with her, too," Trixie added. "Not to mention the other staff who have had her steal kids from their sports teams. They call her Coacher Poacher."

"That can't make for a pleasant atmosphere in the faculty lounge."

"Haven't you noticed?" Trixie raised an eyebrow. "Blair never goes there. She has lunch with her boyfriend, Thor Goodson, in his office in the gym."

Thor was the new PE teacher. He'd been hired a year ago, when the old one finally retired. Since Scumble River High was such a small school, he ended up coaching most of the boys' sports. Thor was another faculty member Skye didn't know too well. Like his girlfriend, he seemed to have no interest in referring kids for her services.

"I wondered why I never saw her in the teachers' lounge, but I figured it was because I'm only here at the high school three or four half days a week."

"Nope." Trixie got up. "Blair's had so many tiffs with the rest of the staff"—Trixie stopped with her hand on the doorknob—"I think she's afraid to eat in the presence of the other faculty."

"Right." Skye snorted. "What does she think? That the teachers will poison her?"

CHAPTER 4

GTG—Got to Go

Thanks, Kathy!" Skye had the receiver wedged between her ear and shoulder as she assembled the material for her eight o'clock parent conference. "Trixie and I really appreciate your help."

"Lucky for you guys, it's a slow news week. I have a big hole on the front page of the *Star*," Kathy said. "Demoting Saxony Station's transfer of their four-hundred-ton transformer from a barge on the Scumble River to the west side of their power plant to the second page isn't a real hardship. They're doing it at midnight, so it's not as if there will be a huge traffic snarl."

"Well, we appreciate it." Skye ran down her

mental list of needed items—legal pad, pen, calendar, and Ashley Northrup's file. Check, check, check, and check. "Trixie has us on a tight schedule."

"I understand her sense of urgency," Kathy said. "I got my golden sheltie, Walter Cronkite, from that shelter. They do good work on a shoestring budget. I'd hate to see them lose their lease."

"The animals are how Trixie roped me in, too." Skye glanced at the wall clock. Three minutes until the meeting. She had to get off the phone. "So I'll e-mail you the article." Skye hit the SEND button. She'd typed in the article while she and the newspaperwoman had been chatting. "Feel free to tweak it."

"Will do." Kathy paused, then added, "I haven't seen you at the shooting range lately. I hope Emmy's little joke didn't scare you away."

"Not at all." Skye frowned. So her suspicion that Emmy had deliberately given her a weapon that had too much kick for a beginner was true. Despite Wally's protestations that the woman wasn't interested in him, and the scene Skye had witnessed between her ex-boyfriend Simon Reid and Emmy, Skye still thought the gorgeous female might have a little crush on Wally.

"I'm glad you feel that way." Kathy's voice was brisk. "Every woman should know how to defend herself." She chuckled. "Especially someone like you, who keeps getting mixed up in murder investigations. I heard that you even solved a case on your honeymoon."

"I just helped the ship's security a little," Skye demurred, then said, "Thanks again for printing the duck race article. Bye." Skye hurriedly hung up, grabbed the material she'd put together for the conference, and stood. She had exactly ninety seconds to make it to the principal's office on time. She'd have to run. It was a good thing she had on her new Tory Burch loafers instead of high heels.

When Skye approached the main office, Opal Hill, the school secretary, was sorting mail into the teachers' boxes. She looked up from her task and said, "Mrs. Northrup is already here, and Mr. Knapik has been buzzing me every five seconds asking for you."

"Sorry," Skye said. Opal was such a fragile soul that Skye had never been able to figure out how she'd managed to work for Homer for so long. "But I still have thirty seconds before I'm officially late."

"Then you'd better get in there right now." Opal's watery brown eyes made her look as if she were about to burst into tears.

"I take it that Homer is in his usual having-to-deal-with-a-parent rotten mood," Skye said as she scooted around the counter.

"Oh, my, yes." Opal's pink nose twitched. "Voices have already been raised."

Skye took a few steps down a dark, narrow hall,

knocked on the principal's closed door, then opened it a crack and said, "Ready for me?"

A gruff voice yelled from behind a massive desk, "It's about time. You're perilously close to being late. Get your rear end in here."

"Okeydokey." Skye took a calming breath. Homer was who he was, and at this stage in his life—which, metaphorically speaking, was about five minutes before he signed his retirement papers—there was no changing him. Pasting a cheery expression on her face, she entered the office.

A wiry-looking woman in her forties with short dark hair was seated on one of the visitors' chairs. Homer glowered at Skye, then waved toward the parent and said, "Oriana Northrup, this is our school psychologist, Skye Denison."

"We've met." Skye held out her hand to the woman. "But it's actually Skye Denison-Boyd now. I got married over winter break."

"Great. Another hyphenated name." Homer rolled his eyes. "Mrs. Northrup is unhappy with her daughter Ashley's program and is requesting placement at a private school."

"Really?" Skye hadn't been expecting that. Mrs. Northrup had been advocating for more services for her daughter since Skye's first encounter with her when the family moved into the Scumble River school district six years ago. However, according to Ashley's file, between the classroom modifications and the special education teacher's support, the girl's freshman year was going well. "Has something happened recently that makes you feel what we're doing here is no longer appropriate for your daughter?"

"Nothing new." The woman's handshake was crushing. "As I explained to Mr. Knapik, I just don't feel that Ashley will ever live up to her full potential without the more advanced services that Thorntree Academy provides for children with Asperger's syndrome."

"I see." Skye glanced at Homer. "With which services were you especially impressed?"

"All of them." The woman frowned. "Thorntree develops a personalized program for every student." When Skye opened her mouth, Mrs. Northrup glared at her. "Yes, you all here claim to do that with your Individualized Education Plan, but we both know that's a load of crap."

"I don't believe that's true." Skye quickly jotted down a note on her legal pad. Clearly, this issue wasn't going to be solved in one meeting.

"Well, I do," Mrs. Northrup continued. "At Thorntree, there's a teacher for every three students. And they promise to maximize learning, not just provide them with an appropriate education." She spit out the last two words as if they were a bug that had somehow crawled into her mouth. "They also provide extra services like social work, occupational therapy, and speech and language."

Skye glanced down at the girl's IEP. "Ashley receives all of those services here. Itinerant therapists from the co-op come in several times a week to work with Ashley."

The Scumble River school district belonged to the Stanley County Special Education Cooperative, an entity that furnished them with programs and personnel, as needed. The cooperative provided social workers, occupational and physical therapists, speech pathologists, and teachers for low-incidence issues such as vision and hearing impairments. The co-op was also the watchdog that dealt with the bureaucratic red tape of special education funding.

"You don't provide services to the degree my daughter needs." Mrs. Northrup crossed her arms. "I've asked and asked for more time, but Ashley never gets it."

"We do need to balance those extras against what she misses in the classroom while she's with the therapists," Skye explained.

"That wouldn't be a problem at Thorntree." Mrs. Northrup's expression was triumphant. "Academic instruction is presented either individually or in small groups, so Ashley would never miss anything."

"We can do that here." Skye felt as if she were wading through a bowl of oatmeal. "But you wanted her mainstreamed."

She sympathized with Mrs. Northrup, but

Scumble River High School was in full compliance with the rules and regulations, and Ashley was doing very well. There was just no way the board would approve the money for a private placement since they weren't required by law to do so.

"You don't understand." Mrs. Northrup scowled. "Thorntree does it all. There's no sacrificing one thing for another. Social skills lessons are part of the daily curriculum, so Ashley's social awareness and communication skills would improve organically." The woman's face reddened as she continued. "She'll develop an understanding of others' feelings, be taught calming techniques, and learn how to seek comfort from people instead of self-stimulating."

"That's exactly what the co-op's social worker and OT are working on with Ashley here."

"In isolation!" Mrs. Northrup shouted. "At Thorntree she can be on an athletic team and fully participate in extracurricular activities rather than be parked on the sidelines. In this school, there's only one club where she can completely take part in the activities. At Thorntree they use the students' strengths to teach them to interpret their environment."

"Yeah. Yeah. Yeah." Homer lumbered up from his desk and said, "We get it." He reminded Skye of the Wookiee from *Star Wars*. Not only because of his lumbering movements and his large frame, but also because of the hair that enveloped him from head to foot. His eyebrows were bushier than her cat's tail, wiry strands poked from his ears like the filaments in lightbulbs, and a coarse pelt covered his arms and hands. Clumps even pushed out between the buttons of his shirt. "This private school is God's gift to all the handicapped little kiddies. How much does it cost?"

"Differently abled student," Skye quickly corrected before Ashley's mother exploded.

"Whatever." Homer waved his hand. "We're providing an appropriate education, correct?" Skye nodded, and he swung his massive head in Mrs. Northrup's direction. "In that case, we're not paying an arm and a leg to send the girl to this fancy school."

"Fine." Mrs. Northrup rose to her feet. "Ashley is going to Thorntree with or without the school's blessing." She flung a sheaf of papers onto Homer's desk. "Here are the signed forms. I expect her file to be transferred before the end of business today."

After the parent had slammed out of the office, Homer sank back into his chair, put his arms behind his head, and said, "That went well."

"Are you out of your mind?" Skye pressed her lips together and ducked her head. *Shoot! Note to self. Just because it comes into my brain doesn't mean it should be allowed out of my mouth.* "What I meant to say was that we're going to get hit with a due-process hearing. You'd better notify our special ed coordinator at the co-op and the district's attorney."

"Nah. Why rock that boat?" Homer narrowed his eyes. "Maybe the mom is willing to pay."

"I doubt it." Skye tapped her fingers on the chair's arm. "I read Ashley's file. Mrs. Northrup is a widow, and she recently lost her only means of support. A while back, the Laundromat she and her late husband owned burned down. There is no way she has the money to pay for a private school."

"You need to let grayer heads prevail." He nudged the paperwork toward Skye. "Take care of this. The sooner the girl's gone, the better."

"I'm telling you this is going to be a problem." Skye flipped through the pages. "Mrs. Northrup is going to hit us with the bill for Thorntree."

"You don't know that." Homer's gaze wandered to the coffeepot and the box of doughnuts on the credenza behind Skye. "Maybe the girl's father had a big life-insurance policy."

"If he did, they need that cash to live on." Skye stood. "Trust me. Mrs. Northrup is going to put her daughter in Thorntree, then take us to due process to pay the tuition. And once Ashley is in that school, if she does really well there, our case against the placement is going to be a whole lot harder to prove."

"I'm not stirring up trouble that only exists in your mind." Homer pointed over Skye's shoulder at his brand-new Keurig. "Make me a cup of coffee on your way out and hand me one of those chocolate long johns."

Skye ignored the principal's food order and heard him yelling for Opal as she hurried down the hall. She had only a few seconds to drop off Ashley's folder and pick up what she needed for her ten o'clock observation. Serving Homer his brunch was not on her schedule.

The rest of the day was busy, and as she had feared, a student crisis reduced her contractually entitled half-hour lunch break to the time it took her to drive to the elementary school. Instead of a shower, she got indigestion from gulping half a dozen crackers down during the three-minute trip, which left her in a bad mood for the rest of the afternoon.

On her way home, she stopped at the pharmacy. She was almost out of her prenatal vitamins and needed to pick up a card for Vince and Loretta's baby shower. Previously, in order to maintain her privacy, Skye had purchased the vitamins in Laurel, but she didn't have time to drive the forty miles, so she had to get them locally. The tricky part would be getting in and out of the store without anyone noticing what she was buying.

Skye headed over to the greeting cards and quickly made her selection from the handful of options available. Once she was done, she headed toward the vitamin aisle. After scooping up the bottle, she covered it with the shower card and made a beeline toward the pharmacy counter in the back. She knew the druggist wouldn't gossip about her purchase, unlike the woman running the front register, who was a friend of her mother. Checking out with one of May's many pals would be like sending a text to the town's rumor mill.

The pharmacist winked at her when she requested that he ring up her order, and Skye put a finger to her lips. He nodded his understanding and slipped her items into a bag before he took her credit card. She signed the slip, and then, feeling smug, Skye turned around to find her mother heading down the aisle toward her.

May was sixty-three but had the energy of a twenty-five-year-old. She kept her house immaculate, exercised at a nearby community's fitness center three times a week, and worked part-time as a police, fire, and emergency dispatcher. Along with her already busy schedule, May's priority was taking care of her offspring. Which would have been understandable if Skye and her brother, Vince, been under eighteen years of age, but not so much when they were both well into adulthood.

May's face lit up when she spotted her daughter, and she hurried toward her. Enveloping Skye in a hug, she said, "I didn't see your car out front."

"I've got Wally's Ford today." Skye gave her mother a quick kiss on the cheek, then edged away from her in the direction of the door. "The brake, parking, and license plate lights aren't working on my Chevy."

"Does your dad know?" May asked. "I'm sure he can fix that."

Skye's heart sank. Her dad's idea of the perfect vehicle was good transportation—paint and fenders were optional. After driving her father's eyesores all her life, she had wanted something a little snazzier when she grew up. Instead, the last time she'd been in need of a car, Jed and her uncle Charlie had found and restored a 1957 Bel Air for her. Although she loved the thought behind the Chevy, Skye hated driving the aqua behemoth and was thrilled to be zipping around in her husband's cool little T-bird convertible.

"I figured Dad was busy getting ready for planting season," Skye hedged. Her father was a farmer, and spring was a busy time for him. "There's no rush."

"It's probably something simple like a loose wire." May followed Skye toward the exit, evidently forgetting she had just arrived and hadn't done any shopping yet. "I'll tell Jed about it after I get off work tonight, and he'll pick up the car in the morning."

"Okay." Skye grabbed the door handle. "Is that a new uniform shirt?" She took a stab at distracting May's attention. "I really like that color on you."

"This old thing?" May straightened the stand-up collar. "You've seen it a thousand times. I was actually thinking of donating it to the church's next clothing drive."

"Oh. Well, it still looks great." Skye took a step backward. "I better get going."

"What did you stop for?" May reached up and put her hand on her daughter's forehead. "Are you sick? You do look a little pale."

"I'm fine." Skye opened the door. "I just needed a card for the baby shower."

"That doesn't look like a card." May pointed to the bag in Skye's hand, her salt-and-pepper hair appearing to bristle in curiosity.

"Uh." Skye stared into her mother's emerald green eyes, the same eyes she saw in the mirror every morning. "Toothpaste," she blurted out. "While I was here, I remembered we needed tooth-paste."

"Stuff like that is too expensive here in town." May *tsk*ed. "Now that you're married, you should buy it at Sam's Club in Joliet. You and I could go over this Sunday and do a massive shopping. I can check your stuff out on my card so you get the really good price."

"Thanks. We'll have to do that sometime." Skye hugged her mom and scooted out the door. "But this weekend isn't good for me. Trixie's decided to have a fund-raiser Sunday. She's putting on a rubber duck race and I promised to help her. Maybe we can go during spring break."

"Dad and I can get you a membership as an

Easter present." May caught the door before it closed and called after Skye, "Because . . ." May's words were muffled. ". . . baby, you'll really need to be able to buy in bulk."

Shit! Skye slid into the car and leaned her head on the steering wheel. Had her mother said *when you have the baby?* No. There was no way she could know. Was there?

CHAPTER 5

☹—Frownie Face

Skye pulled into her garage and parked Wally's T-bird next to the out-of-commission Bel Air. Slipping the straps of her purse and duffel bag over her wrist, she grabbed the pharmacy sack and an armload of files, then exited the car and hurried up the sidewalk. It had taken quite a bit of research, but Skye thought she had finally figured out what form of architecture the big old house represented.

The design seemed to have Colonial, Tudor, and even Victorian features, but she was fairly certain it was actually an American Foursquare to which a previous owner had added a wraparound porch. Strictly speaking, a Foursquare had a quartet of nearly equal-size rooms per floor, and this place didn't, but Skye was pretty sure that before the various additions, it had started life in the traditionally boxy shape.

She wasn't totally certain about the house's origins since she'd inherited the place from Alma Griggs, a woman she'd known only a couple of months prior to receiving the bequest. Mrs. Griggs had taken a liking to Skye after she had stepped in when an unscrupulous antiques dealer had tried to take advantage of the sweet old lady.

And because of a weird birthday coincidence, the elderly woman had decided Skye was the reincarnation of her deceased daughter. Because of this, and since Mrs. Griggs had no close relatives, she'd made Skye her sole beneficiary. Her only request had been that the house be repaired and Skye live in it for at least a year.

The unpaid back taxes and the lack of liquid assets had forced Skye to take out a home-equity loan for the renovations, and a bumpy start with a bad-boy contractor had delayed the restorations, so it had taken her quite a while to get the place fixed up. But she was finally done—at least with the first and second floors. The third story was still completely untouched.

Thank goodness Wally had agreed to live there after their wedding. With everything she'd been through refurbishing the house, Skye wanted to enjoy the fruits of her labor.

It had helped that once they were officially married, the resident apparition had backed off.

Prior to making their relationship legal, Mrs. Griggs, who evidently had never gone toward the light, had done everything in her ghostly power to prevent Skye and Wally from making love. If that had persisted, there was no way in heck they could they have continued to live there. However, Skye took it as a good sign that they hadn't had a visit from the resident spook since returning from their honeymoon.

Unlocking the door and stepping into the foyer, Skye found her path blocked by a large black cat. Bingo sat on the throw rug, narrowed his big golden green eyes, and stared at her accusingly. He had belonged to her grandmother, who had explained that since she could never win the actual game, she had named her cat Bingo so that she could at least shout out the word when she was calling for her pet.

After Grandma Leofanti's death, Skye had rescued the beautiful kitty from her uncle's evil clutches. Dante had been sure the animal was valuable and had wanted to sell him, but Skye knew that an older cat with no pedigree would more likely be abandoned than cause a bidding war.

Evidently, forgiving Skye for whatever real or imagined transgressions had upset his feline feelings, Bingo twined around Skye's ankles, meowing and purring simultaneously. She dropped her stuff on the hall bench and scooped him up, burying her face in his velvetlike fur. He revved his motor and purred louder, kneading her shoulder with his front paws.

A few seconds later, apparently deciding he'd had enough affection, Bingo extended his back claws to indicate his sudden displeasure. Once he got Skye's attention, he leaped from her arms. Landing with a soft *thud,* he strolled away, his tail sticking straight up into the air.

Strangely soothed by the cat's customary welcome-home ritual, Skye picked up her duffel and the pharmacy bag and headed toward the staircase. Stopping in midstride, she sniffed. What was that delicious smell?

It took her a few seconds to remember that Dorothy Snyder made supper for them on Mondays and Thursdays. Along with his gun collection, treadmill, and awesome sports car, Wally had brought something, or she really should say some*one,* else into the marriage—a part-time housekeeper. Skye had been reluctant to have somebody cook and clean for her, but when Wally had pointed out that if she refused, she was putting the woman out of a job, she'd relented.

Skye was still uneasy with having Dorothy work for them. While the woman was an amazing chef and kept the place spotless, she was also one of May's oldest friends. Although Wally had assured Skye that he'd spoken to her about confidentiality and warned her that any leaks to her BFF would result in her immediate dismissal, Skye continued to be a bit uncomfortable with the situation.

Then again, Skye took another whiff of the enticing aroma; she was getting used to coming home to a wonderful meal she didn't have to prepare. What was worse—a lack of privacy or having to cook every night?

Exasperated at her own indecision, she ran upstairs to change clothes. She couldn't wait to get out of the outfit she'd worn for school. When she'd packed it, she hadn't realized that the waistband of the khaki slacks had become uncomfortably tight and the buttons on the blouse now pulled open across her chest. Wally might be thrilled with her larger breasts, but an increase in cup size meant that nothing fit right anymore.

After tucking her vitamins into the master bath's medicine cabinet, she took the last pill from the previous bottle and tossed the container in the trash. Then, finally, Skye took a much-needed shower. Once she was clean, she put on sweatpants and a T-shirt and hurried down the steps. Dashing into the kitchen, she skidded to a stop, letting out a tiny squeak of alarm.

What was Dorothy still doing here? Normally the housekeeper left before Skye got home from work, and on the days she didn't, the cranberry red Cadillac Catera sitting in the driveway gave Skye a heads-up that she was in the house.

Dorothy turned from the stove and said, "Are you early or am I late?"

She was a tall, solidly built woman in her early sixties. She and May had been classmates, and her deceased husband had been in the navy with Jed. The two couples had been close friends, and as a child, Skye had spent a lot of time with the Snyder family.

"I think it must be you, because I even stopped at the drugstore on my way home." Skye hugged the older woman. "Where's your car?"

"Tammy's SUV was in the garage. She needed to run to Laurel to get food for my granddog, so she borrowed the Caddy and dropped me off."

Skye hid a smile. Dorothy's daughter had stated that the only grandchild she was producing for her mom would have four feet. Dorothy had accepted Tammy's declaration much better than Skye's mother would have taken similar news.

Dorothy glanced at the wall clock and frowned. "She should have been here to pick me up over half an hour ago. I hope she's okay."

"Maybe you should call her cell." Skye lifted the lid on one of the pans. Italian sausage simmered in a spicy tomato sauce.

"Yeah." Dorothy reached into the pocket of her jeans and dug out her phone. "I have to get home and get spiffed up. Tonight's my bowling league, and there's a new guy who's a real cutie patootie."

She winked and slid her free hand down her hips. "Rumor has it he's a widower."

Skye gave Dorothy a thumbs-up, then noticed that Bingo had magically appeared at her feet. He thumped her leg with his paw and purred loudly. *Aw, yes.* It was cat chowtime. As the housekeeper talked to her daughter, Skye prepared Bingo's supper. She popped open the tin of Fancy Feast, scooped the contents into his bowl, and set it and fresh water next to the untouched bowl of dry food on a mat that read, KITTY CAT CAFÉ. FEED ME AND I WILL LOVE YOU FOREVER.

Bingo sniffed delicately, lifted his head, and glared at Skye.

"Come on, don't be silly. You've been eating the same stuff for over five years now."

He looked up at her out of slitted eyes, sat back, and stared.

"We've had this discussion before. Grandma may have prepared home-cooked meals for you, but that isn't going to happen in this house." Skye pointed to the back door. "If you're not happy here, feel free to leave." Bingo continued to gaze at her, and Skye added, "You're lucky that I buy you the name-brand cat food."

Bingo blinked as if thinking it over, then took a tentative lick.

"That's more like it." Skye patted the cat's head, turned, and walked to the refrigerator. She grabbed a can of caffeine-free Diet Coke and a container of spinach and artichoke hummus, then took a bag of toasted garlic pita chips from the cupboard and carried her snack to the table.

On a good day, Wally didn't get home until after five, usually closer to five thirty. And since he liked to work out and shower before sitting down at the table, they rarely ate dinner before six thirty or seven. She wasn't fond of eating that late—it felt as if she had just finished supper and it was time for bed—but she was slowly adjusting to her new husband's schedule.

One method of coping was to have a little something a bit earlier to tide her over and then eat less with Wally later on in the evening.

"Tammy'll be here in ten minutes. Walmart was really crowded, and they only had two cash registers open." Dorothy tucked away her cell and said, "I'll put the sausage in the fridge next to the polenta. When you're ready for supper, the salad is in the green Tupperware bowl and the garlic bread is on top of that container wrapped in foil. Put the bread in the oven for fifteen minutes while you reheat the sausage and polenta."

"At three fifty, right?" Skye asked, and when Dorothy nodded, she said, "Thanks. It sounds yummy. But then, all your food is."

"You're very welcome." Dorothy finished tidying the kitchen and started to wash the pan that the sausage had been in. "How's everything with you?"

"Just fine." Skye dipped a pita chip into the hummus. "I can't wait for this week to be over. I'm so ready for spring break."

"It'll be nice for you to have some time at home." Dorothy dried the pan. "You had to go to work the day after you got back from your honeymoon, didn't you? That had to be exhausting."

"A little." Skye took a sip of her soda. "But since you did all the laundry for us, it wasn't too bad." She smiled. "I'm getting spoiled."

"Like May didn't spoil both you and Vince?" Dorothy snickered, then sobered and asked, "Have you been feeling okay?"

"Uh-huh." Skye stuffed a chip into her mouth so she couldn't talk. *Shoot!* Had Dorothy noticed something? Had she told May?

"You don't want to get run down." Dorothy slid the clean pan into the cupboard shelf and walked over to Skye. "The whole putting on a wedding and then starting a new life can be tough." She patted Skye's shoulder. "Now that there's more than just you to consider, you need to take better care of yourself." She opened her mouth to continue, but the sound of a honking horn interrupted her. Grabbing her purse from the counter, she said, "Don't forget to take your vitamins."

Oh. My. Gosh! Skye choked on the chip she'd been chewing. She closed her eyes. Was there any evidence of her pregnancy? *No.* She certainly hadn't bought any maternity clothes or baby items.

Unless Dorothy had noticed the unusually rapid consumption of soda crackers, Skye hadn't left any trace of her morning sickness. She'd even been careful to hide her copy of *What to Expect When You're Expecting*—it had been a pain to stick it in a shoe box at the back of her closet every time she was through reading, but she'd done it.

Skye shook her head. She was being paranoid. No one knew about the baby. Not Dorothy. Not May. Not anyone. And no one would know until she and Wally made the announcement. Reaching for another chip, she relaxed against the back of the chair, then stiffened.

Crap! Had Dorothy opened up the medicine chest and seen the prenatal vitamin bottle or noticed an empty one in the trash can? That would certainly explain her farewell remark. Best-case scenario, she just meant that now that Skye had a husband, she wasn't on her own anymore, and anything that affected her would affect him, too.

Yep. That had to be it. Skye took a sip of soda, then stood and fetched the stack of folders from the hall bench. Until Wally got home, she'd work on the report that Trixie's early-morning visit had prevented her from completing. Feeling virtuous, she spread the papers across the kitchen table, arranged her yellow legal pad at the proper angle, and picked up her favorite pen. *Heck!* Maybe she could even get a head start on the next day's cases.

An hour later, Skye was pondering the meaning of the pattern of subtest scatter on the Wechsler Intelligence Scale for Children—Fourth Edition, affectionately known as the WISC-IV, when she heard a car pulling up in front of the house. Shoving the protocol into the folder, she organized the files that were strewn across the table into a pile, got to her feet, and dashed into the hallway.

Wally had just stepped inside, and when he spotted her, he met her halfway down the corridor, wordlessly gathering her to his chest. He gently cupped her chin and claimed her lips. His kiss was hungry, and she returned it with a reckless abandon that surprised her. They'd been apart for only twelve hours, yet it felt as if she hadn't been in his arms for days.

At the same time that he roused her passion, it was clear that his own was growing stronger, too. He pulled her tighter, her soft curves molding to the contours of his muscular body. Blood pounded in her brain and her knees trembled. Something about her pregnancy had put her hormones, and apparently Wally's as well, into overdrive. They'd been going at it like oversexed rabbits, and she wondered if that was natural. She needed to check with someone about that.

As Skye's world spun out of control, the radio attached to Wally's epaulette crackled and the dispatcher's voice said, "Officer Martinez, there's a ten-ninety-one at the St. Francis parish hall. Please be advised that the ladies are afraid to go to their cars."

Skye jerked out of his arms. Nothing like her mother's voice coming from her husband's shoulder to throw a bucket of cold water over Skye's lust.

May was the afternoon dispatcher for the Scumble River Police Department, and as such, Wally was her superior. The role of boss and son-in-law was a delicate balance—one Skye was trying not to influence. But it was tough with Skye also working for the PD as a psych consultant. That was the bad part of small-town living: There was no way to keep a clear demarcation between professional and personal worlds.

With a sheepish grin, Wally unclipped the radio from his shirt and said, "Sorry about that." He set the receiver on the bench. "I need to remember to turn that thing off once I'm home."

He tried to take her back into his arms, but Skye headed for the kitchen, asking over her shoulder, "What's a ten-ninety-one?" She'd memorized the more common ten-codes, but the meaning of that particular one eluded her.

"A stray animal." Wally followed Skye and took a beer from the fridge. "If it's vicious, I hope Martinez doesn't try to capture it all by herself. Too bad animal control only works nine to five."

Zelda Martinez was the newest police officer and the only woman on the Scumble River force. Zelda had joined the department eighteen months ago. She'd been hired fresh out of college and was still inexperienced in dealing with everyday issues not covered in the curriculum.

"Should you check to see if Zelda's okay? Maybe give her a call?" Skye asked, picking up the pile of folders and carrying them back out to the hallway bench so she wouldn't forget them in the morning.

Once again, Wally followed Skye, and after she'd put down the files, he gave her a light kiss on her lips. "I love how you worry about everyone, but Martinez has to learn these things on her own."

"You're right. I know that. I wouldn't swoop in to rescue one of my students. Well, yes I would, but I know I shouldn't." Feeling oddly self-conscious, she eased out of Wally's reach and said, "It must be the hormones talking, or I'm becoming my mother." She smiled up at him. "Pray for the former."

The puzzled expression on his handsome face was replaced with a grin and he said, "Speaking of hormones, how are you feeling?"

"As usual, once ten a.m. comes and goes, I'm fine." Skye shrugged. "I sure hope the morning sickness doesn't last throughout the whole pregnancy. If it does, I'm never doing this again."

"I'm happy with once." He chuckled. "Or ten times. However many kids you want." Wally put down his beer bottle and unbuckled his leather utility belt, placing it next to the radio and Skye's duffel. Next he loosened his collar and took off his tie.

"That's good." Skye had no idea how many children she wanted. She'd see how they did with this one before she decided. An only child might be lonely, but there were always cousins. Vince and Loretta had already provided one of those. "Are you planning to work out before dinner?"

"If you're not too hungry." He put an arm around her, gave her a hug, then started to free her curls from the French braid she'd put her hair in after her shower. He liked it loose and was forever undoing it from Skye's preferred ponytail or bun. "Sitting behind a desk or in a patrol car all day doesn't do much to keep me in shape, and as an older dad, I need to be in tip-top form."

Wally had eight years on Skye, a fact May had held against him when he'd first started pursuing her daughter. He was also divorced, which had been another mark in her negative column, at least until he'd gotten an annulment. Now that he and Skye were married, May had finally come around, and she was firmly on Team Wally.

"Speaking of exercise," Skye said as Wally continued to unbraid her hair and massage her scalp. "You won't believe what happened to me this morning after my swim."

Wally had finished freeing Skye's hair and started to rub her shoulders, but he stopped and said, "What? Another run-in with Homer?"

"Not then." Skye grimaced. "That came later, after the Trixie part."

"Sounds like you had quite a day." Wally turned his attention to kneading her neck.

"I did." Skye relaxed under Wally's ministrations. "Oh, that feels good."

"How about this?" Wally bent his head to nibble at her earlobe.

"Oh. Yeah." Skye enjoyed the dizzying current racing through her.

Wally's lips seared a path down her throat as he peeled off her T-shirt.

She felt as if she were floating, and for several long moments she mindlessly enjoyed the sensation of her husband's mouth and hands exploring her body. Now that they were married, being with Wally felt different, felt better. Possibly, it was being able to make love without the Catholic guilt of premarital sex or the need to go to confession afterward.

Finally, Skye took Wally's hand and led him upstairs to their bedroom. No need to make out in the drafty foyer when they had a king-size four-poster at their disposal.

Once they had shed their clothes, Wally

stretched out on the bed, drawing Skye on top of him. She nuzzled his chest, then raised her head so she could look into her new husband's eyes as she ran her fingers through the pearl-gray strands at his temples. She liked the way the silver emphasized the midnight blackness of the rest of his hair.

Tracing the smooth olive skin that stretched over his high cheekbones, Skye purred her pleasure. He was such a gorgeous man. And he was all hers.

With her caresses, Wally's brown eyes went from the color of milk chocolate to dark. Finally, he captured her right hand and brought it to his lips, kissing and nibbling his way to her wrist.

She shivered as he nuzzled the sensitive skin there. She responded by kneading the muscles of his broad shoulders while kissing the strong column of his throat. Wally growled and reversed their positions so that she was lying on the mattress. After that Skye lost track of time.

An hour or so later, while Wally and Skye lay cuddling under the sheet, he asked, "So what happened to you at the pool this morning?" After she described her altercation with Blair, Wally said, "Maybe you should just skip your swim for a while."

"Why should I?" Skye got up and started to get dressed again. "From now on, I'll make sure to check the schedule, and there shouldn't be any more problems with her."

"Just be careful." Wally got up from the bed, took Skye's chin in his hand, and tilted her face upward. "She sounds a little crazy, and that can be dangerous."

"Trust me." Skye made a face. "As a psychologist, I know that."

"So you'll avoid her?" Wally headed into the bathroom and turned on the shower.

"I promise." Skye waited for the water to warm up, then joined him underneath the spray. "I'll run the other way if I see Blair Hucksford anywhere near the pool."

"Excellent plan." Wally smiled, slid his hand down her hip, and proceeded to show her how good girls were rewarded.

CHAPTER 6

AWHFY—Are We Having Fun Yet?

Seriously? Again? Skye lay completely still, staring up at the ceiling. When she'd first opened her eyes, she'd made the colossal mistake of turning her head too quickly to check the time on the alarm clock. She'd immediately felt as if she'd just taken a roller-coaster ride after eating a really greasy corn dog.

As she fought to control the queasiness, she ran her schedule through her head. She was supposed to be at the junior high Tuesday mornings, then the high school in the afternoon. And to top it off, she had PPS meetings at both schools. No way could she call in sick.

Just after midnight, Skye had been jerked from a deep sleep by the thunder and lightning of a severe storm passing through the area. It had taken her forever to doze off again, and she'd hoped to finally be able to snooze at least until her alarm sounded, but once again, she'd woken up before dawn. It was barely five o'clock and still pitch-black in their bedroom. The sun wouldn't rise for another ninety minutes, and both she and Wally could sleep for at least one more hour. Well, to be perfectly accurate, he clearly could continue to spend time in slumberland. She, on the other hand, although so tired she could cry, couldn't fall back asleep.

Suddenly, she was burning up. Trying to cool off, she carefully threw back the covers. A few seconds later, she was freezing. In an attempt to avoid another wave of nausea, she tried to grab the blanket without moving her head. Nope. She couldn't reach it. As she stretched her fingers toward the elusive quilt, a sharp pain shot up her spine. She whimpered. *Okay.* This was officially not fun.

"Are you all right, sugar?" Wally's warm voice tickled her ear.

"No." Skye held back a sob, not wanting the poor guy to have to deal with a hysterical wife as soon as he opened his eyes. "I feel awful."

"The doc said the morning sickness might peak at ten to eleven weeks, then diminish between twelve and sixteen." He gently ran his hand over her stomach. "Seems like Junior is right on time."

"Swell. The queasiness better improve at three months, because I don't know if I can handle thirty more days of this." Skye made an effort not to whine, but she didn't succeed. "And now my back hurts."

"Turn over and I'll give you a massage." Wally nudged her, and Skye stiffened.

"I can't move or I'll vomit." Skye froze until the nausea subsided, then said, "I thought this would be the happiest time in my life." A tear ran down her cheek. "But I'm just sick of being sick. I want to be able to eat an English muffin for breakfast again and drink a cup of coffee without feeling as if I'm going to hurl."

"It won't be too much longer." Wally stroked her forehead. "You can do it."

"I'm disappointed in myself," Skye confessed. "I thought I'd be stronger."

"You are. You're the toughest person I know." Wally pressed a kiss to her lips. "I'll go get you a cup of ginger tea and some crackers. You just lie here and relax."

Wally hurried away, and Skye tried to doze. A

few seconds later her eyelids flew open. *Great!* Now she had to pee. Maybe she could hold it. She concentrated on clenching her muscles and thinking of something dry like the sun beating down on the desert sand.

Nope! Her visualization wasn't working. It was get up now or change the sheets later. She eased herself off the mattress and hurried to the bathroom. After using the toilet, she sank to the floor and hugged the bowl, waiting for last night's ice cream sundae to stage a comeback.

When Wally returned, Skye said weakly, "One thing being pregnant has taught me—evidently you can keep puking long after you think you've finished."

"I'm so sorry, darlin'." Wally stroked her hair. "You know I'd go through this for you if I could."

She made a noncommittal sound, not entirely convinced her handsome husband was telling the complete truth. After she sipped her tea and nibbled on a saltine, her queasiness finally subsided enough that she was able to stand.

When she reached into her duffel for her bathing suit, Wally frowned. "I thought you were going to avoid the pool for a while."

"I promised that I'd avoid Blair, not skip my swim." Skye took off her nightshirt and panties. "Before I left the high school yesterday, I checked, and the area isn't reserved this morning. Besides, the swim really helps the morning sickness."

"Maybe I should go with you." Wally leaned against the bathroom door, watching her. "It would be fun. Like on our honeymoon."

"Well, technically"—Skye shimmied into her maillot—"since you aren't an employee of the school district, you would need to get a pass from the superintendent's office in order to use the facility."

"It sounds as if you don't want me there." He narrowed his eyes.

"It's just that if Blair does show up, she's such a stickler for the rules, I'm afraid your presence would cause more problems than it would solve." Skye headed back into the bedroom to gather her outfit for the workday. She glanced at Wally, who had followed her, and added, "So it's not that I wouldn't love having you with me. I just want to avoid stirring up any more trouble with the woman."

"If she's there, do you promise not to talk to her?" Wally's jaw clenched.

"Of course." Skye finished packing her things. "Oh, you distracted me last night"—she wiggled her brows and gazed at the bed—"before I could tell you that we're going to need to make an announcement about our impending happy event soon."

"I thought we agreed to wait until a few weeks after the first trimester."

"Unfortunately"—Skye pointed to her belly—"Juniorette is starting to show."

"Yes, he is." Wally beamed and touched Skye's spandex-covered baby bump. "But you should be okay in your regular clothes."

"Not for much longer." Skye pulled on her sweat suit. "*She* is growing by the day." It was too soon to know the baby's gender, and they had been teasing each other with the possibilities.

"So, we make the announcement after Vince and Loretta's shower on Saturday?" Wally asked. "We can phone everyone first thing Monday."

"Yes." Skye walked down the stairs carrying her duffel. She stopped at the hall bench to stuff the files and her purse inside before snapping the padlock, then said, "There's a good chance Dorothy has an idea about what's going on, and when I saw Mom at the drugstore yesterday, she said something that makes me think her pal might have shared her suspicions." Skye paused at the front door. "Or at least gave her BFF a clue."

"Should I talk to Dorothy?" Wally asked, then gave Skye a good-bye kiss. "Confidentiality was a part of her employment agreement."

"Not yet." Skye stepped out onto the porch, but turned and said, "One more thing. Dad will be by today to take a look at the Bel Air, so if it's gone, don't think it was stolen." She waved and muttered as she hurried toward the garage, "Worse luck."

It was exactly six o'clock when Skye pulled the T-bird into the high school driveway. At first she thought that, like yesterday, the lot was empty. Then she noticed a black Miata tucked near the athletic-equipment shed. It wasn't an official parking spot, but its proximity to the gym's emergency exit would be convenient for anyone who had a key that shut off the alarm. Besides Homer and the custodian, the only faculty members with keys were the coaches.

Shoot! Was that Blair's car? Skye pulled Wally's Ford into an open slot but didn't turn off the engine. Maybe she should just drive on over to the junior high. A wave of nausea hit her. *No.* The pool wasn't reserved, and she needed to swim. Everyone else might be intimidated by the volleyball coach, but Skye refused to join their ranks. Besides, the Mazda could belong to Thor Goodson.

As soon as Skye unlocked the entrance and walked inside, she noticed the auxiliary lights. *Heck!* Last night's storm must have knocked out the power again. She hoped the custodian had reported the outage to Commonwealth Edison. If it wasn't restored before school started, classes might have to be canceled.

Luckily, she didn't need electricity to swim. Taking her morning dip in the pool now felt like a holy quest, and she was too stubborn to turn back. Skye walked down the hallway, through the gym, and into the girls' locker room. Just to be on the safe side, she rechecked the calendar taped to the door. The schedule hadn't changed from when she'd looked at it yesterday afternoon. The last reservation for the pool had been for Monday evening from nine to ten.

Dropping her duffel on the bench, she stripped off her sweat suit and exited the locker room. In the near darkness, the view of the pool area through the blue opaque safety glass wall was a little eerie. She rounded the corner and strolled over to the ladder.

After adjusting her swim cap and goggles, she started to climb down, then caught sight of something at the bottom of the pool. Without the normal subaquatic lights, she couldn't tell if there really was anything there or not. She shrugged. It was probably just a shadow.

Easing off the ladder and into the water, she realized that it was a lot colder than usual. She mentally slapped her forehead. Of course it was cooler; no power meant no heater. Shivering, she dove underneath the surface, hoping that fully submerging would help her acclimate more quickly to the chilly temperature.

She swam a few feet, then went deeper and paddled along the bottom of the pool. Seeing the shadow she'd noticed earlier, she hesitated. There really was something down there, but without the lights, it was difficult to see exactly what. Swimming closer, she reached out to touch whatever it was and almost screamed.

Choking from the water she'd swallowed, Skye shot to the surface. Unless this was a very elaborate practical joke and the prankster had access to an extremely realistic-feeling dummy, there was a body at the bottom of the pool.

CHAPTER 7

BRB—Be Right Back

Skye gasped, trying to get her breath, then kicked frantically and swam as fast as she could toward the side of the pool. She had to get out of the water. She was shivering uncontrollably, and that couldn't be good for the baby. Reaching the edge, she grabbed the ladder, then hesitated. What if the person was alive? Their skin had felt ice-cold, but then again, so did hers. She was a trained lifeguard. She couldn't just leave them to die.

Murmuring a prayer that she wasn't endangering her unborn child, she turned back and dived down to the bottom. Thankfully, the water's buoyancy made it relatively easy to bring the person to the surface. Getting them out of the pool was an entirely different matter.

Although she was ninety-nine percent certain there was no one else around, Skye screamed for help. She continued to shout as she moved the drowning victim toward the ladder and used the strap of her goggles to secure the individual to the step.

Climbing out of the water, Skye lay down with her head and shoulders over the pool edge, hooked one leg through the ladder railing for leverage, and untied the fastenings. Finally, inch by painful inch, she hauled the person up onto the concrete apron.

She was grateful she'd started lifting weights in the home gym Wally had installed in one of the extra bedrooms. She still didn't have much upper-body strength—she'd barely passed her last lifeguard recertification test. But two or three months ago she would have never been able to boost someone out of the water without the aid of a shepherd's crook, a rescue tube, or a backboard.

Heck! Before the weight training, she was lucky to get herself up the metal rungs, let alone someone else.

Turning the casualty over, Skye squeezed her eyes shut. It was Blair. Considering the Miata parked outside, she'd known there was a good chance it might be the science teacher, but she'd purposely stopped herself from contemplating the drowning victim's identity.

Giving the person a name made the situation too real. And if it was real, she was afraid she wouldn't be able to do what needed to be done.

Because if she thought too much about what was happening, it might immobilize her.

Struggling to stay calm, Skye pretended this was just a routine training exercise and Blair was a CPR manikin. She immediately checked the teacher's throat for blockage, then pinched her nose shut and blew into her mouth while she watched to see if Blair's chest rose. When there was no movement, Skye readjusted the woman's head so that the chin was pointing upward and tried the rescue breaths again. The chest still didn't rise, so Skye started compressions.

The movies and television made it seem that a drowning victim should be turned on his or her side to get the water from their lungs. But in reality, CPR was more effective, and the chest compressions would also pump out the fluid.

Skye wasn't sure how long she tried to resuscitate Blair, but after what seemed like forever, she had to admit that the teacher was dead. There was nothing Skye could do to bring her back. She needed to inform the powers that be, starting with her husband.

Having discovered bodies before—too many times for comfort—she knew the drill. But instead of moving, she heard herself whimper and realized she was perilously close to a total breakdown. This was no time to lose it. She dug her fingernails into her upper thigh, and the sharp pain shocked her back into focus.

She didn't have the luxury of giving in to her feelings. She had to notify the authorities and then contact Homer. She glanced at the wall clock. It was 6:36. The staff would begin to arrive in less than forty-five minutes and the students half an hour after that. Decisions had to be made. If the school was going to be closed for the day, the parents and the bus company had to be alerted sooner rather than later.

But Skye remained kneeling beside Blair, a voice inside her head whispering that she'd just had a fight with this woman the day before. Her last thoughts about the teacher had been hateful ones. The queasiness returned, and her stomach roiled. Suddenly, she gagged.

Stop it, Skye ordered herself. *You are not only a consultant for the police department, but you're a psychologist. You've been taught to remain unemotional, to dissociate yourself from the situation, and to disconnect your emotions.* She swallowed hard, got to her feet, and thought about the measures she needed to take.

First, get her cell from her purse. Second, call Wally. Third, get out of the wet swimsuit, put on some clothes, and wait for him to arrive. She bit her thumbnail. Was there a fourth item on her to-do list?

Still in a near trance, she staggered to the locker room, dug out her phone, and dialed her home number. It rang four times and then went to voice mail. She got the same response when she tried Wally's cell.

Well, hell! Where was he? He didn't start work until eight, and although he often went in before his shift officially began, this was early even for him. Maybe he was in the shower. Skye frowned; then, just in case there had been an emergency and he'd been summoned to the police station, she tried his private line. When he didn't answer, she gave up and dialed 911. At least her mother wasn't on duty. She really didn't want to have to deal with May's maternal fussing.

"Scumble River police, fire, and emergency," Char, the dispatcher who covered the midnight-to-eight stint, answered on the first ring. "How can I help you?"

"This is Skye. Can you send an officer to our house and have him tell Wally that I need him at the high school right away?" She paused. There was no use tying up the town's lone ambulance since she was certain Blair was beyond any help they could provide. "And Wally should probably contact the coroner to come, too."

"Honey, are you okay?" Char's concerned voice soothed Skye.

"I'm fine. Just get Wally here right away."

Without waiting for a response from Char, Skye pushed the OFF button, then quickly pulled the towel from her duffel, dried off, and slipped on her sweat suit. Tucking her cell into the pants pocket, she secured the locker door behind her, then headed toward the entrance to let Wally in when he arrived. She was chilled to the bone, and she wondered if she'd ever feel warm again. Certainly not anytime soon.

As she waited, she briefly wondered where Cameron was during all of her screaming. Cameron Unger had been the elementary school custodian, but after his mother was killed, he transferred to the high school position, and Skye had grown used to seeing the young man when she came for her early-morning swims.

A few seconds later Skye remembered that at their last meeting, in an attempt to cut costs, the board had eliminated the third shift. The building was now empty from eleven p.m. until seven a.m. Which probably meant that nobody was aware of the power outage either.

Skye immediately fished her phone from her sweatpants pocket and scrolled through her contact list. *Shoot!* She didn't have Homer's home number. She'd have to call Uncle Charlie. As the board president, he'd certainly know how to reach the principal.

Before she could dial, she saw Wally's squad car screech to a stop in front of the school. That had been quick. Had he gotten one of her messages, or had an officer already been in the area? There sure hadn't been enough time for anyone to get to their house with a message.

Wally burst out of the cruiser and flew up the sidewalk, a look of alarm on his face. Although he wore his uniform, his tie was missing and his wet hair stood on end, as if he'd shoved his fingers through it.

Skye pushed open the door and met him on the steps. He gathered her into his arms, then ran his hands down her back and sides as if checking her for injuries.

Finally, his voice husky, he said, "Darlin', are you okay?"

"I am now." She snuggled against him for a moment, then kissed his cheek and withdrew from his embrace, tugging him inside and down the hall. "When I dove into the pool, I found Blair Hucksford's body on the bottom."

"You're sure she's dead?" Wally asked as he walked beside Skye.

"Yes." She unlocked the door, led him through the dressing room and into the pool area. "I managed to get her out of the water and performed CPR." Skye lurched to a stop, and her voice quavered when she admitted, "I hope I didn't hurt the baby by doing that, but I couldn't just leave her if there was a chance she might survive."

"Do you feel any abdominal pain?" Wally's brow furrowed, and he tipped up her chin, examining her face. "Any cramping or spotting?"

"No." Skye shook her head. "I actually feel better. Less nauseated."

"Then I'm sure you're fine." He started to turn toward the body but hesitated and said, "But if you have even a twinge, you need to call the doctor ASAP."

"Definitely." She bit her lip. "I'm sorry if you think I shouldn't have taken the chance with our baby."

"That's who you are, sugar." Wally hugged her. "You could no more turn your back on someone in need than you could scale Mount Everest."

"Thanks." Skye frowned. "I think." She poked him in the chest. "And I'm sure I could climb a mountain if I had the right equipment."

"Uh-huh." Wally had clearly already learned the appropriate response to his new wife's statements. He gave Skye a final kiss on the cheek, then crouched next to the body and pressed two fingers to the side of Blair's throat. "Tell me exactly what happened. Start with when you pulled into the parking lot this morning."

"Okay." Skye gathered her thoughts. "The first thing I saw was that except for a black Miata parked near the athletic-equipment shed, there were no other cars. I figured it belonged to one of the coaches, since it was near the alarmed gym exit and they all have keys to that door."

"So you went inside." Wally waited a few more seconds, then removed his hand from the woman's neck. "Did you see anyone in the building?"

"No," she answered quickly. "But I did notice

that the building's power was out. Fortunately, the emergency lights were working."

"Why didn't you leave then?" Wally laid his ear on the victim's chest.

"I figured that I was already in my bathing suit and I didn't need it to be that bright to swim." Skye watched as Wally lifted his head and picked up Blair's wrist, checking for a pulse. "I put my things in the locker room, took off my sweat suit, and walked into the pool area. I thought I saw a shadow at the bottom of the pool, but it was hard to tell without the subaquatic lights." Skye's voice cracked. "So I climbed into the water."

"I know this is tough." Wally straightened and took her back into his arms.

"The water was cold, so I dove down, trying to warm up." Skye spoke into his chest. "That's when I saw it wasn't a shadow at the bottom." Her voice broke. "But I still couldn't determine what it was until I reached out, and that's when I realized it was a person."

"Then what?" Wally pulled her closer and smoothed his hand over her hair.

"Then I dove back down and brought her to the surface. I shouted for help, but no one was around." Skye explained about the elimination of the midnight shift from the custodian's schedule, and when Wally nodded his understanding, she continued. "Once I got the drowning victim out of the pool, I saw it was Blair, and I tried to resuscitate her." Skye bit back a sob, but a tear rolled down her cheek. "But it wasn't any use."

"It's okay, baby." Wally kissed her temple. "I wish you hadn't been the one to find her. Try not to think about it anymore."

"Right." Skye was fairly sure she wouldn't be forgetting the last hour anytime soon. "Then I tried calling you at home, on your cell, and on your private line. Finally, I just dialed nine-one-one."

"I was in the shower." He held her for a few more minutes. "By the time I got out and heard your message, Anthony was at the front door, ringing the bell like he thought I might be deaf."

"He must have been close by to get there so fast," Skye murmured, drawing strength from her husband's touch. "Did you notify Simon?"

"Yes." Wally frowned, clearly unhappy. "He's on the way. In fact, you'd better go let him in the front door. I'll stay with the body."

Skye cringed. Simon Reid, her ex-boyfriend, was the county coroner, not to mention the owner of both the local funeral home and the bowling alley. She hadn't seen him since her wedding reception, where he'd told her that even if her feelings for him had changed, he would always love her. She wondered if things between them would be awkward.

She didn't have long to worry about it because the hearse was just pulling in behind the squad car when Skye returned to the entrance. Simon exited the driver's side, carrying a black satchel. He walked to the rear of the vehicle and took a collapsible stretcher from the back.

As he wheeled the contraption up the sidewalk, Skye noticed that not a strand of his short auburn hair was out of place. His cheeks were freshly shaven and his black wing-tip shoes were so perfectly polished he could use them to check if his tie was straight.

Instantly, she was aware of her own rumpled appearance. She hitched up the drooping sweat-pants and tugged the navy sweatshirt down. If anyone would notice her baby bump, it would be her ex-boyfriend.

Holding the door open, she said, "Hi, Simon. Sorry to get you out so early. The body is in the pool area. Follow me."

"Hello, Skye. No problem about the time." Simon smiled. "You know I'm an early riser. When we were dating, you liked to sleep until noon. I wonder what changed your habits." He lifted an auburn brow, then followed her down the hallway and asked, "Has the deceased been identified?"

"Yes. By me. Her name is Blair Hucksford." Skye led Simon through the locker room and out to the edge of the pool. "She's the junior and senior science teacher here, as well as the girls' volleyball coach. I found her at the bottom of the pool. She must have been swimming alone and drowned."

"That isn't a very safe practice." Simon and Wally exchanged businesslike nods. "I warned you about that when we were dating."

Skye opened her mouth to snap at Simon, but Wally shook his head and murmured, "You don't have to worry about Reid's opinion anymore."

"Right." Skye smiled at her husband and stared impassively at Simon.

Wally nodded his approval, then turned and said something to Simon that she couldn't hear. The two men exchanged spots, and Simon set his satchel on the ground. He took out an elaborate camera and began to photograph Blair from various angles. He then turned her over and repeated the process. Finally, he made a small incision below the ribs on the right side of the body and inserted a thermometer deeply into the cut.

Rising, he stuck a different thermometer in the pool water and waited until it registered. Then he took his phone from the inner pocket of his suit jacket, brought up the calculator, and did a quick computation.

Finally, he looked at Wally and said, "Taking into consideration the temperature of the water and that the temperature of a dead body decreases at about one-and-a-half degrees per hour, Ms. Hucksford's liver temperature indicates she died somewhere between eleven p.m. and midnight."

"I wonder what she was doing swimming alone so late at night," Skye said.

"She wasn't alone." Wally pointed to two marks on Blair's neck. "See those punctures? I noticed them when you went to let Reid inside."

"Don't tell me you think she was killed by a vampire." Skye rolled her eyes. They'd had some odd deaths in Scumble River—one by chocolate, another in a mud bath, and a third involving a steamroller—but she refused to believe that this one implicated Count Dracula.

"No." Wally shoved his hands in his pockets. "Those are wounds caused by certain types of Tasers and stun guns. When the trigger is pressed, two darts shoot out and attach to the target. At that point, the person's immobilized and loses muscle control."

"So you're saying Blair was murdered." A wave of nausea swept over Skye.

"I'm saying it's a strong possibility, and we need to treat it as such." Wally reached for his cell and dialed. "I'm calling in the crime-scene techs. Will you go meet them at the door, darlin'?"

"As soon as I finish throwing up."

CHAPTER 8

FWIW—For What It's Worth

Huddled under a blanket, sipping oversugared tea, Skye sat in the principal's office watching Charlie and Homer argue. Her eyes kept drifting closed, only to jerk awake as her chin sagged forward onto her chest. It was seven thirty in the morning, her head was pounding, and even though neither man was paying any attention to her suggestions or requests, they wouldn't let her leave the room.

After announcing that he suspected Blair was murdered, Wally had called in several of his officers. Once they'd arrived and placed crime-scene tape over the doors to the gym, locker rooms, and pool area, Skye had finally been allowed to contact Charlie. Homer hadn't answered his home phone and he refused to own a cell, so Charlie had called the district superintendent. Dr. Wraige had declared that it was the principal's decision whether or not to close the school, and they would just have to wait until they located him to find out what he wanted to do.

By the time the principal was tracked down, having breakfast at the Feed Bag, most of the faculty had already attempted to enter the building. They had all been turned away by the officer securing the school's entrance. They were currently milling around on the front sidewalk, using their cell phones to spread what little news they had gleaned from the police.

Now, as Homer and Charlie debated the pros and cons of calling off school, some of the more rural students, who were picked up as much as an hour before the first bell rang, were already on their buses en route to the school.

Calls from worried parents were flooding into the school's answering machine, and the continual ringing of the telephone in the outer office was not helping Skye's headache one little bit. When she refocused on the two quarreling men, she saw that, evidently, Charlie had won the dispute, because he was grinning and had appropriated Homer's chair and desk to make some phone calls.

Homer stomped over to Skye and declared, "Since the cops have only cordoned off the gym, and some of the little brats are already on their way to school, and the teachers are sitting on their butts in the parking lot, we're opening for business as usual." He jerked his thumb at Charlie and said, "According to our esteemed board president and local meteorologist, the weather is supposed to be halfway decent today, so PE classes will be held outdoors and the kids will wear their street clothes."

"What about crisis intervention?" Skye wrinkled her brow. "Both the staff and students will be upset when they hear about Blair's death."

"Wally tells me that the police are keeping the victim's identity quiet until they can notify her next of kin." Charlie covered the receiver with his hand and answered the question Skye had directed to Homer.

"Like that's going to happen." A stubborn look settled on Skye's features. "You know darn well that someone will leak that info."

"That's your husband's problem, not ours." Charlie ended his telephone conversation and crossed his arms. "Cell phones aren't allowed to be used in school, so even if the gossip mill finds out, no one in this building except the three of us should know."

"Right." Skye got up and stretched. "Someone is bound to sneak a peek at their phone and see a text from an anxious parent or spouse."

"Collect all the phones before classes start." Charlie leaned his elbows on the desk. "That way no one can break the rules."

"Except those who don't turn in their cells." Skye rolled her eyes. "And can you imagine the mess trying to give them all back at the end of the day would be?" She glanced at Homer. "Who's going to do that?"

"Good questions." Homer rubbed his neck. "Any suggestions, Mr. President?"

"You'll figure it out." Charlie rose, marched to the door, and said to Skye, "Now, quit arguing with me and do as I told you."

"I wasn't arguing," she protested. "I was just explaining why I'm right."

"Well, stop it." Charlie kissed the top of her head. "I gotta get back to the motel." He owned and operated the Up A Lazy River Motor Court. Waving, he said, "Call me if you need me."

Homer waited until Charlie marched out the door and was out of sight, then stated, "Next time we're screwing things up my way."

"Okay." Skye lengthened the word. Did Homer know what he'd just said? Mentally shrugging, she suggested, "Instead of trying to make this a big secret, which will only stir up rumors, let's make an announcement during homeroom that there was a fatal accident and the police are trying to figure out what happened." She flipped open her notepad. "That should be enough for today, but tomorrow, once everyone knows it's Blair and that she was murdered, we need to have a crisis strategy in place."

"That's your job." Homer reclaimed his desk. "If you can't handle it, call the special ed co-op. We certainly pay them a fortune for their 'expertise.'" He put air quotes around his last word. "We might as well get something for our money."

"You know darn well the special ed coordinator

won't come out here or allocate resources on just my say-so." She was cranky and itchy and had had enough. "I'll put together a plan, but you need to make a call and tell him I'm acting with your authority."

"Fine." Homer ignored her bad temper. "But don't go crazy with power."

"I'll try to control myself," Skye muttered. Suddenly the lights went on, and she said, "It looks as if the electricity is back."

"Cameron must have figured out what was wrong." Homer stuck a finger in his ear and dug around. "ConEd claimed there were no problems on their end."

"Hmm." Skye scrunched up her face and mused, "I wonder if the killer somehow sabotaged the power supply, hoping that would interfere with any investigation."

"I'm not convinced Blair was murdered." Homer glowered. "I know you're like the grim reaper of Scumble River and tend to find homicidal maniacs wherever you go, but occasionally an accident does happen."

"But . . ." Wally wasn't releasing the details, so she trailed off without explaining about the Taser wounds. Instead she said, "The coroner has ruled it a suspicious death and the police are treating it as a murder investigation, so I wouldn't count on it being an accident. You need to let the police know about the electricity."

"Sure." Homer waved her away. "Now, go let the staff into the building and tell them that our little darlings will be arriving on schedule."

"After I do that and call to let Neva know I won't be at the junior high today, I'm going home to take a shower and put on something more appropriate." Skye glanced down. "Once I get out of this sweat suit and wash the chlorine off, I'll be more able to function."

"You'll have to make up the time," Homer warned. "Or I'm docking you an hour."

"Be my guest." Skye took her keys from her purse and moved toward the door. "I'll submit an overtime claim the next time an IEP conference runs late."

"Hey." Homer glared. "If I had my way, those meetings wouldn't last more than fifteen minutes. After that, all we're doing is rehashing the obvious and listening to the parents bitch and moan."

"What we have to say regarding their children is hard for many folks to hear. They need an opportunity to process it and ask some questions." Skye knew she was wasting her breath with Homer, but she felt the need to defend the parents involved in the often emotional and always complicated special education procedures. "I'll be back in an hour or so." As she left, she said, "Call me if all hell breaks loose while I'm gone."

"You'll be the first to know." Homer waved her away, then added, "On your way out, tell Opal to go over to Tales and Treats and get me a couple of sweet rolls. I didn't get to finish my breakfast before your godfather dragged me out of the restaurant, and my blood sugar is dropping."

Once Skye showered, dressed, and ate a couple of saltines to appease her churning stomach, she returned to the high school and headed for the faculty lounge to gauge the mood of the staff. There was a lot of curiosity as to what had happened at the pool and who had died, but no one seemed distressed. And none of the teachers Skye spoke with reported noticing any troubled or upset students.

Skye spent the rest of the day mostly sequestered in her office, working on a crisis plan and coordinating with the social workers and psychologists from the county special ed co-op. Both while patrolling the hallways during passing periods and on her occasional revisits of the teachers' lounge, she observed that the day seemed to progress in a fairly typical manner. Wally had told Skye that he planned to ask Simon to put Blair into a body bag before he allowed anyone else into the pool area. He'd also requested that the deceased be driven directly to the county hospital and turned over to the medical examiner.

Evidently, the security measures had been successful, because when the dismissal bell rang at 3:25, the identity of the victim was still unknown. Skye was sure the information embargo wouldn't last more than a day at most. Someone at the ME's office was bound to blab, and all it would take was one leak before everyone in town knew the victim was Blair Hucksford. And soon after that, they'd learn she'd been murdered.

Luckily for Wally's plan, there were several teachers out sick, so Blair's absence didn't raise a red flag with anyone. Overhearing Blair's boyfriend, Thor, remark that it was odd she hadn't called him to tell him she was going to take the day off, Skye had quickly hinted that it might be that time of the month for Blair. Thor had turned red, muttered his understanding, and fled the faculty lounge so fast he nearly knocked over Opal, who had been just entering the room.

Skye smiled at the recollection of the physical education teacher's hasty retreat, then glanced at her locked office door. She had put out the DO NOT DISTURB sign, which the staff knew meant she was unavailable except for an emergency. She'd been reluctant to cut herself off from the faculty, but one of the most difficult parts of Skye's day had been dodging Trixie.

Her friend would want all the details the police were currently keeping confidential. Ever since Trixie had decided to write a mystery, the budding novelist had been fascinated by all things criminal. Rather than having to refuse to answer her BFF's questions, Skye had taken the coward's way out and avoided her.

It was relatively easy to evade the librarian during the school day. The tricky part would be getting to her car without Trixie nabbing her. Skye would have to try to slip out the back door.

But before she left, she wanted to see if Wally planned to be home at his regular time. She picked up the receiver and dialed his private line, and as she listened to the telephone ring, it occurred to her how easily she and Wally had slipped into the roles of wife and husband.

There were some aspects that still felt a little odd, but waking up every morning with him beside her and drifting off to sleep in his arms was heavenly. Just his presence in the house was strangely comforting. Even when he wasn't in the same room with her, she loved hearing his music playing or his footsteps overhead while she relaxed in the sunroom.

"Hello?" Wally's silky baritone brought her back to the present.

"Hi, sweetie." Skye flipped open her calendar and asked, "Do you need me at the station this afternoon for the Hucksford case?"

"Not yet." Wally's voice was strained. "Until the ME and crime-scene tech's preliminary reports are in, there's nothing much to do. Once we get those, I'll have a better idea where to aim the investigation."

"Speaking of the CST, are they still processing the gym?" Skye noted the appointments she needed to cancel for tomorrow and closed the planner.

"They called and told me that they finished about twenty minutes ago," Wally answered. "The gym, locker rooms, and pool area are once again available for the school's use."

"Good." Skye sent Homer a quick e-mail as she asked, "Do you know if you'll be working late?"

"I doubt it." Wally sighed. "Best-case scenario, the ME and CST get back to me tomorrow, but it could be the day after or even longer. I hate not being able to do more while the trail is fresh, but I don't want to talk to the vic's friends or colleagues until after I get ahold of her parents."

"You haven't reached them yet?" Skye asked.

Holding the receiver between her ear and shoulder, she sent e-mails to the elementary and junior high principals informing them of the high school emergency and of her absence from their buildings the next day. Both women would be unhappy, and she fully expected a call or two of complaint. Each principal thought her school deserved the majority of Skye's time and attention.

"I had to leave a voice mail," Wally said. "Blair's emergency contact number in the school's file turned out to be a landline."

"And both parents probably work." Skye gathered her things. It was time to make a run for her car. "Blair was in her late twenties, so her folks might only be in their midforties or early fifties."

"Right." Wally spoke to someone, then said, "I've got to go. I'll call you if I'm going to be later than five thirty. Love you."

"Love you, too." Skye smiled, absurdly pleased that Wally had started to end all their conversations by declaring his affection. "Bye."

Skye hefted her tote bag over her shoulder, turned off the lights, and slipped into the deserted hallway. It was nearly half past four, and the teachers were allowed to leave at 3:35. There must not have been any after-school activities or detentions today, because the corridor was empty and the building was silent.

By heading out the back exit, she was able to avoid passing the library, so if Trixie was still around, she wouldn't see her. Skye warily looked both ways as she stepped outside. Once she was on the grass, she hurried toward her car, rummaging through her purse as she walked.

Heck! She should have had the keys in her hand before she left her office. *Ah.* There they were. Triumphantly, she fished the ring from the bottom of her bag, lifted her head, and shrieked.

"Surprised to see me?" Trixie stood, blocking Skye from the T-bird.

"What are you doing here?" Skye glanced around. Trixie's Honda wasn't anywhere near where Skye had parked. "Are you having car trouble?"

"Nope." Trixie poked Skye in the chest. "I'm having friend trouble."

"Oh." Skye backed up. "I have no idea to what you're referring."

"Sure you don't." Trixie snickered. "I can always tell when you have a guilty conscience because you suddenly start using impeccable grammar."

"Are you saying that I usually don't speak well?" Skye edged around her pal, opened the driver's door, and threw her tote bag and purse on the passenger seat. "I'll have you know that I minored in English and never received less than an A in those classes."

"Don't try to change the subject." Trixie grabbed Skye's arm before she could slip into the car. "You're not getting away that easily."

"Sorry." Skye shook off her friend's hand. "But I really have to run."

"Not so fast." Trixie threw herself between Skye and the T-bird.

"I'll see you tomorrow." Skye hip-checked her BFF. At times like this, being taller and heavier than the tiny librarian came in handy.

"You're not leaving until you talk to me." Trixie moved behind the car.

"Seriously, I need to leave," Skye stalled,

wondering if there was room to drive forward instead of backing out of the space.

"I hear Blair Hucksford was murdered." Trixie smiled in triumph and hopped on the trunk. She patted the blue metal surface next to her and said, "Sit down and tell me everything."

CHAPTER 9

FAQ—Frequently Asked Questions

S on of a buck!" Wally's frustration hissed through the Thunderbird's interior like a drop of oil on a hot cast-iron pan.

Skye held her cell phone away from her ear, waiting for him to stop swearing and calm down. As soon as she'd escaped from Trixie's interrogation, she'd driven into town, parked, and immediately phoned Wally—who was now ranting about loose lips sinking ships.

Dodging most of Trixie's questions, Skye had admitted only to finding Blair's body and being the one to call 911. Since she had no idea who wanted Blair dead or why the teacher was killed, she had been able to honestly tell her BFF that she didn't have any inside knowledge about the murder.

Oops! Wally had finally stopped cursing, and there was now an ominous silence coming from her phone, so Skye quickly said, "According to Trixie, no one else knows about Blair, and I pinkie swore her to secrecy. But I thought I'd better warn you that there was a leak, and to be prepared."

"How on God's green earth did she find out the victim's identity?"

"Apparently, in the name of research for the book she's writing, Trixie has cozied up to the ME's administrative assistant, aka his wife."

Skye was sitting in front of the dry cleaner's, and as she talked to Wally, she watched a woman maneuvering a gigantic stroller over the business's threshold and through the narrow doorway. The baby's screams could be heard through the T-bird's closed windows.

Putting her hand on her stomach, she wrinkled her brow. Although she'd considered many aspects of motherhood, she'd never really thought about the everyday difficulties of navigating life completely responsible for another human being's every need. Suddenly it seemed like a really tough job, and she wasn't sure she was up to the challenge.

"Don't that just beat all?" Wally interrupted Skye's thoughts. "You buy 'em books and you buy 'em books and they're still so ignorant they just chew on the covers."

Skye's lips quirked upward. She loved it when her husband reverted to his roots and started speaking like the Texas boy he was at heart.

"I'm about to put a rattlesnake in that doc's pocket and ask him for a quarter." Wally ground his teeth so loudly Skye could hear it. "All those precautions and we're done in by pillow talk."

"On the good-news front, when Mrs. ME phoned Trixie, she had just finished typing her husband's preliminary report." Skye tried to cheer up Wally. "Once her husband signed off on it, she planned to send the report to you right away. Have you checked your e-mail recently?"

"Not in the last half hour." Wally paused, and Skye could hear the clicking sound of him typing on his computer keyboard. A few seconds later, he said, "Yep. It's here."

"That's a relief." Skye dug through her purse, looking for the receipt for her dry cleaning. "Have Blair's parents contacted you yet?"

"No." Wally grunted. "But they live in California, so they're two hours behind us. It's only two forty-five there, which means they're probably not home from work yet. I left my cell number on their machine because I didn't want to have to hang around the PD, waiting for them to call me."

"Good." Skye got out of the Ford. "Then I'll let you go so that you can read the ME's report." \ She walked across the sidewalk and through the Clean Bee's door. Just before clicking off her cell, she said, "I'm running some errands, but I'll see you at home about five thirty."

Warm solvent-scented air washed over her as

Skye entered the dry cleaner's. She got into the back of the line and looked around. It was the after-work rush, and five customers were in front of her. As she waited, she mindlessly stared at the back of the guy directly ahead of her. After a couple of minutes, she noticed that the white printing on his black T-shirt was superimposed over a bright red volleyball and read, SCUMBLE RIVER STILETTOS. 2006 CLASS 5A CHAMPIONS.

The man was in his early forties, wearing jeans and a baseball cap. Skye chewed her thumbnail. She was fairly certain that the championship shirts weren't widely available for sale, which meant that he was probably a parent of one of the players. She tilted her head, considering. Or at least a big supporter of the team.

Noting that the line was stalled by a woman who couldn't find her receipt or, apparently, even remember exactly what clothing she'd brought in to be cleaned, Skye managed to catch Mr. T-shirt's eye and said, "Gee, I sure hope this doesn't take too long. I stayed late at school to get some work done and now I'm running behind schedule."

"Are you a teacher at the high school? I don't think I've seen you at the PTO meetings." He smiled. "My daughter's a junior."

"I'm the district psychologist." Skye fished a card from the outer pocket of her purse and handed it to him. "I work at all three buildings."

"Ah. That's why we haven't met." The man shook his head. "My Roxy hasn't needed your services. She's well-adjusted, and she always makes the honor roll."

"Grades like those are quite an accomplishment. You must be thrilled for her." Skye pointed to his shirt. "And I'm guessing she's also on the volleyball team."

"She's the captain." He hitched up his pants and beamed proudly. "She's up for a scholarship at Southwest Illinois University."

"Wow! That's terrific." Skye nodded enthusiastically, then asked, "Are there any other schools besides SWIU interested in her?"

"No. She was lucky to get noticed by that one." He rubbed the back of his neck. "There aren't too many volleyball scholarships for women. The men's athletic programs get all the money."

"How did SWIU discover her?" Skye doubted Scumble River High School's athletes were on too many college scouts' must-see list.

"Her coach went to school there and knew someone." He was starting to look at Skye as if wondering why she was asking so many questions. "We were lucky that Ms. Hucksford came to Scumble River, or Roxy might never have had the opportunity."

"How long has she been coaching?" Skye knew Blair had been at the high school for a few years, but she wasn't sure when the teacher had taken over the volleyball team. "I haven't had much interaction with Ms. Hucksford."

"This is her second year." He noticed that the line had moved and edged forward. "Ms. H has done an amazing job with those girls."

"Oh. Wasn't the team very good before?" Skye wished she knew more about the sport. "How did Ms. Hucksford improve their performance?"

"Well . . ." The guy shoved his hands in his back pockets, his expression guarded. "There were a couple of very talented players—Roxy and Keely Peterson, to name names—but the problem was that none of them had team spirit until Ms. Hucksford took over."

"That's impressive," Skye said, glad that Blair's death hadn't yet been made public. No way would this guy talk as freely about the volleyball coach if he knew she'd been murdered. "And I imagine not easy to achieve."

"Exactly." His eyes shifted away from Skye for a moment, but when he looked back, he said, "Some of the parents couldn't accept the time and commitment that accomplishing that goal took."

"Interesting," Skye said, starting to get a glimmer of an idea.

"Looks like it's my turn." He stepped up to the counter and said, "Nice talking to you. You should come to a game next year."

"I'll sure try to." Skye smiled. "Lovely chatting with you, too."

After Roxy's father completed his transaction, took his plastic-wrapped clothes, and left, Skye stepped up and handed the clerk her receipt. While she waited for the woman to locate Wally's uniforms on the revolving rack, Skye thought about how nice it was to hear something positive about Blair. Maybe the other teachers hadn't liked her, but at least one volleyball parent had been a big fan of the dead woman. Someone in Scumble River would mourn her.

Skye stood in the master bathroom, luxuriating under the soothing spray of the newly installed eight-inch rainfall showerhead. It was her second shower today, but the first one had been more of a hurried rinse so she could get back to school than a true scrub. She had plenty of time. Wally had phoned to tell her he wouldn't be home until six thirty.

When her fingers started to prune, she stepped out of the stall, toweled off, and reached for the moisturizer. Still feeling itchy from her recent coatings of caked-on chlorine, she applied and reapplied the lotion until her skin was shiny and slick.

As Skye dried her curls, a little voice carped at her. Should she bow out of this investigation? Although her doctor had assured her that going back into the pool to bring Blair to the surface hadn't put the baby at any risk, Skye still felt guilty. The nagging voice in her head sounded a lot like her mother's, but maybe she should listen anyway.

While mentally debating her participation in the case, she finished styling her hair, then applied bronzer and mascara. Wally would understand if she chose not to work this case. Heck, he might even encourage her to sit out this one. But did she really want to turn into that kind of woman?

She wiggled into a pair of black jeans—thankful for the touch of spandex when she could barely zip them. Flipping through the hangers in her closet, she chose a ballet pink knit top that displayed her amplified cleavage to its full advantage. She usually greeted Wally wearing sweats and sporting a ponytail, but he'd had a rough day and deserved a little treat.

Hearing the sound of the front door closing, she hurriedly slipped on her pink Coach flats. Then she stole an additional second to put on lipstick and take one last glance in the mirror before going to greet her new husband. After passing her own inspection, she flew down the steps, into the foyer, and rushed up to Wally.

Her welcoming smile faded a little as she noted his exhaustion. Although he was only an hour later than usual, the poor guy was obviously dog-tired. She reined in her out-of-control hormones. *Heck!* Wally was forty-four. She didn't want her pregnancy lust to kill him. Clearly this wasn't the best time to seduce him or, for that matter, to discuss her reservations about continuing her role as the PD's psych consultant.

Wally silently shed his jacket, hung it and his gun belt on the foyer's coatrack, then said, "It seems like years since I kissed you good-bye this morning at the pool." Without waiting for her response, he swept her into his arms and added in a lower, huskier tone, "Dang it. I miss you so much when we're apart."

As his mouth claimed hers, Skye caught a glimpse of his expression. Passion and something she couldn't quite read swirled together in his deep brown eyes. Was it apprehension? But why would he be uneasy? Unless, of course, his concern was about the case.

Mentally shrugging—she'd figure it out later—Skye twined her arms around his neck and buried her hands in his thick black hair. She loved the crisp feeling of the strands as they feathered through her fingers. His lips sent her heart into a wild disco beat, and she pressed herself closer, reveling in the sensations he aroused.

Wally deepened the kiss, his tongue stroking hers. He tasted sweeter than her favorite chocolate-dipped shortbread cookie, and she wanted to gobble him up. She forgot about the murder, the baby, and all her other qualms, and enjoyed the moment.

Wally's fingers were cold as his hands crept under the hem of her shirt, and she shivered. But his touch immediately warmed up when he unhooked her bra and cupped her breasts. She ran her palms down his back, stroking the muscles and dipping below his waistband. She had no idea how long they stood there, absorbed in each other, but when they finally broke the kiss, both of them were gasping for breath.

He wrapped an arm around her waist and started to guide her toward the stairs, but when his stomach let out a loud growl, Skye stopped and raised an inquiring eyebrow at him. He twitched his shoulders, denying his hunger, and tried again to lead her up the steps. But when his stomach rumbled a second time, Skye refused to budge. She turned and shoved him in the direction of the kitchen.

"Did you eat today?" Skye asked as she pushed him into a chair.

"I didn't have time to go out and pick up anything," Wally said. "And I left here this morning without packing a lunch. But I had a can of root beer from the machine and a couple sticks of beef jerky."

"Why didn't you ask someone to go through Mickey D's drive-through for you?" Skye asked, opening the refrigerator and examining their options for supper. Too bad this wasn't a Dorothy day.

"You know I don't like to take advantage of my position as chief."

"I didn't propose that you order an underling to pick up your dry cleaning—'cause I did that." Skye brought Wally a bottle of Sam Adams. "Just ask a friend for a favor. Or even call Mom. She brings Vince lunch every day at his hair salon. I'm sure she'd be thrilled to feed you, too. Heck, once she knows I'm pregnant, maybe she'll add me to her list of meals-on-wheels beneficiaries."

"You must be hungry, too, or feeling light-headed." Wally twisted off the beer cap and took a healthy swig. "Because you have to be pretty woozy to suggest involving May in our lives even more than she already is. I thought our goal was to keep our independence."

"You're right." Skye scrunched up her face. "I just hate the thought of you going hungry." She wandered over to the pantry. After examining the nearly empty shelves, she turned to him and said, "Our choices for dinner are leftovers from last night, an omelet, or frozen pizza."

"Leftovers." Wally took another swallow of beer. "That'll be the quickest."

"Okay." Skye returned to the fridge, removed a glass casserole dish, and popped it into the microwave. "Tomorrow I'll try to get to the supermarket after work. But whether or not I have time depends how the kids and staff react to the news of Blair's murder."

"I'd do it, but I doubt that I'll have a chance, either." Wally got up and started to set the table. "Why don't we draw up a list and have Dorothy do the grocery shopping? She'd probably be happy to earn a little extra cash. We can even ask her to make dinner."

"Well . . ." Skye filled a glass with ice and caffeine-free Diet Coke. "Let me think about it."

She was torn. They were both extremely busy, and having Dorothy help them out would be marvelous, but Skye wasn't used to having discretionary income. Seven years ago, when she'd returned to Scumble River, she'd been beyond broke. Having made several foolish decisions that had maxed out her credit cards, she'd been deeply in debt. The only thing standing between her and living out of her car had been the generosity of her family. She'd worked hard and scrimped to pay off her obligations, but that fear of losing everything again hadn't gone away.

Now that she and Wally had combined salaries, they were comfortable and could afford a few luxuries. In fact, they could actually have almost anything they wanted, because although no one from Scumble River knew it, Wally's father was a millionaire. And Wally's mother had left him a hefty trust fund when she died. Skye had only recently found out about his affluence herself.

Because he wanted his wealthy background and hefty bank account to remain a secret, Wally had always been careful to live within his means. And if anyone noticed that his father seemed to have more money than he should, the story that Wally had carefully spread around town was that Carson Boyd's boss was a very generous billionaire.

It was probably silly to refuse the help, and after the baby came she'd need even more, but—the microwave beeped, interrupting Skye's inner debate. Taking out their meal, she put the dish on the table and Wally fetched the salad. As they sat down to eat, Skye still hadn't made a decision.

Digging in to their dinner, Skye felt a warm body press against her calf. Glancing down, she saw that Bingo had mysteriously appeared out of nowhere and was gazing up at her with a pitiful expression of hunger on his furry little face. She snickered and said to the cat, "You've already had your supper."

"It's the law of dinner-table attendance." Wally chuckled. "Cats must be present at any meal where there is anything even remotely appetizing being served."

"Well, Bingo's not getting any scraps." Skye shook her finger at the beseeching feline. "His vet says he's gaining weight again and somebody must be feeding him extra." She tilted her head at Wally. "Either it's you or Dorothy, because it isn't me."

"I plead the Fifth." Wally kept his eyes focused on his plate.

"Tell that to the veterinarian at Bingo's next checkup." Skye ate a couple of bites, then asked, "Did Blair's folks ever return your call?"

"Yes. Just as I was leaving the station, which is why I was late."

"When are they flying out here to pick up their daughter's body?" Skye asked.

"They aren't." Wally shook his head. "It seems they were estranged from Blair. Once the ME releases her, they'll arrange her burial, but that's it."

"Oh." Skye put down her fork. The polenta had formed a lump in her stomach. "Did they say what happened to make them feel that way?"

"They refused to discuss it. All they would say was that her actions had forced them to disown her."

CHAPTER 10

TMI—Too Much Information

After they'd eaten, Wally went upstairs to change out of his uniform, and now, as he entered the sunroom where Skye was sitting, she asked, "What in the world did she do?"

"Who?" While they cleaned up the kitchen, their conversation had turned to family and household matters, so at her abrupt question, Wally looked puzzled.

"Blair." Skye chewed the inside of her cheek. "I've been trying to think of what I could possibly do that would make my parents not only disown me, but refuse to bring my body back home."

"All Mr. Hucksford would say was that his daughter's behavior was unacceptable to them."

"Hmm." Skye thought about all that statement could imply. "What do Mr. and Mrs. Hucksford do for a living?"

When Wally headed for his recliner, Skye tugged him down onto the settee and cuddled against the soft fabric of his T-shirt, inhaling the scent of Downy.

"He's the principal of Hucksford Christian Academy and she's the kindergarten teacher," Wally said. "Blair's sister, Bernadette, is the school secretary, and her husband is the PE instructor."

"So it's a family endeavor." Skye pursed her lips. "Maybe the estrangement was because Blair took a job at a different school."

"That would be a fairly extreme reaction to a career choice."

"Maybe not." Skye held up her index finger. "First, taking the Scumble River job meant she lived thousands of miles away from home." Skye added another finger. "Second, she chose to work in a secular versus religious school, which, depending on her parents' beliefs, might be reason enough to shun her." Skye wiggled three fingers at him. "And last, she . . . ah, fine, I don't have a third reason, but I still think her teaching at Scumble River High versus Hucksford Christian Academy is important."

"Possibly," Wally conceded, but he sounded far from convinced. "Would you be up to calling Blair's sister, Bernadette, to see if you can get her to tell you why her parents renounced Blair?"

"Sure." Skye laid her head on his shoulder. "Do you have her number?"

"It's upstairs in my shirt pocket." Wally put his arm around Skye. "I'll put it in your purse before we go to bed tonight."

"Was there anything in the medical examiner's preliminary report that might help the investigation?" Skye had held off discussing the case until Wally was fed and had had a chance to relax, but he appeared okay now.

"Not that I could see right off." Wally scraped his hand over his face, clearly discouraged. "The ME concurs with Reid's estimation that the vic died Monday night sometime between eleven and midnight—give or take a little on either end, since we aren't sure how fast the pool cooled off after the power outage."

"That reminds me of something I wanted to ask you but forgot to mention when I called you after school," Skye said. "Did Homer tell you that ConEd claimed there were no problems on their end?"

"No." Wally frowned. "Knapik never spoke to

me at all. As far as I know, he didn't have any contact with the police or the techs."

"Even though he said he would, I was afraid he wouldn't bother to inform you since, when I brought it up to him, he insisted the information wasn't important. But it made me wonder if the killer somehow monkeyed with the electricity, hoping that would interfere with any investigation."

"Son of a buck! Homer Knapik is a useless piece of crap. That could be a vital piece of the puzzle." Wally leaned forward and searched around the coffee table until he found a pen among the clutter scattered across the glass top. He rummaged through the flotsam and jetsam until Skye reached into a magazine rack by her side of the love seat and handed him a legal pad. Flipping to a clean page, he smiled and said, "Thanks for checking up on Knapik, darlin'. You always know exactly what I need."

"I try." Skye smiled fondly at the man she loved more each day that she was married to him. She was so fortunate to have made the right choice of husbands.

Wally scribbled, then said, "The problem with finding any forensics in the gym/locker room/pool area is that unless the murderer is someone who has no business in the school, their prints and DNA have a legitimate reason for being in those places."

"But only the custodian has any reason to be in the boiler room."

"Exactly." Wally nodded. "I need to call the crime-scene techs and get them over to the school ASAP, before any evidence that might be there is lost." He got up to use the telephone in the kitchen. Cell reception was poor in the big old house. "I'll be right back. Do you want anything?"

"No." Skye shook her head. "I'm still full from supper." She hesitated. "Well, maybe some ice cream." As he took a couple of steps, she added, "With some caramel sauce . . . and whipped cream."

His laughter floated back toward her as he walked away. While she waited for her dessert, she thought about how lucky she was. She'd never expected to find such a wonderful guy or to be this happy.

Picking up the remote, she turned on the television to see tomorrow's weather forecast. Just as the meteorologist appeared on the screen, Bingo leaped onto the TV stand. Skye got up and nudged him, but the big black cat refused to budge. She tried to push him aside, but he dug his back claws into the wood.

She was still trying to shove the cat out of the way when Wally returned with two dishes of ice cream. He grinned at her efforts and asked, "What's going on?"

"Bingo is blocking the television." Skye gave

up, clicked off the TV, and took a seat next to her husband.

Wally handed Skye her bowl, then dug into his. As he ate, he looked from where the unperturbed feline was sitting with his hind leg extended straight into the air while he washed his nether regions and said, "Darlin', I'm pretty dang sure that Mr. Cat doesn't think he's blocking the view. He thinks he *is* the view."

"You're probably right." Skye laughed, then asked, "Anything else from the ME's report? Trixie didn't have any specifics, or at least none she admitted to knowing."

"Cause of death is drowning, but the chlorine would have washed away any other physical evidence, so there wasn't much to go on." Wally blew out a frustrated breath. "There were some gouges in the vic's scalp. The ME's working theory is that at some point after being Tasered, Blair regained some muscle control, at least enough for her to make her way to the surface of the pool. And at that point, the killer held her head under the water until she stopped struggling."

"Was she raped?" Skye's stomach clenched at the thought, but she had to ask. "Or would the chlorine make it impossible to tell?"

"You're thinking because she was there so late that she was with someone," Wally said.

"Yes." Skye wrinkled her brow. "Maybe a date that went wrong."

"There were no signs of forced sex. No tearing or bruising," Wally said in a clinical tone. "And any evidence of consensual intercourse would have been lost because she was in the water so long. First thing tomorrow I'll be checking to see if the boyfriend has an alibi and if their relationship was exclusive."

"Today at school, Thor seemed worried about her." Skye told Wally what the physical education teacher had said about Blair's absence.

"Did he seem sincere?" Wally put down his empty ice cream bowl and made another note, then looked at Skye and asked, "Or did the guy seem more like he was trying to establish his innocence?"

"Hmm." She tapped her chin. "He seemed sincere at the time."

"Anything else you overheard or noticed at the school today?"

"Not today." Skye savored the last bite of caramel-covered ice cream. "But according to Trixie, Blair wasn't very popular with most of the other staff. Some of the faculty disliked her because she poached kids from their sports teams, and others weren't fond of her because of her abrasive personality." Skye hesitated, then added, "Again, according to Trixie, some parents had problems with Blair, too. And she never ate lunch in the teachers' lounge."

"That's good info. Since we wanted to keep the

victim's identity a secret, we weren't able to question the teachers today about Blair. I'm sure tomorrow, when we start interviewing her colleagues, we'll get an earful." Wally smiled as he wrote down Skye's observations. "Any idea what the parents' issues with the vic might have been?"

"When I stopped at the Clean Bee," Skye said, tilting her head, "I had an interesting conversation about that with the man in front of me in line. His daughter's the captain of the volleyball team, and he gave me an earful about Blair and the other parents."

"Seriously?" Wally chuckled. "You really have to love a small town."

"Well, I'm not sure how helpful this will be, but the man mentioned that Blair had really turned the volleyball team around." Skye's face lit up. "It was nice hearing something positive about Blair, since my own experience with her was so negative."

"What did this guy say about the parents who didn't like her?" Wally asked.

"All he said was that even though she'd improved the team's performance, some folks were unhappy with her methods because she demanded so much of the girls' time." Skye twitched her shoulders. "But my guess is that in addition to that issue, there were parents whose daughters got cut from the team who were unhappy with her decisions. Especially since I sincerely doubt she was nice when she informed the girls they hadn't made the squad."

"Sounds a lot like my experience playing baseball and football in high school." Wally rolled his eyes. "Parents can be extremely competitive about their kids' participation in sports."

"So I hear." Skye made a face, then used her finger to get the last of the whipped cream from the bottom of her dish. Catching Wally's amused look, she blushed and put the empty bowl next to his.

"It's really helpful having you in the school, where you can gather information. What you've told me tonight might be the lead we need to find the killer." Wally went back to making notes. "At least now we have somewhere to start the investigation."

This was it. Skye needed to talk to him about her worries. She cleared her throat and said, "I've been thinking about whether or not I should change some things now that I'm pregnant."

"Oh." Wally put down the notepad he'd been using, turned toward her, and kissed her on the cheek. "What kind of changes are you thinking about making?"

"Like maybe I should take a leave of absence from the PD until after I have the baby." She rested her palm on her stomach. "I don't want to do anything that might be a risk for Juniorette."

"Of course not. And I don't want you to either." He stroked her belly with his fingers. "You need to do whatever makes you comfortable."

"I called my doctor this afternoon," Skye confessed. "She said that bringing up Blair's body from the pool and doing CPR didn't endanger the baby. She said it was okay for me to continue with all my normal activities."

"That's great." Wally caressed her jaw with his thumb. "Calling her was a good idea."

"Do you think I shouldn't take part in this investigation?" Skye looked at him from under her lashes, trying to gauge his reaction. "It's your baby, too, so you should have an equal vote."

"Pregnant or not pregnant, I never want to see you in danger."

"I know." Skye kept her face down so he couldn't read the uncertainty in her eyes. "And I appreciate how you've always tried to keep me safe, without smothering me or being over-protective."

"But I don't think it's in your nature to be indifferent to others' problems." Wally cupped her cheek. "You need to help people. To be involved in life. Neither of us wants to go down that slippery slope of becoming a helicopter parent or turning into your mother. We'll just make sure that you have plenty of help with the baby. Maybe hire a nanny."

"Maybe, but I'm not ready to think about that

yet. Once we announce that I'm pregnant, we can figure out the rest." Skye turned her face and kissed his palm. This was a big part of why she knew she loved Wally and not Simon and why she had married him. Simon's insistence that she be as coldly logical as he was drove her nuts. Wally accepted her for who she was, with no desire to change her, and that made her feel cherished.

When she didn't speak, Wally continued. "Regarding your role as psych consultant to the PD, how about we play it by ear? Do only what you're comfortable with on this case. Take a pass on anything that makes you nervous without any feelings of guilt."

"That sounds good." She could barely force the words past the lump in her throat. Wally was so sweet. He always knew what to say and how to say it to comfort her. She smiled and tried to lighten the moment. "But I'm Catholic, so I always feel guilty."

"Not a totally bad thing." Wally grinned. "Keeps you on the right path."

"You are so not funny." Skye whacked him on the arm, then turned serious and said, "Making calls and keeping my ears open at school is no problem. I just don't want to get into a situation with a suspect that might turn physical or get out of control."

"We'll just make sure to do any suspect

interviews I'd like your help with at the PD." Wally nestled Skye against his side.

"Good." Skye let out the breath she'd been holding. "I may not have liked Blair very much, but no one should be able to get away with murder."

CHAPTER 11

FYEO—For Your Eyes Only

Seven a.m. the next morning, Skye slid into her Bel Air and pulled out of the garage. Worst luck, the Chevy's faulty lights had been easy to fix. *Darn!* It had taken her father only a couple of hours to find the short and repair it, so she was once again forced to use her own car. After tooling around in Wally's cool T-bird, driving the '57 Bel Air felt like she was maneuvering a float down Fifth Avenue in the Macy's Thanksgiving Day Parade.

On the bright side, she didn't feel nauseated. When she'd woken up, it had taken her a few minutes to realize she wasn't queasy. But after getting out of bed, and for the first time in a couple of months not having to race to the bathroom, she'd felt as if she'd won the lottery. And not a puny scratch-off—the multimillion-dollar Powerball.

Skye wiggled happily on the roomy bench seat of the Bel Air. Maybe the morning sickness was over and she was finally into the glowing part of the pregnancy that she'd read so much about in romance novels.

It was good to have something encouraging happen at the beginning of what would be a tough day. She allowed herself to enjoy the sensation for a few seconds; then her monkey mind whirled into action and she thumped her hand on the steering wheel. *Hell's bells!* She'd forgotten to order the rubber duckies for Trixie's race.

Okay. She'd do it as soon as she got to her office. What else had she overlooked in the aftermath of yesterday's turmoil? Let's see . . . She had an after-school meeting with the student newspaper staff to rope them into helping with the race, but that was it. There wasn't anything more that she'd promised to do for the fund-raiser. Right?

She certainly hoped not. Today was already going to be a busy one without adding any more items to her to-do list. After talking to Blair's parents, Wally had released the identity of the victim and given a brief statement to Kathy Steel, who had hurriedly squeezed the breaking news into today's *Scumble River Star*.

Just their luck that the weekly newspaper came out on Wednesdays and Kathy had been able to get the item in before the issue went to press.

Everyone with a subscription would read about the murder over breakfast. Those folks would immediately phone any friends who didn't get the paper delivered to their doorstep and fill them in on the latest gossip. That meant by now most townspeople knew that Blair was dead and that foul play was suspected.

Thankfully, after a student's death a few years ago, Skye had written up a crisis-intervention procedure. Since before Skye had been hired, neither a social worker nor a psychologist had ever remained in the employment of the Scumble River school district for more than a year, no one had ever bothered to create an emergency plan. At the time of that earlier sad incident, Skye'd had to make it up on the fly. At least now she had a strategy in place to handle the shock and grief of the staff and students.

Both now and during that earlier crisis, Homer saw no need for such an intervention, but then again, he wouldn't. As she had before, Skye insisted on providing services. She'd pointed out that with any deaths associated with the school, many of the students could suffer emotional trauma.

For the majority of kids, it was their first taste of mortality. And although most of the teens would act as if the death didn't bother them, if the situation wasn't handled properly, studies showed that the students would be vulnerable to suicide attempts, substance abuse, and other risk-taking behaviors.

On this occasion, with the passing of a teacher rather than a fellow student, fewer of the kids might be affected by the death. But it was likely that the faculty would be more upset. Even staff members who weren't fond of Blair would probably have a reaction to her passing. Feeling ashamed that they hadn't liked her could be just as hard to deal with as grieving. After all, guilt was almost as powerful an emotion as affection. Maybe stronger.

Skye's current plan was to ask the social worker from the special ed co-op to handle the faculty while she saw the students. She figured that the teachers might be less inhibited with someone they didn't have to face in the lounge every day. And she was definitely more comfortable dealing with the kids. In order to inform anyone who hadn't heard the news about Blair, Homer had agreed to get the teachers together at 7:20. When Skye arrived at school, she had ten minutes to get organized before the meeting, and she didn't want to be late.

Hurrying through the front door, Skye found Risé Vaughn waiting in the lobby, balancing several bright pink-and-orange bakery boxes in her arms. She and her husband, Orlando Erwin, owned Tales and Treats, the local bookstore and café. And although the store didn't usually deliver,

Skye had called Risé and asked her as a special favor to bring over an assortment of pastries for the gathering, figuring that the sugary snacks would help offset the staff's feelings of shock.

After paying the shopkeeper and thanking her for her help, Skye rushed to the home-ec area. The meeting was being held in that classroom because it was one of the few spaces big enough to hold the entire faculty. The other choices were the lunchroom—but students who arrived at school early were seated in that area—and the gym. How-ever, considering that Blair had been murdered in the PE wing, using the gymnasium hadn't seemed like a good idea.

Skye laid out the goodies on a back table, along with the napkins she'd brought from home. Paper plates would have been better, but she didn't have enough on hand and she hadn't made it to the store to buy them.

A lot of the teachers were already assembled, and because she didn't want to answer their questions or start the meeting until everyone had arrived, Skye distracted them with the pastries. She pointed out the varieties and praised Tales and Treats for providing the baked goods on such short notice.

While Skye waited for everyone to select their snack, she suddenly felt her own grief and despair fighting their way to the surface. Her experience with Blair had been negative, but the death of anyone, especially someone who had barely begun her life, was almost too much to bear. Who knew what the young woman might have accomplished or how much she might have grown and changed if she'd had the chance to live to a ripe old age?

Pushing her sorrow away, Skye stepped up to the front of the room and said, "For those of you who haven't heard, there's some sad news that I need to share with you. Blair Hucksford's body was found yesterday morning at the bottom of the pool." There was no reason to announce that she was the one who had found Blair, since that fact hadn't been released. "It has been determined that she died under suspicious circumstances. As of this morning, the police are investigating her death."

Skye waited for the whispers to die down, then resumed the speech she'd rehearsed in front of her bathroom mirror. "If you feel a personal sense of loss and think you can't handle your classes, please let me know immediately. I'll inform Homer, and he'll make other arrangements to cover your absence."

Skye paused, but no one came forward. She had noticed that Thor Goodson was not present, and after Trixie's account of Blair's relationship with the other staff, Skye hadn't expected anyone else to be overcome with grief. Although some of the teachers might feel the need for help dealing with their emotions later, right now there was a good chance they were still processing both the event and their feelings.

Skye continued. "Because we're a small school, when the bell rings to signal the beginning of classes, we'll assemble all the students in the cafeteria. I will announce Blair's death and give the kids what little information we have regarding the circumstances surrounding it. At that point, all teachers should return to their homeroom assignments. Any students who want to talk more about Blair's death will be asked to stay in the cafeteria. The rest will be dismissed to their classes."

Skye added, "As the need arises, kids will be seen in small groups or individually. A social worker from the special ed co-op is scheduled to arrive before the student assembly. He or she will be available exclusively for the staff and will be in the library office."

Most of the teachers looked as numb as Skye felt. One or two had tears rolling down their cheeks. Skye paused to let everyone absorb what she'd said, then asked, "Any questions or concerns?"

"If Blair was murdered, how do we know the rest of us are safe?" Pru Cormorant demanded, narrowing her watery blue eyes. "There might be a serial killer who targets teachers running loose in Scumble River High School."

Skye took a breath before answering. Most of

her interactions with Pru were like being poked in the eye with a sharpened number two pencil. The English teacher regularly sent parents insulting notes—a recent one had included the unforgettable line, "Your child might be an honor student, but you're still an idiot."

Pru had also flat-out refused to have children with special needs in her classes. She was the speech and debate team sponsor and preferred to deal only with the intellectually gifted and extremely motivated students.

Pasting on a fake smile, Skye said, "There is no indication of any risk to the rest of us." She saw that other faculty were now murmuring their concern and assured everyone, "Blair's assault showed no signs of the kind of ritualistic behavior associated with a serial killer." Skye crossed her fingers, hoping the information she'd gleaned from *Criminal Minds* and *CSI* was accurate. "If we were in danger, I'm sure my new husband, *the police chief*"—she didn't hesitate to emphasize Wally's title—"wouldn't have let me go blithely off to work today without an armed escort."

"Now that Chief Boyd has been married to you for several months, I think he might be glad to be rid of you," Pru muttered, raising an overly plucked brow.

"Don't believe everything you think," Skye retorted, then stared at the annoying women.

Finally, Pru ran her fingers through her stringy dun-colored hair, harrumphed, and turned away.

Noting that the rest of the staff appeared to be reassured, Skye dealt with the usual inquiries, such as who should say what to the students. Then she announced, "A letter with information about Blair's death and what the school is doing in response to the tragic event will be sent to all parents this afternoon via e-mail. A duplicate message will go home with the students to ensure that those families without Internet service are also kept informed."

Asking again if there were any more questions, Skye waited while the teachers shuffled their feet and looked at one another. When no one spoke, she dismissed the staff, boxed up the remaining refreshments, took them to the faculty lounge, and hurried to her office.

She had three things she wanted to do before the day started. First, order the doggone rubber ducks before she forgot about them again. Second, find out if the crime-scene techs had found anything of interest in the boiler room. Wally had gone into the PD early to check on the results of the search, and she had just enough time to give him a call. And third, make sure that the co-op social worker had arrived and was ready to see clients.

Ten minutes later, the ducks were ordered and the social worker had been installed in the library office space that he would be using for his counseling sessions, but Skye hadn't been able to reach Wally. He wasn't picking up either his private line or his cell, and she was reluctant to go through the dispatcher. She really didn't *need* to know right away, and if Wally was busy, she didn't want to bother him.

As she hurried toward the lunchroom, she wondered if the fact Wally wasn't available was a good or a bad sign. Had the CSTs found a useful clue that he was busy following up on? Or had that lead been a dead end, returning the investigation to ground zero?

When the students filed into the cafeteria, there was none of the joking, laughter, or raised voices that Skye had come to expect at an assembly. The kids found seats at the picnic-style tables without the usual fuss of who was next to whom and sat there silently, staring at her.

Wishing she'd thought to grab a bottle of water, Skye forced herself not to fidget. Her mouth was dry and the butterflies in her stomach had formed a conga line. Normally, public speaking didn't bother her, but this was different. She was about to face four-hundred-plus kids who might or might not already know one of their teachers had been murdered in their own school.

Skye stood near the serving window where food trays were usually handed out and waited for the stragglers to find a seat. The pea green cinderblock walls were hung with posters advertising the seven basic food groups and nutritionally balanced meals.

Many had been altered with Magic Marker and teenage humor. Skye blinked and hid a smile. Was that cucumber wearing a condom? How had Homer missed that little piece of adolescent wit and artistic flair?

A heavy odor of burnt cheese and canned green beans hung in the airless room, and Skye felt her tummy roll. *Shoot!* Was her morning sickness back? She took a shallow breath. *No.* She was fine. She opened her mouth, but suddenly she couldn't remember her planned remarks. The students' unnerving stillness and intense gazes were giving her the heebie-jeebies. Had one of them killed their teacher?

There were a lot of tough parts to her job as a school psychologist, but this might be the most difficult. In order to create an atmosphere in which the students would feel safe to expose their feelings, she needed to keep her own emotions under control. If her demeanor wasn't self-possessed, unflustered, and relaxed, the kids would feel scared and insecure.

It was a struggle, but she held on to her composure and said, "Most of you know me, but for those who don't, my name is Mrs. Denison-Boyd and I'm the school psychologist." Skye paused. "A lot of you have probably heard the sad news that Ms. Hucksford was discovered dead yesterday in the school swimming pool. The police are investigating her death, and we'll share with you any information they provide to us in the future. But one thing they already know is that there is no reason to believe there is any danger to anyone else."

Skye examined the expressions of the teens. Most were staring back at her silently, but she could hear whispers, so she quickly continued. "When Mr. Knapik rings the bell, you should go to your first-hour classes. But if anyone feels too upset to go to class, you are welcome to stay here and we'll talk some more. I would also like all the volleyball players to remain."

When the students were dismissed, Skye counted how many had decided to linger. Twenty-six kids were left behind. Skye assumed the nineteen clustered together were the volleyball team. The seven other students were scattered among the tables either singly or in pairs.

Twenty-six kids were way too many for an effective group intervention. She would have to send some of them to see the social worker. As it had seemed that none of the staff was anxious to use the man's services, she'd put him to work with the students.

After some thought, Skye decided to send the social worker the non-volleyball players. However, before she dismissed that group, she wanted to get a sense for who was distressed with the idea of death and who was distraught over their personal loss.

Skye scanned the faces of the students. Although with recent world events, she was sure things had changed, but back when she'd been in graduate school, her program hadn't provided much training for this type of incident. After the last crisis, she had supplemented her knowledge and skills with articles she'd read online or in the *Communiqué*, the National Association of School Psychologists newsletter.

Still, this wasn't in her usual wheelhouse, so crossing her fingers that she was on the correct path, she said, "Before we break into smaller groups, I'd like each of you to tell me a little bit about how you knew Ms. Hucksford."

The teens clustered together at the front table whispered among themselves. Then a girl with her hair in a long black braid raised her hand.

Skye pointed to the student and asked, "Would you like to go first?"

"I've known Ms. Hucksford since she started coaching us. She helped me become a better player."

Skye thought she heard someone say, "Not out of the goodness of her heart."

No matter what the tragedy, and despite the old saying, people often spoke ill of the dead. Skye thanked the girl, then nodded to the other young women in the bunch around her. "Were you all on the team, too?"

They bobbed their heads.

A young man sitting with the only other male who had remained in the lunchroom caught Skye's attention, and she walked over to him and asked, "Were you in one of Ms. Hucksford's classes?"

"I was. She was helping me with my college applications. I want to go to U of I and major in physics."

"That was really nice of her." Skye smiled reassuringly. The boy seemed okay. A little upset with the loss of his teacher but far from distraught.

"How about you?" Skye indicated the other young man. "Was Ms. Hucksford helping you, too?"

"Yes." He nodded. "She helped the whole football team with our science classes."

Skye talked to the rest of the kids, ending up with one last girl who was sitting in the back all by herself. She had a long brown ponytail whose end appeared to have been dipped in red ink, three earrings in each lobe, and wore a headband decorated with tiny pink skulls. She was staring into space and seemed startled when Skye approached her and asked about her relationship with Blair.

"My name's Keely Peterson, and at one time," the girl said slowly, "I thought she was wonderful."

Skye looked at her quizzically.

The girl rose from her seat. Her hazel eyes blazed. "But then I found out what she was really like. Which makes it hard for me to feel sorry that she's dead."

CHAPTER 12

RUOK?—Are You Ok?

It was eight fifteen and the first-period bell had just rung as Skye led the volleyball players into her office. Nineteen was really too large for a normal group session, but because they were teammates, she thought it would be best for them to be seen together. None of them appeared to be overly upset, although a few were noticeably sadder than the rest of the group.

While Skye had seen the others around the school, she knew only one of the girls. Juliette Inslee was a sophomore and this was her second year on the school newspaper's staff. While Juliette made an effort to come across as unintelligent, Skye had found her to be a lot smarter than she pretended.

Juliette had shown a real talent for writing insightful pieces about everyday adolescent life, recently tackling the subject of favoritism in the school system. At the time Skye had figured the girl had been the victim of favoritism in one of her classes. Now she wondered if Blair's coaching style had been what inspired Juliette's article.

Since Blair hadn't forced Juliette to choose between working on the *Scoop* and playing volleyball, the coach must not have thought being on the paper's staff was a threat to the bond she wanted her team to form. Either that, or the girl hadn't informed the possessive woman about her other extracurricular activity.

As the volleyball players settled into the folding chairs that Skye had asked the custodian to set up, she was glad that her room at the high school could accommodate such a large number. In her grade school or junior high office, two or three kids were maximum occupancy.

Once all the girls had found seats in the double circle, Skye asked them all to introduce themselves. The young woman with the braid turned out to be Roxy Alvarez, the team captain and the daughter of the guy Skye had chatted with at the dry cleaner's.

Skye concentrated on trying to remember all the names, but because so many wore similar clothes and hairstyles, her efforts were probably as pointless as trying to judge the winner of a karaoke contest. Teenagers claimed to want individuality, but few had the nerve to stand out. It was a shame she couldn't ask them to wear name tags.

Looking around the circle, Skye announced, "Everything we discuss here today is private. That means none of you should talk about it to anyone outside the group or within earshot of anyone outside the group. I'll keep whatever is said in this session confidential unless I feel that there is a danger to someone. Do you all understand?"

They all nodded. A few glanced at each other with raised eyebrows and giggled.

"The only other rule is that we all be respectful of each other." Skye's voice was firm. "You may not feel the way someone else does, but that doesn't make how they feel any less important."

"Like if I was sad, but Keely was mad," a bubbly blonde offered, darting a glance at the girl with the red-tipped ponytail.

"Exactly." Skye looked at Keely, who sat in the back row as far from the rest of her teammates as the small space allowed. "Do you want to talk about why you changed your mind about Coach Hucksford?"

"Maybe later," Keely said, chewing on the end of her hair. "For now let's just say that I'm a flamingo in a flock of pigeons."

"That's fine," Skye assured her. "And if you'd like to talk to me alone, we can set that up, too. No one has to share if they're uncomfortable doing so."

"Then why are we here?" Roxy asked, her tone

conveying utter boredom. "I have a test third hour and this period is my study hall."

"You and anyone who doesn't feel like they need to talk are free to leave," Skye said evenly, thinking that it was interesting that the captain of the varsity team was the first to want to go.

Suddenly, Skye recalled that a week or so ago—she wasn't exactly sure of the timeline—she'd overheard a group of girls in the school hallway talking about the team captain arguing with the volleyball coach. Back then she hadn't thought much about what they'd said, but with Blair's murder, the conversation took on more significance. She'd have to remember to tell Wally about it.

Tucking that info into the back of her mind, she pointed to a stack of passes she'd prepared yesterday afternoon and said, "Anyone who doesn't want to be here can take one of those and return to class."

When no one else stood up, Roxy gazed sullenly at Skye, then said, "I'll stick around. The test will probably be postponed."

"You could be correct about that. Today's schedule is certainly out of whack. But I have no idea what the faculty plans to do about tests and assignments, so be prepared to take the examination." She checked out the girl's reaction. Something was bugging her, so she asked, "Did you have Ms. Hucksford for science class?"

"I'm a junior. Of course I had her." Roxy crossed her arms. "It's not as if there is more than one teacher for chemistry."

"Right." Skye nodded slowly. "Then all of the varsity players had Ms. Hucksford, and you've all lost both your coach and a teacher."

Expressions ranged from indifference to sadness to the dawning realization of what Blair's death really meant. A couple of the girls drew in a sharp breath and whispered to their neighbor.

"With that in mind, what I'd like to talk about now are your feelings regarding Ms. Hucksford's passing." Skye leaned forward and made eye contact with each of the girls, trying to gauge where to start. "What were your reactions when you first heard the news?"

"We aren't going to kill ourselves, if that's what you mean," Roxy sneered. "We feel bad about the coach, but we're not going to throw ourselves on her funeral pyre or drink poisoned Kool-Aid."

The others murmured their agreement, but Keely hunched her shoulders and said, "I wouldn't put it past some of you. But only if the coach left exact instructions in her will for how you should do it."

"Hey, you know the team rule." Roxy stared at Keely. "Keep it cute or keep it mute."

Skye was dying to know what was behind Keely's snarky comment and why Roxy had immediately shut her down. Sadly, questioning either girl wouldn't result in any kind of honest answer. Instead, after waiting a beat to see if Keely would ignore her captain and continue, Skye responded, "So, Keely, you feel that some of the others were more influenced by Ms. Hucksford's wishes than you were?"

"This whole school thing is just a big circus, and the volleyball team is the freak show." Keely gestured contemptuously around the circle. "Coach tells them to jump into the water, and no one even stops to think if they can swim; they just head into the pool."

"And how do you all feel about what Keely claims?" Skye asked. Although she was surprised that the girl had mentioned the swimming pool—the place Blair had died—for now she was willing to see where the discussion led. "Does anyone agree that perhaps you were overly eager to please your coach and didn't think through her requests?"

"Keely is being melodramatic." Roxy seemed to have appointed herself spokesperson of the group. "She resents the rest of us because she's not a team player like we are."

"Perhaps, but how do you feel about what she said?" Skye asked. "Remember, we're talking about our own feelings, not someone else's."

"I didn't always agree with Ms. Hucksford." Roxy shook her head emphatically, making her long black braid swish from side to side across her back. "But when we signed on for the team, we knew that the only way for us to shine was to do what our coach told us to do. Good things come to those who wait."

"Too bad those things are usually the stuff left behind by those who got there first," Keely muttered.

"So, Keely," Skye intervened. "You didn't feel the way Roxy did?"

"Truthfully," Keely said with a sigh, "I did at first, but then I changed my mind."

"Oh?" Skye murmured encouragingly, hoping the girl would explain. When she remained silent, Skye asked, "Would anyone else like to share something about their experience with Ms. Hucksford?"

Finally, the floodgates seemed to open for the others, and all the girls began to speak up. Skye sat back, allowing the teenagers to talk and process the events for themselves. She occasionally clarified or refereed, but mostly she observed for the rest of the time.

There were only a few minutes left in the period when Roxy asked Skye, "Do you know who's going to take over for Ms. Hucksford?"

"It's probably too late in the school year to hire a new science teacher." Skye hid a smile. She'd been wondering just how long it would be before the typical teenage narcissism kicked in. It was perfectly normal for adolescents to be self-involved and put their own needs before those of anyone else, and Skye had been speculating at what moment one of the girls would start to realize how Blair's death would affect their lives. "So most likely, Mr. Knapik will just hire a sub for the rest of the term."

"How about volleyball?" Juliette asked. "Who will coach us?"

"Since volleyball season isn't until the fall"— Skye shrugged—"my guess would be that the position won't be filled until then."

"But we train all year." Roxy's voice cracked. "We can't just opt out until September. Some of us have to be at our best."

"Yeah." Keely's gaze was hard. "Wouldn't it be a damn shame if after all you've done to get a chance at that scholarship, you lost it now?"

Before Roxy or Skye could respond, the bell rang. As the teenagers filed out of her office, Skye made sure each girl knew that if they were interested, she was available for an individual counseling session. None of them appeared eager to take her up on her offer.

Once they were gone, she headed over to the library to see if the social worker wanted any help, but he declined her offer. He had seen the seven students Skye had sent him, as well as the solitary teacher who had sought his assistance, and was currently helping Trixie plot her next book. The social worker agreed to stick around for another hour, but if no one else came to see him for counseling, he'd return to his regular co-op duties.

Like the volleyball players, whom Skye had worked with, none of the social worker's counselees had asked for any individual sessions. Evidently, very few of the staff or students of Scumble River High School were *that* upset by Blair's death.

It was close to nine thirty by the time Skye left the library and headed toward the faculty lounge. She'd bet her last package of Thin Mints—the ones hidden at home in the back of the freezer—that although some of the teachers might want to talk, several wouldn't be willing to seek out formal therapy.

However, if she were there, say getting a cup of tea or waiting in line to use the attached restroom, they might start a conversation about how they were feeling. It wouldn't be the first time she'd held an impromptu counseling session at the old stained Formica tables in the faculty room.

Skye was concentrating on making it to the staff bathroom for a much-needed pit stop, when the school secretary came dashing toward her. Normally Opal reminded Skye of a mouse, but today, as she sprinted down the corridor, she looked more like a cheetah.

"Skye! Skye!" Opal shouted while she ran. "Where have you been?"

"My office until nine." Skye waited for the

winded woman to catch up, surprised that the normally timid secretary would yell in the hallway. "Then the library for the past half hour or so. Why?"

"Mr. Knapik is in with the superintendent and has ordered me not to disturb them, but the cops are here. What should I do?"

Opal had fallen into the habit of consulting Skye when Homer was absent because she was one of the few staff members not responsible for a classroom full of students who couldn't be left on their own. There was no other administrator, so the secretary considered Skye the next best thing.

"What do the police want?" Skye asked. "Are they planning to arrest someone?"

"I have no idea." Opal dabbed at her forehead with a lace-edged hanky.

"You didn't ask them?" Skye turned on her heel and marched toward the office, trailed by the secretary. "What did they say?"

"They asked for Homer." Opal panted as she trotted next to Skye.

"Then my advice would be to get Homer immediately." Skye paused before reaching the lobby and faced the hyperventilating woman. "Truly, if the police want to talk to him, you have no choice."

"No. I can't." Opal sagged against a locker. "He'll get mad at me if I bother him."

"Fine." Skye knew arguing was useless. Opal

had been Homer's secretary since he took over as principal back when the kids had to fight off saber-toothed tigers on their walk to school. It had been a different time, and at her age, Opal was not going to be able to change her view of the world or how male authority figures were to be treated. "I'll get Homer myself. He's usually angry with me anyway."

Wally and Sergeant Quirk were standing in the main office. Skye greeted them as she walked past and asked them to wait a minute while she got the principal. She hurried down the short hallway to Homer's door, knocked, and identified herself. No answer. She knocked again and leaned her head against the wood. Not a sound. She tried the door. It opened easily, but no one was in the room.

Skye went back to the outer office and said to Wally, "Did you see Homer leave?"

"No. No one has been in or out since Opal went to find you." Wally tapped his fingers on the counter. "If he's not available, you and Opal can help us round up the teachers and students we need to interview."

"We really need Homer for this. He should make that kind of decision." Skye asked Opal, "When was the last time you saw Mr. Knapik?"

"When I showed Dr. Wraige into the principal's office." The secretary twisted her fingers. "It was nine a.m. on the dot, because the bell had just rung, and I never left the front desk until I went to get you."

"Then where are they?" Skye walked back to Homer's office, looked around. *Heck!* She'd forgotten about Homer's secret exit. Behind his desk, concealed by floor-length drapes, was a door designed to look like a window from the outside of the building. She knew he'd used it before to escape the building without being observed.

Opal had followed Skye and said, "Mr. Knapik and Dr. Wraige must have decided to go for coffee." She added, "Or to play golf. It's the first warm, sunny day we've had this spring."

"You've got to be kidding! A teacher dies and they go hit a bucket of balls?" Skye returned to where Wally and the others were waiting. "It appears that Homer is AWOL. Opal will call you when he comes back. I don't have the authority to give you access to students."

"How about if Quirk and I talk to the teachers first?" Wally asked.

"Sure." Skye wrinkled her brow. "But I sort of thought you'd want me in on those conversations and we'd do them after school."

"This will be more of a general weeding out." Wally smiled. "We're hoping to narrow down the suspect pool today. Then later, when we know who had motive and opportunity, I'll bring you into the mix."

"Are you planning to talk to the whole faculty?" Skye asked.

"No. Today we'll just speak to the folks Blair would have been in contact with the most. The other coaches, extracurricular activity sponsors, and the science teachers." Wally flipped open the folder he carried and handed Skye a list. "And right now the only students we're interested in questioning are the girls on the volleyball team."

"I'll start phoning their parents while you speak to the staff." Skye glanced at Opal. "Can you call in a sub to float between the classrooms while the faculty is being interviewed by the police?"

"Not without Mr. Knapik's authorization." Opal retreated behind her desk.

"Sweet mother of Jesus." Skye threw up her hands. "What is the procedure if a teacher is called out from class for an emergency?"

"We have whoever has a free period cover their children." Opal opened a file cabinet drawer, pulled out a sheet of paper, and thrust it toward Skye. "Here's the schedule. You decide how to do it."

"No." Skye took the page and gave it to Wally. "How about you all just talk to the teachers during their free period instead of shuffling them around?"

"Works for me." Wally scanned the paper. "I'll let Opal know if we're keeping someone longer than the time they have off."

"Good. Our school nurse is assigned to the

151

junior high on Wednesdays, so Sergeant Quirk can use the health room, and since Trixie will be thrilled to help out on an investigation, I'm sure she'll let you use the library workroom."

Skye pulled Wally aside and told him about overhearing that Roxy Alvarez had argued with her volleyball coach. He thanked her and made a note of it.

Before leaving for her office, Skye said to Opal, "Please notify me the minute Homer returns. He and I need to have a chat about exactly what my duties include."

CHAPTER 13

LD—Link Dead

Opal buzzed Skye after the third lunch period to tell her that Homer had finally returned. Skye hurried to the main office, and after a perfunctory knock on Homer's door, she walked in without waiting for his permission. He was seated behind his desk on his cushy leather chair with his head leaning back. Chain-saw snores buzzed from his partially open mouth.

Skye stepped over to him, poked his shoulder with her index finger, and demanded, "Where were you?" She waited for his eyelids to pop open, then said, "When the police arrived to talk to teachers and kids about Blair's murder, you were nowhere to be found."

"Dr. Wraige and I were at a county board of education meeting in Laurel," Homer snapped, slowly sitting up. "Opal should have had it on my schedule. Not that it's any of your business."

Skye ignored his bark, crossed her arms, and asked, "Then I have to wonder why you two used the window exit instead of leaving via the front door."

"The custodian had just polished the lobby floor and we didn't want to mess up the wax." Homer tottered to his feet. "And I don't like your attitude. I'm your boss, not the other way around."

"Of course you are." Skye kept her voice cool. Although she thought he was lying through his big white false teeth, she could hardly accuse him of not telling the truth. Homer was what those who worked in education called a seagull administrator—a principal who flew into the school each morning, made a lot of noise, then crapped all over everything and left before any-one could shoot him. "I never meant to imply other-wise."

"That's more like it." Homer smirked. "And don't you forget it. Because right this minute, I'm not in the mood for your sass. I'm having one of those days when I'm mighty tempted to let my middle finger provide all my answers to everyone's stupid questions."

"Seriously?" Skye shook her head, then said, "Anyway, back to actual school business. When the police arrived, intending to interview our staff and students, Opal asked me what she should do. As you pointed out, I'm not the boss, so I had to ad-lib. Perhaps it's time for you to get a cell phone."

"Nope." Homer strolled over to his mini fridge and pulled out an orange soda. "I see no reason to be at everyone's beck and call."

"Then who exactly is in charge when you're not here?" Skye looked longingly at the can. Her throat was parched, and she hadn't had time to get to the lounge to buy a soda from the machine.

"Technically . . ." Homer tilted the ice-cold can, drank deeply, burped, and continued. "Pru Cormorant is assistant principal, but . . ."

"Right." Skye shuddered. The annoying English teacher was about the only thing she and Homer agreed on. Better no one at the helm than Pru. "How did she get the job? Why doesn't anyone know she has it? And what are her duties?"

"She has the most seniority." Homer had the grace to look a little sheepish, a first for him. "We always allow whoever's closest to retirement to be the assistant principal so they can maximize their pension benefit. No one knows she's assistant principal because she has no duties. It's an in-name-only position rather than an actual one."

"Of course." Skye sighed. The joy of small-town politics never ended. She made a face, and when Homer glared, she feigned innocence and said, "Darn! Did I just roll my eyes out loud?"

"Anything else?" Homer took her elbow and pulled her toward the door.

"The chief and Sergeant Quirk are talking to the faculty during the teachers' free periods, and I've phoned all the parents of the students they want to interview. Luckily, I was able to reach almost all of the volleyball team players' parents. You see how handy cell phones are, Homer?" Skye couldn't believe she was the one insisting someone else needed a cell when she'd been so reluctant to get one herself. "I'll keep trying to touch base with the two or three I haven't contacted." Skye paused for a breath. "The ones who are concerned are coming in to be with their daughters during their meeting with the police."

Ignoring her dig about the phone, Homer said, "Why did you do that? Now we'll have a bunch of parents running around here and interfering with us." Homer sneered at Skye. "I suppose you felt compelled to defend the little brats' rights."

"It also protects the school district from a lawsuit," Skye pointed out. "You could be held liable."

"No way." Homer shook his massive head from side to side, looking a lot like a buffalo trying to get rid of an annoying fly. "I assume full responsibility for my own actions, but not those that are someone else's fault." He paused and smacked his rubbery lips together. "Which are most of them."

"And that's why I called the parents." Skye blew out an exasperated breath.

"Yeah." Homer jeered. "Right. You're a real peach and deserve a medal. Now, as long as all the classes are covered, I don't give a rat's ass about the rest of it." Homer nearly pushed Skye out of his office.

When Skye heard the lock click behind her, she stood staring at the closed door. Evidently, Homer was indifferent to what had been happening in his absence or what was currently occurring in his school. She had half a mind to go home and let him cope.

It was a shame that if she jumped ship, he wouldn't be the only one to suffer. Squaring her shoulders, she headed down the hallway at a jog. She could see a light at the end of the tunnel, and really hoped it was the bathroom.

Once she'd taken care of her most urgent need, she washed her hands, then went into the faculty lounge, bought a soda from the machine, and went back to her office to eat her lunch.

By three fifteen Wally and Quirk had talked to everyone on their list. Before leaving, Wally stopped by Skye's office and said, "I'm heading back to the PD now. Don't wait dinner for me. I have no idea when I'll be home."

"Did you find out anything?" Skye asked.

"Just that everyone claims to have alibis, but most are from spouses or significant others, so not too reliable. Nothing new about motives." Wally paused in the doorway. "But the crime-scene guy did get a couple of unidentified prints from the electrical panel in the boiler room. They don't match either of the custodians, so we're hopeful they belong to the killer."

"Well, that's good news." Skye frowned when Wally didn't smile. "Isn't it?"

"It will be once we have a suspect." Wally shrugged. "Unfortunately, there isn't a match to anyone on IAFIS."

"Oh." Skye nodded. IAFIS was the Integrated Automated Fingerprint Identification System used by the police to find perpetrators who already had a criminal record. "Right."

Knowing Wally had been at the school all day and that he hadn't had any lunch, Skye reminded him to eat something; then she kissed him good-bye and headed down the hallway. She was running late for the newspaper staff's after-school meeting. They met in the library because that was where the computer lab was set up.

She and Trixie got the kids settled down and on task, and then Skye updated her BFF on everything she knew about the murder. Or at least everything Wally had told her she could share. Trixie didn't have a chance to ask too many questions because the newspaper staff was wrapping up the April issue and both she and Skye were kept busy helping the kids meet their deadline.

A couple of hours later, when they'd completed the monthly edition, Skye announced that she was looking for volunteers to assist with the rubber duck race. Fortunately, they were all good kids and happy to pitch in to support Trixie's fund-raiser.

Once the students said good-bye and left, Trixie turned to Skye and beamed. "See. Easy-peasy. The kids all agreed to help number the ducks."

"Big surprise." Skye raised a brow. "After you showed them all the sad puppy and kitten pictures, how could they say no?"

"Yep." Trixie hooked her thumbs into the material of her shirt on either side of her chest. "The idea of putting together an album of the adorable shelter animals was pure genius on my part."

"When did you have time to do that?" Skye moved around the computer lab tidying up the space. "You only told me about the race two days ago."

"You know that when I get an idea in my head, I can't rest."

"True." Skye wasn't certain whether she admired

her friend's energy or if she should suggest that Trixie be evaluated for hyperactivity.

"Well, you're usually a pushover, so when it was so hard to persuade you to help me, I knew I'd need to bring out the big guns in order to get everybody else on board." Trixie twisted a short strand of hair around her finger. "Monday afternoon, while I was surfing the net looking for ideas to help inspire me on ways to publicize the event, I popped over to I Can Has Cheezburger?"

"You were hungry?" Skye threw away some trash and stared at her friend.

"No." Trixie shook her head, then shrugged. "Well, yes. I'm always hungry, but ICHC is a website with pictures of mostly cats, but other animals, too. And all the photos have funny captions."

"O-kay." Skye stretched out the word. Where was this leading? "And?"

"This site gets as many as a million and a half hits per day."

"You're kidding me." Skye had grown fonder of technology, but clearly she still didn't quite grasp the enormous impact of the World Wide Web.

"Nope." Trixie hopped to her feet and started putting the chairs on top of the tables so the custodian could vacuum more easily. "Which made me realize that there's nothing more persuasive than cute animals."

"And that's when you dropped everything, drove over to the shelter, took the pictures, and came back here to make up the scrapbook," Skye guessed. Between the newspaper and yearbook committees, all the equipment Trixie needed to print photos and create an album was available in the school's computer lab.

"Exactly." Trixie beamed. "And it's worked like a charm. I put together several copies, and the GIVE kids have been using them to solicit prizes for the race and to sell ducks. We already have a savings bond from the bank, dinner for six from the Feed Bag, a mani-pedi from the spa, a hundred-dollar check from the Fine Foods Factory, a book and muffin basket from Tales and Treats, and a case of wine from the Brown Bag Bar and Liquor Store."

"Extremely impressive for two days of effort." Skye slid the last chair into place. The library was ready for the next school day. "Have you gotten the permit from the city council yet?"

"Of course." Trixie pumped her fist in the air. "How could you doubt me? As of three p.m. we are an officially sanctioned event."

"That's amazing." Skye started to walk toward the door, but Trixie blocked her path. Skye frowned and said, "I need to get going."

"Just a second." Trixie gripped Skye's arm as if she were afraid her friend was about to make a run for it. "There's one more thing."

"Oh." Skye didn't like the fact that her BFF couldn't look her in the eye.

160

"Actually"—Trixie's cheeks reddened—"getting the permit turned out to be harder than I thought. Your uncle is a total jerk."

"Tell me something I don't already know." Skye tried to free herself from Trixie's grasp. "Dante is the king of the skunks."

"And I was getting sort of desperate." Trixie continued as if Skye hadn't spoken. "When one of the GIVE kids came up with a solution."

"That's great." Skye started to pry Trixie's fingers off her arm. "The whole point of extracurricular activities is for the students to learn problem solving and enhance their social skills."

"Precisely." Trixie refused to allow Skye to escape her hold. "Anyway, the girl said that her pop could get the permit for us."

"Is her dad on the city council?" Skye asked, trying to recall which member had children in high school. After a second, she still couldn't come up with anyone. They were mostly in their fifties and sixties. Maybe the councilman was the girl's grandfather.

"No." Trixie shook her head. "Considering the family, I didn't ask too many questions. Normally, I might not have even agreed to request this parent's help, but I was getting desperate."

"Oh. My. Gosh! You can't be freaking serious!" Skye yanked her arm free, not caring if she got scratched in the process, and rushed toward the exit. "Tell me the father you're talking about isn't—"

"Miz Skye, as I live and breathe. I ain't seen you since your weddin' reception."

Earl Doozier strolled into the library, a huge grin in his toothless mouth. Earl was the top dog of the Red Raggers, an assorted family of misfits who always seemed to be around when there were nefarious activities brewing. They didn't usually make the first move, but they were quick to take advantage of any opening to beat the crap out of someone or exploit a profitable situation.

Dooziers didn't have savings accounts—they had jars full of cash buried in their backyards. Their kids took chemistry in school not because they were premed, but so they could make pipe bombs. Skye was sure that if they won the lottery, they'd invest the money in a trip to Las Vegas, a lifetime supply of Pabst Blue Ribbon, and a trailer truck full of Marlboros for the men and Virginia Slim Menthols for the ladies.

Despite all this, through her job as a school psychologist, Skye had established a good relationship with Earl. She'd worked to ensure his many children, sisters, brothers, nieces, and nephews made it through the public-education system with as few problems as possible.

And in turn, Earl and his kin had managed to save Skye on a few occasions. By now they treated her almost like one of their many pet hound dogs—with casual affection and neglect.

That is unless someone bothered her. Then it was all-out war.

How in the world had Earl managed to get the permit from the city council for Trixie's fundraiser? Skye cringed. Did she really want to know? Before she could decide, a woman with blond hair from a box of Clairol, a Pamela Anderson bust, and the personality of a honey badger barreled into the room.

Skye groaned. Earl's wife, Glenda, had arrived.

Ignoring Skye and Trixie, Glenda glowered at her husband and screeched, "What in the hell is takin' you so long, Earl Doozier?"

Earl, evidently having a death wish, said, "Aw, ain't that sweet? She misses me."

"Like I miss cramps once my period's over with." Glenda put her hands on her hips and narrowed her eyes. "You said you'd only be a second, but I listened to Kenny Chesney sing 'Beer in Mexico' and Craig Morgan belt out 'International Harvester,' and you still ain't back."

"But, honey pie, I gots myself a little lost. The hallways confused—"

"Don't make me break a nail slappin' some sense in you," Glenda shrieked.

Skye's gaze was drawn to the bright orange talons Glenda was using to poke at her husband.

"I said I'd be a minute." Surprisingly, Earl didn't seem afraid. There was a stubborn expression on his typically slack-jawed face when he said,

"This is important to Bambi, and I ain't lettin' her down. Besides, I's got a plan for our future."

"The last time you told me you was plannin' for our future, you bought two cases of beer instead of the usual one." Glenda tapped a safety-cone-orange stiletto on the worn carpet. "I'm countin' to three and you better have your skinny butt out of here and back into the Buick or I'm leavin' you to walk home. It's clear you don't care about me."

"But sweet cheeks, you's knows that my love for you is like diarrhea." Earl clasped his hands to his heart. "I just can't hold it in."

"Well . . ." Glenda hesitated.

"'Cause you're prettier than a beer truck pulling up in the driveway."

"You say that to all the girls." Glenda batted her false eyelashes at her husband.

While the lovebirds were cooing at each other, Skye murmured to Trixie, "Bambi Doozier is a member of your community service club?" Bambi was the last of Earl and Glenda's brood—at least so far—and this was her first year attending Scumble River High School. She was a quiet girl and one of the few Doozier offspring who hadn't been referred for any special education assistance—thus Skye hadn't had much to do with her.

Tugging at the crotch of her skintight jeans, her low-cut tank top exposing a large expanse of chalk-white cleavage, Glenda glared at Skye and said, "What are you implyin'? That we ain't civic-minded?"

Skye made sure she was out of reach of Glenda's claws and said, "Of course not. It's just that few freshmen are interested in helping others."

Earl looked from his wife to Skye and back. "Two seconds. I promise."

Glenda scowled, nodded her agreement, then squawked at Earl, "Okay, Mister. Give Miz La-Di-Da Skye her precious permit, but if you ain't in the Regal by the time the next song is over, come lovin' time, I'm gonna learn from your mama's mistakes and start using birth control."

"Give me the permit now." Skye held out her hand. She so didn't want to hear about Earl and Glenda's sex life.

"I gotta explain somethin'." Earl shot Trixie a crafty look. "Right, Missus Frayne?"

"Dinner ain't gonna cook itself, and possum takes a long time to bake or it's tougher than your old leather work boot," Glenda announced, and stomped away.

Skye was uncertain as to why Earl would need a work boot since as long as she'd known him, he'd never had a job, but she said, "We don't want to keep you and Glenda from your dinner."

"We got time." Earl scooted farther into the library and carefully closed the door.

As he scouted the perimeter, Skye took a good

look at the skinny little man dressed in camo sweatpants and a torn T-shirt. He almost looked like a ten-year-old boy, until you noticed the dense tattoos up and down his forearms and the basketball-shaped gut hanging over his trousers.

"What's going on?" Skye glanced between Trixie and Earl. "What's to explain?"

"You tell her, Missus Frayne." Earl took off his dirty baseball cap, revealing muddy brown hair that formed a horseshoe around a bald spot the size of a cantaloupe. "You know what I need."

Trixie shuffled her pink-and-black-high-top–clad feet, sucked in a lungful of air, and finally blurted out, "Earl graciously agreed to use some infor-mation he knew about the mayor to get the permit for the duck race."

"So Earl blackmailed Dante?" Skye lasered the little man with a hard look. "What's in it for you?"

Trixie glanced sideways at Skye and answered for Earl. "If I agreed to let him run a teeny-tiny little cornhole tournament as part of the event."

"Cornhole?" Skye knew, or at least hoped, it wasn't what it sounded like.

"Beanbag toss," Trixie clarified. "It's very popular right now."

"And you want to have a competition?" Skye asked Earl. "Why?"

" 'Cause it'll be fun." Earl widened his blood-shot eyes innocently.

"And?" Skye prompted. "I know you, Earl. Your idea of fun is scamming the city slickers, starting fights, and drinking beer."

"Now, don't be that way, Miz Skye," he whined. "You got me all wrong."

"I sincerely doubt it." Skye knew Earl was up to something; she just couldn't figure out what. "Describe this cornhole tournament."

"It's nothin' special." He scratched his head. "Just good clean fun for the whole family."

"It's up to you, Trixie." Skye gave up. Getting the truth out of a Doozier was harder than squeezing the last bit of toothpaste from a tube and a lot more frustrating. "Your decision."

"I have no choice." Trixie held out her hand to Earl. "You've got a deal."

Earl shook, gave Trixie the slip of paper, and put his cap back on. "I'll just skedaddle before Glenda skins me alive." Over his shoulder, he added, "I'll see you ladies on Sunday."

"Terrific." Skye waited for him to leave, then said to her friend, "You do know that Earl's up to something, right?"

"Uh-huh." Trixie shrugged. "But I'm sure it's nothing Team Skyxie can't handle."

Skye winced. She really needed to get off that team.

CHAPTER 14

F?—Are We Friends?

After saying good-bye to Trixie, Skye got into her Bel Air and watched her friend's Honda roar out of the school parking lot. In order to make ends meet when she and her husband had had some unexpected expenses, Trixie had sold her beloved Mustang. But the high-spirited librarian drove as if she were still behind the wheel of a hot rod and was competing for first place at the Route 66 Raceway.

As Skye put on her seat belt, she wondered how the investigation into Blair's murder was going. Earlier that afternoon, when Wally had popped into her office, he'd been in too much of a hurry to bring her fully up to speed, but he had promised to fill her in when he got home.

It was good to know they'd found some fingerprints on the electrical panel, but she'd forgotten to ask if they'd talked to Thor Goodson. According to the police shows on television, when a woman was murdered, the husband or boyfriend was usually the killer.

Her stomach growled, and Skye checked the time. It was nearly five thirty. *Hmm!* Wally wasn't going to be around for supper. Maybe she'd treat herself to a meal at the Feed Bag—Scumble River's only sit-down restaurant. She never had made it to the supermarket or written a list for Dorothy, and she was too tired to go grocery shopping right now. Besides, it had been quite a while since she'd been to the diner, and it would be nice to relax and read a book instead of going home and scrounging for something to eat.

A couple of minutes later, Skye pulled her car into one of the few remaining spots in the diner's parking lot. Hopping out of the Chevy, Skye hurried inside. She hoped there would still be an available table.

It was well into supper rush hour at the Feed Bag—Scumble River was a rural community whose hardworking citizens ate at daybreak, noon, and five. No late-night, leisurely dining for them. By six o'clock they were in front of their televisions ready for the news, and a half hour later they were settled into their recliners watching *Wheel of Fortune*.

While she waited to be seated, Skye scanned the crowd. People who came to the Feed Bag felt as if they were part of an extended family. For the elderly, it was a comfort knowing that the staff would notice if they varied from their normal routine and that someone would check up on them if they didn't show for their customary coffee, bowl of soup, or game of chess.

For the young families, it was reassuring that no

one would frown if their kids were loud or messy. Not to mention that when the check arrived, they wouldn't have to take out a second mortgage to pay it.

And for the singles, it was a safe place to go on a first date. Or a comfortable spot to meet up with other like-minded people looking for a love match.

Lost in her thoughts, Skye didn't notice the Feed Bag's owner, Tomi Jackson, until the tiny woman asked loudly, "You meeting the chief?"

"Unfortunately not." Skye shook her head ruefully. "It's just me tonight. Wally's too busy with the murder investigation." Thanks to the *Star*, there was no use being discreet. By now there wasn't a man, woman, child—and maybe even pet—in Scumble River who hadn't read and thoroughly discussed the case.

"Poor guy still needs to eat," Tomi grumbled as she led Skye to a booth recently vacated by a couple who still stood close by, chatting with friends. It was near the wall of windows and a prime spot to observe everyone in the place. "When you're ready to leave, I'll fix up something to go for him and you can drop it off at the station."

"That's a great idea." Skye threw her tote bag onto the bench seat and slid in beside it. "I'm sure he'd love your fried chicken basket."

"Will do." Tomi handed Skye a menu. "Do you need a couple of minutes?"

"Uh-huh. I want to check out the specials before I decide on an entré." Skye flipped open the laminated pages until she found the center insert. "In the meantime, I'll have a caffeine-free Diet Coke with a slice of lime. I did a lot of talking today, and I'm dry as a bone."

"Coming right up." Toni stuck her pen into her platinum-blond beehive, a style that added several inches to her height. Ageless, she had been a part of Scumble River for as long as Skye could remember. "If you have a taste for something exotic, the meat loaf and mashed potatoes platter is fair to middling tonight. Cook's been watching the Food Channel and got sort of daring. He added curry powder to his usual recipe and made it into little individual loaves."

"Thanks for the tip." Skye watched the owner as she tottered away in five-inch heels. How Tomi worked twelve-hour shifts wearing stilettos was beyond Skye. But the high-heeled shoes and the hairstyle were the older woman's signature look, and she hadn't changed either since the restaurant opened forty years ago.

A few seconds later, when Tomi returned with her soda, Skye—having deciding to skip the meat loaf since she had never been fond of hamburger in any form except a patty—asked for the smothered chicken plate. After the older woman left to convey the order to the cook, Skye sipped her drink and gazed around the restaurant.

Tomi had redecorated the place in the eighties, using lots of mauve and brass, and hadn't touched it since then. More than twenty years of hard wear and tear were catching up with the interior. Rips in the vinyl seats had been repaired with duct tape, smudges on the walls had been dabbed with a color that didn't quite match the original paint, and the ivy in the planters along the backs of the booths was long dead and replaced with plastic flowers that hadn't been dusted in recent memory.

Still, the only ones who noticed the dated decor were the occasional tourists who wandered in on their drive down Route 66. And most of them soon learned that trash-talking a beloved Scumble River institution like the Feed Bag was not a good idea for their continued well-being. Vehicles had been known to develop sudden engine problems, flat tires, and mysterious scratches to their pristine paint jobs if their titleholders were too vocal or too persistent in their criticism of the restaurant.

Speaking of people making disparaging remarks, Skye dug through her tote bag for the mystery she was currently reading. A pompous author had just been killed after disparaging small towns in his speech to a book club, and she was anxious to see how the amateur sleuth would manage to insert herself into the investigation.

She knew firsthand that looking into a murder with no authority was tough, which was why she'd been happy to accept the position as the psychological consultant to the Scumble River Police. The pay was minuscule, but there were other compensations. Not the least of which was sleeping with the police chief.

A chapter and a half later, Skye's visit to a fictional rural community in Missouri was interrupted when Tomi brought her a fresh soda and apologized. "I'm real sorry it's taking so long. I have no idea how, but we ran out of potatoes. I sent a busboy over to Walt's Supermarket to buy some more and he just got back. It'll probably be another fifteen or twenty minutes. Is that okay?"

"Sure." Skye tapped the cover of her book. "This will keep me occupied, and there isn't any place I have to be, so I'm in no hurry."

"I sure wish everyone felt that way." Tomi grimaced. "Around here, patience doesn't seem to be a strong point for a lot of folks."

As Tomi darted away to soothe her hungry customers, Skye smiled in sympathy. She could empathize with the business owner. Most of the people she worked with weren't all that understanding of delays either, and everyone thought their problem should be her priority.

Before Skye could focus back on her mystery, the front door opened, and she glanced toward the entrance. It was now well past the accepted Scumble River suppertime, so she was curious as to who was eating so daringly late.

Somehow Skye wasn't surprised when Emerald,

aka Emmy, Jones glided inside the restaurant. Emmy, a beautiful woman in her late twenties or early thirties, had moved to town to teach dance classes in the studio her mother co-owned with Skye's aunt Olive.

Emmy had been involved in some unspecified trouble while living in Las Vegas and had been sent to Scumble River for a fresh start, but she hadn't quite adjusted from Sin City to small-town America. Dining early, dressing to blend in, and not rocking the boat were just a few of the customs to which she was still becoming accustomed.

Skye watched as Emmy spoke to Tomi, who shook her head. Frowning, Emmy scanned the room. When she spotted Skye, she waved, then pointed to herself and the empty bench at Skye's table. Putting her hands together as if in prayer, she mouthed the word *please*.

So much for a quiet dinner reading her book. Skye forced a welcoming expression onto her face, nodded, and waved the shapely blonde over. Skye wasn't at all sure how she felt about Emmy. She'd initially met her during a murder investigation that took place the week before Skye's wedding, so bridal jitters could certainly have influenced the surge of jealousy that had zipped through her psyche when she'd first laid eyes on the woman.

Not only was Emmy stunning, but she was a

member of the same gun club as Wally. He'd admitted that the dancer had hit on him when she'd originally moved to town, but he'd assured Skye that once Emmy was aware he was engaged, she'd treated him as no more than a friend. However, Skye still had her doubts.

She noticed that as the gorgeous performer sashayed toward her, she shamelessly flirted with every man she passed. Emmy playfully tapped their arms, patted their shoulders, or touched their cheeks, teasing one with, "I haven't seen you in a while," and another with, "We missed you at the last gun club competition."

Wives and girlfriends scowled, but the men preened under her attention. Dressed in a high-waisted, formfitting red pencil skirt and a tight black blouse, she reminded Skye of a fifties pinup girl, which made Skye recall the burlesque routine that Emmy had performed at Wally's and her bachelor/bachelorette party. It had been fairly innocent, but that seductive dance might be why Skye still had a lingering feeling of wariness toward the stunning woman.

"Hi, Emmy." Skye pasted on a smile. "Care to join me for dinner?"

"That's so sweet of you." Emmy slid onto the bench opposite Skye. "Tomi said they'd had some sort of supply snafu so it would take a while for any tables to free up." Emmy pouted. "And I'm starved."

"If you put in your order right away, it'll probably come out when mine does," Skye suggested, then asked Tomi, who had just walked up, "Right?"

When Tomi nodded, Emmy shoved away the menu and said, "Great. I'll have the ribs, coleslaw, and a loaded baked potato."

"Coffee?" Tomi gestured with the pot she held in her left hand.

"I guess so." Emmy giggled. "If you served drinks, tonight I'd say, 'Step aside, java. This is a job for alcohol.'"

After Tomi filled Emmy's cup and left, Skye searched her mind for a topic of conversation.

Before Skye could think of anything, Emmy wiggled in her seat until she was comfy, then said, "How are the shooting lessons going?"

"I decided to put those off for a while." Skye reflexively placed her hand on her stomach, then quickly removed it. They really did have to announce the pregnancy soon, before she inadvertently did something to spill the beans.

"Oh. Yeah. About that. I hope you weren't mad about the whole recoil thing." Emmy's expression was a little sheepish. "It's sort of a joke we play on all the newbies. I promise not to do it again."

"I wasn't upset," Skye assured her. So Kathy Steele had been right. Emmy *had* given that gun to her on purpose. She would need to keep that in mind in dealing with the mischievous dancer.

"The lessons just aren't convenient right now."

Emmy glanced around. "Is that handsome husband of yours here?"

"Nope." Skye fought to keep the smile on her face. "He's busy on a case."

"That's a shame," Emmy purred. "He hasn't been out to the club in quite a while either."

"Well . . ." Skye gave Emmy a long look. "You know how it is with newlyweds." She wasn't sure if she was making casual conversation or warning the strikingly sexy woman away from her man. "Since I haven't been interested in shooting, he'd rather stay home with me than go fondle some pistol or rifle by himself."

"There I go again. Sorry about that." Emmy blew out a frustrated breath. "Sometimes I forget to take off my professional persona."

"Do you have a stage name?" Skye examined the tall, lithe woman, hoping that by *professional* she meant *burlesque* dancer, not something else.

"I'm considering Willow St. André." Emmy tossed her ponytail. "What do you think?"

"Nice." Skye nodded. "Classy, yet provocative. I like it a lot."

"Thanks." The lovely dancer beamed, then wrinkled her brow when ZZ Top's "Sharp Dressed Man" started playing from her purse. She fished a cell phone out of the black alligator clutch and swept her finger across the screen. Frowning, she tapped a few keys with her thumbs, sighed, then quickly touched another icon and tapped again.

Skye viewed the whole process with suspicion. She had figured out texting, although with the old-style keypad on her cell, it was a tedious process. And she'd seen some of the more advanced devices that some of the students possessed, but what in the heck was Emmy doing?

"Look." Emmy held out her phone. "See what I just posted on Open Book."

"Open Book?" Skye squinted at the tiny screen. She didn't see anything that looked like a book. Next to a teeny picture of Emmy were the words: At the Feed Bag with my friend Skye Denison-Boyd. Can't wait to hear ALL she has to say about a certain ex-boyfriend of hers.

Emmy swept the screen with her finger, and Skye saw photos of people she didn't recognize, cute animals, and even a few flowers. Next to each miniature picture were random comments about the weather, elaborate recipes, and cats.

"What in the world is all that?" Skye asked, confused at what she was seeing.

"You're joking, right?" Emmy arched a feathery brow, and her sapphire blue eyes narrowed in disbelief. "You aren't on Open Book?"

"I guess not." Skye shrugged. "It's hard to be 'on' "—she arched her fingers in air quotes—"something you've never heard of."

"Oh. Yeah. I forgot." Emmy wrinkled her cute

little turned-up nose. "Wally mentioned that you aren't really into the whole Internet thing."

"That's not completely true," Skye protested, wondering just when her husband had mentioned that little tidbit to the beautiful dancer. "I'm catching up."

"Well, Open Book is an online social networking site," Emmy explained. "Some brainiacs at a big university created it so people all around the world could meet, share interests, and express themselves."

"And anyone can see what you write or the pictures you put up?"

"Sort of. I don't really understand all the technicalities." Emmy bit her lip. "I do know that there are ways to limit who can look at your posts, but most people don't bother to do that." She shrugged. "Like the whole point of putting up a profile, writing status updates, and taking photos is for other people to see them."

"Aren't there privacy concerns?" Skye asked, appalled. "I mean, if you took a picture of us together and put it up but I didn't want my photo on this site, could I make you take it down?"

"I have no idea." Emmy's eyes widened. "Why wouldn't you want people to see your picture or know you and I were together at the Feed Bag? I get lots of gigs for my burlesque routine that way."

"Not everyone wants to live their lives in full view of the public eye." Skye mentally slapped her forehead. Of course a performer would love something like Open Book. Someone with those types of aspirations had to have at least a little bit of an exhibitionistic tendency or they'd never be able to face an audience.

"I suppose." Emmy didn't look entirely convinced. "Anyway, Open Book is fun, and it's a good way to subtly let someone know something you don't want to come right out and tell him."

"Oh?" Skye caught a hint of spite in Emmy's voice. "Like what?"

"Like, say someone didn't show up for a date. You could post a picture of yourself with someone they would prefer you weren't alone with."

"Are you referring to Simon?" Skye asked, hiding a smile. Emmy was dating Skye's ex-boyfriend, and he was as straitlaced as they came. Simon wouldn't be fond of Skye and his new girlfriend exchanging feminine secrets or making comparisons about him.

"Yes." Emmy pushed out her bottom lip. "I think he's starting to take me for granted. We were supposed to meet here at six fifteen, and now I just got a text from him saying he can't make it. I figured that when he wasn't here when I arrived, he was standing me up again. He always puts business before me."

"Well . . ." Skye trailed off, not knowing what to say. "Simon is like that."

How much time were the bubbly blonde and

the somber funeral director spending together? Were they getting serious? Emmy seemed to be a younger version of Simon's mother, which would drive him crazy. Then again, the embrace Skye had witnessed had seemed off the chart in sensuality, and men could forgive a lot if the woman was hot and the sex was even hotter.

"And it worked like a charm." Emmy ignored Skye's statement and pointed to the entrance.

"Good gravy!" Skye grimaced. Simon had pushed through the glass doors and was scowling in their direction.

CHAPTER 15

STAN—Stalker Fan

Simon strode purposefully toward their table. He greeted various folks along the way but ignored anyone's attempt to detain him and start a conversation. As always, he wore a perfectly tailored dark suit, a crisp white shirt, and highly polished black oxfords. He pointedly gazed at Emmy as he slid in next to Skye.

Shoot! Why did I scoot over for him? Skye scowled. The whole polite thing wasn't working for her. She had to quit being so nice.

Once Simon was seated, he said, "Are you ladies having a nice chat?"

Emmy tossed her long blond hair back and retorted, "We were."

Skye kept her mouth shut. Simon's presence was awkward on a couple of different levels, and she wasn't about to add to any of them. She really didn't want to witness a lover's quarrel between another couple, especially one involving an old boyfriend. And judging from the exasperated look on Simon's face and Emmy's defiant expression, they were about to have a doozy of an argument.

Worse, Wally would not be happy when he heard that she'd had dinner with her ex-beau. He wouldn't care that Emmy was also there. With Skye and Simon's history, the gossip would be relentless. And before long, Simon and Emmy's squabble would be turned into a fight caused by Simon's unrequited love for Skye.

While Emmy stared at her boyfriend, Tomi hurried over and asked, "What can I get you, Simon? The girls' meals will be out any second, so if you all want to eat at the same time, I recommend the prime rib, the meat loaf, or the turkey dinner."

"Just coffee." Simon glanced at Emmy. "I only have a couple of minutes."

"How about a slice of pie with that?" Tomi pulled over one of the cups already on the table and poured from the pot in her hand.

"Your lemon meringue is hard to resist, but no thanks." He smiled at the older woman.

"At your age, you shouldn't worry about avoiding temptation." Tomi raised an eyebrow. "Because when you get older, it will avoid you."

"And how would you know that?" Simon tilted his head appraisingly. "Surely not from experience."

"Sweet talker." Tomi tapped Simon's shoulder. "Let me know if you change your mind."

"Will do. But I haven't been getting much exercise lately, and I need to lose a little weight." Simon patted his waistline.

"Me too, honey." Tomi winked and said over her shoulder as she strolled away, "But the only way I'd ever drop a few pounds is if I visited London."

"I'm sorry that I had to break our date." Simon leaned slightly forward toward Emmy. "As I said in my first text—the one I sent you at six so you wouldn't waste your time driving to the restaurant—there was an urgent state of affairs that needed my attention. And as I said in my second text—after you disregarded my original message—had to attend to the situation immediately and I was still unable to meet you here."

"What was the big emergency? A dead body was about to come back to life if you didn't embalm it right away?" Emmy said mockingly. "Are you saving us from the zombie apocalypse?"

Skye was getting increasingly uncomfortable and decided dinner wasn't worth sitting through this scene. "Excuse me. Could you let me out?" she asked. She was trapped between a wall on one side and Simon on the other, and he didn't budge. He acted like he hadn't even heard her.

"Of course not." Simon's voice was low. "Mr. and Mrs. Hucksford asked if they could arrange their daughter's funeral via Skype. They live in California and aren't able to travel to Scumble River. Since I've never used Skype, I needed to download the software onto my laptop and figure out how to work it before their appointment at seven."

"Why didn't you tell them you'd talk to them tomorrow?" Emmy thrust out her lower lip. "The woman's dead. What's the hurry?"

Skye had the same question, and now that Simon was discussing Blair, she wasn't as eager to escape. Wally would definitely want to know why the Hucksfords were moving so quickly. Especially since their daughter's body hadn't even been released by the ME yet.

"Tonight at seven is the only time their attorney was available," Simon explained. "He's leaving for Australia tomorrow morning and will be gone for several weeks."

"Why do they need a lawyer to arrange her funeral?" Emmy asked.

Another good question. Skye flipped open her book, pretending disinterest, but kept her ears open. She didn't have to get involved. Emmy was doing just fine getting information from Simon.

"Something about the deceased's estate." Simon took a sip of coffee.

"So you decided to blow off your date with me in order to accommodate a couple of strangers." Emmy curled her lip. "People who don't care enough about their daughter to fly to Illinois to get her body?"

"It's not my place to question how people mourn." Simon's expression was somber. "Everyone demonstrates their emotions differently. Something I've tried to explain to you on my own behalf on several occasions."

"Don't get me started." Emmy narrowed her eyes. "You know that I don't have brakes."

"Well, if you're going to insist on living on the edge, you better make sure you're wearing a seat belt, because you're headed for a crash." Simon glowered back.

Emmy's lips parted as if about to argue the point; then they snapped shut. A second later, in a deceptively casual tone, she said, "But you found time in your busy schedule to come have coffee with us when you saw that I was here with Skye. Didn't you?"

"I . . . uh . . . well—"

Simon was saved by the arrival of Emmy's and Skye's food. Tomi put their plates in front of the women, along with a fresh glass of soda for Skye. She topped off Emmy's and Simon's coffee and asked Simon again if he wanted anything to eat.

After making sure that no one needed anything else, Tomi told them to enjoy their meal and hurried away to handle the line that had suddenly formed at the cash register.

As Skye forked a bite of grilled chicken breast topped with grilled green peppers, onions, mushrooms, and mozzarella cheese into her mouth, she watched Emmy tear into her barbecued spare ribs. For such a slim woman, Emmy appeared to have a big appetite.

A few seconds went by, and then Emmy paused in mid gnaw and said, "You never answered my question. Why did you rush down here?"

"I have no idea," Simon admitted. "Maybe because I was looking for an excuse to see you tonight, even if it was for only a couple of minutes." He took Emmy's hand—the one not holding the spare rib. "I felt that I had to cancel the date and oblige the Hucksfords in their time of grief, but I truly was sorry to miss seeing you tonight. I'd been looking forward to it all day long. I guess I should have told you that in the text, but I didn't know how to say it."

A lump formed in Skye's throat. That was one of the sweetest things she'd ever heard Simon say. She resolutely ignored the teeny twinge of jealousy. No reason to be a dog in the manger. She didn't love Simon and was happy he'd found someone else.

Noticing that Simon and Emmy were staring

soulfully into each other's eyes, Skye tried to give them as much privacy as the situation allowed by concentrating on her food. But considering she was less than a foot from Simon's side, she couldn't avoid overhearing their conversation.

Emmy murmured, "Nobody cares how well you waltz. But you have to eventually just get up and dance."

"I try." Simon's voice was husky. "For you, I'll try harder."

Skye had decided it would be a good time to go to the restroom, but Simon's watch suddenly began beeping. He quickly slid out of the booth and stood up. Stepping over to Emmy, he leaned down and whispered something in her ear.

She giggled, pursed her lips, then said, "Okay, but only because I already packed my costume."

Simon kissed her cheek and shook his finger at her. "And no more personal info on Open Book."

"We'll see." Emmy looked up at him through her eyelashes. "Depends how good you are tonight."

His ears red, Simon said a stiff good-bye to Skye and hurried out of the restaurant.

As soon as he was gone, Skye said, "I take it he's forgiven and you're meeting up after his Skype appointment?"

"Yep. He said the five most important words in any relationship." Emmy smiled as if she'd just won Wimbledon. *"You were right. And I apologize."*

"Which was your strategy all along," Skye guessed.

"I love it when a plan comes together." Emmy held up her hand for a high five.

Skye slapped the other woman's palm. Emmy seemed like the perfect match for Simon. She was able to stand up to him in a way Skye never had quite been able to manage. Emmy could help him chill out, relax, and get more pleasure out of life. Evidently, lots more pleasure, if his blushing about their late-night plans were any indication.

Skye and Emmy enjoyed the rest of their meal, and afterward Skye felt a little better about the stunning blonde. Maybe they'd even be friends someday. That is, if Emmy could stop flirting with Wally.

It was after seven by the time they finished eating, paid their bills, and Skye took the to-go box from Tomi. Emmy and Skye walked into the parking lot together, and once Emmy had gotten into her car and driven away, Skye checked her cell to see if Wally had left her a message. There were no texts or voice mails from him indicating he was home, so she headed over to the PD. What in the world was keeping Wally there so late?

The police station shared a large redbrick building and parking lot with the city hall and town library. During the day, finding a spot could be tricky, but since it was so late, Skye had her choice of slots. She pulled the Bel Air between her mother's white Oldsmobile and the ugliest car she'd ever seen—a purple 1973 Gremlin.

When Skye pushed open the PD's glass door, a series of chimes announced her arrival. She waved at her mom, who stood at Skye's right— bulletproof glass reached from the counter to the ceiling, separating her mother from the reception area.

May waved back, then buzzed Skye through the security entrance on the far wall. Once she was through the door, Skye took a step and poked her head around the corner to greet her mom.

"Hi." May didn't take her eyes from the computer screen. "Did Wally call you in? I thought he said he was going to wait until tomorrow."

"Nope." Skye held up the carryout box. "I had dinner at the Feed Bag, so I brought him some supper. I forgot you'd be working or I would have gotten you a slice of that chocolate cake you like so much."

"I'm glad you didn't. Tomi's desserts are too hard to resist." May grimaced. "And I'm still trying to lose those five pounds I gained on the cruise." She glanced at Skye. "Looks like you are, too."

"Not really," Skye said coolly, then asked, "Is Wally in his office?"

"No. He's with a suspect." May made a face, then turned back to the computer. She was expected to type data into the computer, monitor the radios, and answer the phones simultaneously.

"But he's been in there a while, so he might be almost done."

"Who's he talking to?" Skye asked. "Is it someone connected to the murder?"

"No. McCabe brought in Banjo Bender. Wally's been wanting to talk to him about all the buildings that have burned in the past few months," May said, finally facing Skye. "He thinks they may not have been accidental. The fire department is hemming and hawing about whether someone torched all those businesses or Scumble River is just having a run of bad luck." May narrowed her eyes. "Apparently, it's not as easy to spot arson as those television shows would have you believe."

"Yeah, Wally tells me that's true about a lot of the forensic stuff they show on TV." Skye pursed her lips. McCabe's presence explained the purple Gremlin. It was a car only the inept county deputy would drive and/or think was cool. "But why is McCabe's personal vehicle parked in the lot? Was he undercover?"

"Yeah. Right. Undercover as the biggest dork on the planet—himself." May snickered, then explained. "Wally asked the county to keep a look-out for Bender, and McCabe spotted him sitting at the Bunny Lanes bar. The deputy was bowling on his regular Wednesday-night league, and there was Banjo—big as life and twice as tipsy."

"Who's on duty here tonight?" Skye asked as the telephone rang.

"Anthony's out patrolling," May said, then answered the call. When she hung up the phone, she added, "He's making the circuit."

The circuit was from one end of Basin Street to the other. It was patrolled mainly to keep an eye on the numerous bars that were scattered down its length. Even on a weeknight, the taverns were hopping, and the drunks sometimes spilled out onto the sidewalks.

"Guess I'll go upstairs and wait for Wally in his office," Skye said.

"When he finishes with Banjo, I'll let him know you're there." May turned back to answer a radio call.

Skye said good-bye and strolled down the short hallway that led past the coffee/interrogation room. The blinds were closed, but she could hear a voice baying, "I ain't no firebug." From the sounds of Wally's laughter, Skye could tell he didn't believe the man.

Continuing on, she climbed the steps to the second floor and paused on the landing. She glanced nervously to her right. A year ago, her uncle had ordered that an opening be cut in the wall between the city hall and the police department. Now, whenever she was there, she was always half afraid Dante would pop out through the archway like the scary clown in a jack-in-the-box.

When she saw His Honor's door was closed, she relaxed. However, since there was light seeping out around the jamb, she hurried down the hall toward Wally's office. Juggling her purse, tote, and the carryout box, Skye fumbled with the knob. Why wouldn't it open? Wally never bothered to lock up until he left for the day.

After groping through her shoulder bag for her key ring, she unlocked the door and stepped inside. As she looked up from stashing away the key, she gasped. Otto McCabe had his feet up on Wally's desk. He was leafing through a folder while he chewed on one of the special sticks of beef jerky that Skye had bought her husband on their honeymoon cruise. She was incensed. Divine Bovine was both pricey and hard to find.

Skye and McCabe stared at each other for a second. Then he tossed down the file, leaped from the chair, and started choking. Throwing down the jerky, he clutched his throat, coughing and sputtering. Just as Skye was afraid that she'd have to perform the Heimlich maneuver— or worse, mouth-to-mouth resuscitation—the deputy spat a chunk of meat into the trash can and scowled at her.

"You pert near scared me to death." McCabe tugged at his green-and-orange aloha shirt, then fingered the huge watch on his wrist.

"I had no idea you were in here." Skye wrinkled her brow. It seemed strange to see him in something other than his tan Stanley County uniform. Shaking her head at his clothing choice, she glared. "And speaking of that, what are you doing with your feet on my husband's desk, eating his expensive snacks?"

"The chief said I could wait for him here." McCabe scowled, and his hand went to his hip, most likely searching for the comfort of the gun that was usually there. "He told me to make myself at home."

The high-strung skinny deputy bore an unfortunate resemblance to Barney Fife from the old *Andy Griffith Show.* Skye wondered if, like Barney, he was allowed to have only one single bullet. If so, did he keep it in his shirt pocket like the TV character?

When Skye didn't comment, McCabe glowered at her and said, "You got no business sneaking in like that. I could have shot you dead."

"Only if you had your gun." Skye stood her ground. "And I doubt Wally meant for you to make yourself quite as at home as you were."

"Says you." McCabe hitched up his pants and bristled. "The chief appreciates me."

"Uh-huh." She peered at the tab on the folder he'd been perusing. It was marked BLAIR HUCKSFORD. "Why were you reading that file?"

"I was bored." He smoothed his greasy hair back into its pompadour.

"Was it interesting?" Skye was curious what, if anything, McCabe had seen and if he'd been looking for any specific information.

"I can't discuss official police business with you." The deputy puffed out his thin chest and straightened his narrow shoulders.

"You do recall that I work as the police department psychological consultant?" Skye said impatiently. They'd had this discussion before, but for some reason McCabe chose not to remember.

"Sure. Nothing gets past me. I got my ear to the ground and my eye on the prize." He thrust his head forward, looking like a pigeon in search of a tasty bread crumb. "You working the murder?"

"Of course."

"Well, it's a mess." McCabe shoved his hands in his pockets. "The chlorine in the pool water ruined any possible evidence, you know."

"Uh-huh."

"And no one seemed to like the vic, except maybe her boyfriend." He leaned a skinny hip against the desk. "And he's missing."

"Really?" Skye said slowly. That was interesting. She'd meant to ask Wally about the physical education teacher but had never gotten a chance to bring him up. "So Thor Goodson hasn't been questioned?"

"Nope."

"That's definitely a problem," Skye murmured to herself. "The clock is ticking."

"Where's the gall-darn fire?" McCabe frowned. "The vic's not going nowhere."

"Come on. You know that the more time that

goes by, the less likely the case is to be solved." Skye rolled her eyes. They'd had this conversation before, too. "We need to be on top of things."

"Don't be lecturing me, missy." McCabe moved into her personal space. "I'm a professional peace officer, and you're nothing more than the chief's trophy wife."

Skye hid a smile. She never thought she'd hear herself called that.

"The rest of us had to work hard to join the force," McCabe bellowed, his Adam's apple moving up and down like a bobber on a fishing line.

Skye backed up a step. The alcohol on the deputy's breath made her dizzy.

"While you and that other woman the chief had to hire to be politically correct didn't do nothing but grow a pair of boobies."

"That's not only untrue but offensive." Skye realized the deputy was inebriated, and he was starting to scare her a little bit.

"You and Martinez shouldn't be on the force." McCabe backed her against the desk and grabbed her by the shoulders. "The chief should have hired me."

"I—"

Before Skye could respond, a voice from the doorway thundered, "Take your hands off of my wife or you're a dead man."

CHAPTER 16

GNOB—Good Night Open Book

"I can't freaking believe he dared to touch you." Wally's face was dangerously red. "I should have separated his head from his shoulders."

"It really wasn't that serious," Skye protested. "I can handle McCabe."

They'd been home for several minutes and Wally still hadn't calmed down. Once the deputy had scuttled away, apologies and excuses trailing behind him like toilet paper clinging to his heel, Wally had made sure that Skye was okay. Once she assured him that she was fine, he whisked her out of his office and down the stairs.

They'd both plastered normal expressions on their faces as Wally told May he was leaving for the day. Then they said good-bye to her and hurried into the police garage. Wally had insisted on driving Skye home, which meant the Bel Air was still in the PD's lot and he'd have to take her to pick it up in the morning.

They'd made the short trip in silence, but once they entered the house, Wally had returned to obsessing about McCabe's behavior. As she guided Wally into the kitchen, Skye continued to reassure him that she was okay. She continued to tell him that she was fine while she transferred his dinner to a plate, placed a plastic dome over it, and slid it into the microwave.

Wally was probably overreacting because of her pregnancy, but she was worried that her new husband was about to have an aneurysm. Pushing him onto a kitchen chair, she fetched a Sam Adams from the refrigerator and handed him an opener along with the beer.

He viciously levered off the cap and downed a quarter of the bottle in one gulp. The bright fuchsia of his complexion faded to a dull brick and he said, "To misquote Clarence Darrow, I've never killed a man, but I sure would read McCabe's obituary with great pleasure."

Skye laughed, then repeated for the fiftieth time, "Truly, it was no big deal." She snickered. "And the look on his face when you stomped in reminded me of a bulldog that had just swallowed a wasp."

"What stirred up the little polecat anyway?"

"He's not a fan of women's equality." Skye poured herself a caffeine-free Diet Coke.

"Huh?" Wally loosened his tie. "You two were discussing equal rights?"

"Not exactly." The microwave beeped, and Skye checked to see if the chicken and potatoes were hot. Satisfied, she put the dish in front of Wally and turned back to get the bottle of ketchup from the fridge.

"So?" Wally poured Heinz over his French fries, then bit into a leg.

"McCabe's upset you hired Zelda and not him when there was an opening." Skye stole a fry. She seemed to be hungry all the time. "I'm not real clear why he's ticked off that I'm the psych consultant, since I'm pretty darn sure he couldn't do that job."

"He's been bugging me to hire him now that Zuchowski's gone and there's another slot open." Wally scratched his head. "I know McCabe's not the sharpest crayon in the box, but I didn't think he was completely cracked. Did he really think manhandling my wife would move his application to the top of the pile?"

"I doubt thinking had anything to do with it." Skye grabbed the Styrofoam container of coleslaw and Wally's fork and took a bite. *Okay.* She really needed to stop eating. "If the odor from his breath was any indication, McCabe was drunker than a frat boy on spring break."

"That's no excuse." Wally threw down the leg bone and picked up the thigh. "I just never thought he was quite that stupid."

"You know," Skye said, staring longingly at Wally's plate, then mentally giving herself a shake, "there's always one more imbecile than you counted on."

"Well, I do have to give McCabe credit for spotting the arsonist we've been after. Banjo shaved off his hair, grew a beard, and put on twenty pounds since his last mug shot."

"Did he confess?" Skye asked, snatching a piece of crispy chicken skin.

"Not yet." Wally finished the thigh and started on the breast. "But he's got a rap sheet a mile long for torching buildings, and he was seen in the area of a couple of the fires, so I'm sure he's good for them."

"Great." Skye yawned. It had been a long day, but she needed to let Wally know about her evening at the Feed Bag, because someone else was bound to tell him if she didn't. "Oh. Before I forget. You're going to hear that I had dinner with Simon tonight."

"Oh?" Wally's eyebrows formed an angry V over his nose. "Do tell."

"I was there alone," Skye explained. "But when Emmy showed up, all the tables were full. She asked to join me, and I couldn't exactly say no."

"Though you would have liked to." Wally's gaze was perceptive.

"Maybe," Skye mumbled, her cheeks pink. She wasn't proud that she was jealous of the gorgeous dancer. "Anyway, it turned out that Simon had stood her up for a date, but she put something on the computer that made him come rushing over, so he had coffee while we ate."

"It sounds like Emmy has him running around in circles." Wally chuckled.

"I'd say so. And it was really fun to see it." Skye grinned, then added, "But the reason he canceled their date is the most interesting part. Blair Hucksford's family set up an appointment to Skype with Simon regarding her funeral arrangements."

"Why is that so interesting?" Wally pushed away his empty plate.

"Because the reason it had to be tonight was that their attorney was leaving the country for several weeks and he needed to be present." Skye tipped her head. "They told Simon the lawyer needed to be a part of the discussion because of something to do with Blair's estate."

"Son of a buck!" Wally slammed his hand down on the table. "I specifically asked about the vic's will, and her parents denied any knowledge."

"So either they lied to you," Skye murmured, "or they weren't aware of the issue at the time you spoke to them."

"Speaking of Blair's family, did you get ahold of her sister?"

"Shoot!" Now Skye hit her forehead with her palm. "I forgot all about it. I'll call her during my break at noon tomorrow. That will be ten o'clock in California. If she's the school secretary, that should be an ideal time to talk to her— after the first bell and before the lunch craziness starts."

"See if you can find out anything about Blair's

estate from the sister." Wally got up from the table, scraped his plate into the trash, then put it the sink and turned on the hot water. "I'll do the same with her folks."

Skye followed Wally upstairs. They were both beat. It had been a long, hard day, and tomorrow probably wouldn't be any easier. A little reading and cuddling in bed, and they'd be ready to go to sleep.

She changed into her nightgown, then went into the bathroom to wash her face and brush her teeth. Wally turned on the shower, then leaned against the counter while he waited for the water to heat up.

"What did you get from the teacher and student interviews? You said you'd tell me more tonight," Skye asked as she put away her toothbrush and recapped the paste.

"There's not much more to tell. The vic didn't have any fans on the faculty," Wally said, stepping under the spray. "And although the members of the volleyball team all said the right things and Roxy maintained that she was not arguing with her coach, there's something they're not talking about. It almost felt like they had Stockholm syndrome."

"I saw those same girls earlier in the day." Skye rubbed her chin. "And now that you mention it, there was an odd vibe. I can't be specific due to confidentiality, but I definitely got the feeling that

201

there was something causing a schism among the players."

"I understand you can't name names, but let me go through my notes and see if I can pick out the ones on opposite sides." Wally adjusted the water temperature. "Once I narrow it down, I'd like to have you sit in on the interviews tomorrow afternoon."

"Hmm." Skye hesitated. Was it ethical for her to do that after establishing a counseling relationship? It wasn't as if she were seeing any of them individually or that they'd revealed any deep, dark personal secrets in the forty-five-minute group session. "I'll have to make it clear to the girls that this is a different setting and I'm not acting as their school psychologist."

"Sure," Wally agreed.

"Speaking of relationships and teachers . . ." Skye raised her voice so Wally could hear her as he shampooed and then rinsed out his hair. "What's this I hear about Thor Goodson being missing? Why didn't you mention that when I saw you at school earlier today?"

"Opal reported that he took a personal day, and he's not answering his phone." Wally picked up a bar of soap and lathered his chest. "Quirk went to his apartment, and his roommate said that Goodson went hiking near Starved Rock. Evidently, he often does that when he's upset. There's spotty cell coverage in that park area, so I asked the rangers to keep an eye out for him up there. I left a message with his roommate for him to call the PD as soon as he gets back."

"But nothing as of eight thirty, when we left the station?" she asked. As he stepped out of the shower stall, Wally shook his head, and Skye added, "I'm guessing he's a prime suspect, so if he doesn't check in soon, you'll put out an APB for him and his car."

"Right." Wally snagged a towel from the rack. "I wish we had his prints. Too bad the Illinois State Board of Education doesn't require teachers to submit a Fingerprint Clearance Card." Wally finished drying and pulled on a pair of sleep pants. "If Goodson doesn't show up by tomorrow, he changes from a person of interest to number one on my list of possible murderers."

It was a good thing that the alarm in Bingo's stomach went off, because the one on the nightstand didn't. The cat's persistent meowing broke through Skye's nightmare, and she struggled to surface from the awful dream. It took her several minutes to fight her way to full consciousness, and her head still felt as if it were wrapped in cotton batting when she staggered into the bathroom, turned on the shower, and stripped off her nightgown.

What had she been dreaming? She had a vague impression of a computer monitor with arms reaching out toward her, trying to pull her into the screen, but that was it. As she dried her hair and put on her makeup, Skye kept trying to recall the details of the nightmare, but finally gave up. Whatever had been scaring her had evaporated like dewdrops in the hot morning sun.

Slipping into a comfortable pair of black knit slacks, a tunic, and flat shoes, Skye chuckled. Most people dressed for success, but she had to dress for recess. She was going to the elementary school today, where she was often called out to the playground to observe a behavior not seen in the classroom, and she had ruined one too many outfits when she'd had to sit on a dirty swing or kneel on the grass to interact with a student.

By the time she was ready to go, Wally was awake and in uniform. He looked as foggy as she felt, and they were mute as they went downstairs and headed toward the coffeemaker. While it was perking, Skye fed Bingo and gave him fresh water.

As soon as she had discovered that she was pregnant, Wally had taken over cleaning the litter box. While he performed that chore, Skye put two English muffins in the toaster and took peanut butter from the cabinet and marmalade out of the refrigerator. This was her second day without morning sickness, and she'd woken up starving.

It was fortunate that she no longer felt queasy, because she wasn't sure when she'd be able to face the high school pool. She might have to wait for the weather to warm up enough to swim at the recreation club before she was ready to venture into the water again.

Wally returned from the utility room, washed his hands, and fixed himself a bowl of cereal. Skye poured cups of coffee for them both, and they sipped in companionable silence, waiting for the caffeine to take effect.

She had asked her obstetrician whether she could continue to drink coffee, and the doctor had assured her that as long as she limited her intake to less than two hundred milligrams per day—or one medium cup of coffee—it was fine. Good thing she already drank caffeine-free soda.

"What are your plans for today?" Skye asked after they had finished their breakfast and she was piling their dishes in the sink.

"Talk to Mr. and Mrs. Hucksford." Wally transferred the last of the coffee into a travel mug and put the carafe in with the rest of the dirty plates. "Bring in Thor Goodson for a conversation and go over Martinez's report. She and Quirk searched the vic's house yesterday."

"And you want me to come by after school to help with the student interviews?"

Skye checked the kitchen one more time to make sure it was tidy. Today was Dorothy's day to work for them, and although Skye knew it was silly to clean before the housekeeper arrived, she didn't want her mother's friend to think they were slobs. Or, worse yet, report that information to May.

"Unless you don't feel well enough or are too tired." Wally took her in his arms and kissed her on the cheek. "You and the baby come first, but if you're up to it, that would be very helpful."

"I feel great." Skye headed down the hallway toward the front door. "But I might need some doughnuts or maybe a cupcake from Tales and Treats. No." She licked her lips. "Make it one of Orlando's famous cranberry and white chocolate scones."

The sound of Wally's laughter followed Skye out the front door, and he continued to tease her about her newly insatiable appetite until he dropped her at the PD so she could pick up her car. She still had a smile on her face when she arrived at the elementary school for their weekly PPS conference.

After the meeting, Skye spent a couple of hours administering various evaluations to a second grader who, despite a high average score on a group intelligence test, was having difficulty with the academics. She had observed the boy in his classroom, and his attention and behavior were fine. So now, as she asked him various questions from the individual IQ assessment, she was looking for any hint of a learning disability.

Skye made sure he was focused and then read, "How can you delay milk from turning sour?"

"Keep it in the cow."

She hid a smile, wrote down his response, and asked the next question. "Explain one of the processes by which water can be made safe to drink."

"Flirtation makes water safe to drink," the boy answered. "It removes the large pollutants like sand, gravel, and fishermen."

Skye blinked, made another note, and went on. This child definitely had a unique way of thinking.

When she finished with the student, Skye checked her watch. She had just enough time to call Blair's sister before she had to be at the junior high for a parent consultation.

Sitting in her car, Skye dug through her purse until she found the paper with the woman's number. Powering up her cell, she made the call.

"Hucksford Christian Academy, how may I assist you?" a cheerful voice chirped in Skye's ear.

"Is this Bernadette?" Skye asked, realizing she hadn't planned what to say and didn't know the woman's married name.

"Yes, it is." Bernadette's tone was cautious. "And who is this?"

"My name is Skye Denison-Boyd. I worked with your sister at Scumble River High School. I'm the psychologist there." Skye hesitated, unsure what to say next. Finally, she just dived in with, "I'm so sorry for your and your family's loss. It must be very difficult to be so far away when you lose a loved one so tragically."

"Thank you," Bernadette answered slowly. "We're still in shock."

"I can imagine." Skye contemplated how she'd feel if it were her brother, Vince, who had been murdered. "Were you and Blair close?"

"We used to be." Bernadette's voice broke. "Before she went to college."

"I'm curious as to why she went to an Illinois university when she was from California." Skye had wondered how Blair had chosen SWIU.

"Southwest Illinois University offered her a volleyball scholarship." Bernadette's tone hardened. "Father begged her not to go there."

"Why's that?" Skye asked. "Because she would be so far away?"

"Well, of course that was one consideration, but more importantly, he didn't want her to spend four years in a heathen institution."

"I see." Skye knew that SWIU had a reputation as a party school, but she suspected that wasn't Mr. Hucksford's concern. "I'm surprised Blair didn't return to California once she got her degree. Scumble River is a small town, and most of our teachers grow up somewhere fairly close by. Few are from out of state."

"By then Father had disowned her," Bernadette

said sadly. "The apostate influences had corrupted her, and her behavior was no longer Christian."

"In what way?" Skye asked.

"Why did you say you were calling?" Bernadette asked, a note of suspicion creeping into her voice.

"As I said, I'm a school psychologist." Skye took a breath. Clearly, the woman was losing patience, so it was now or never. "But I also work as a consultant for the police department. I'm helping to investigate your sister's murder. And we need to know what Blair did that was so heinous that your father washed his hands of her."

"She turned into an exhibitionistic pervert." Bernadette spit out the words as if they tasted like ashes. "Someone who was willing to sell her soul because of a stupid game."

CHAPTER 17

TTYL—Talk to You Later

Skye stared at her cell phone. Bernadette had muttered good-bye and hung up before Skye could ask anything else, so she'd never gotten to introduce the subject of her sister's estate. And what had the woman meant by Blair selling her soul for the game? She might have been referring to her sister attending a secular university versus a Christian institution. But what exactly had Blair done that made her an "exhibitionistic pervert"? Were the SWIU volleyball uniforms that immodest?

Glancing at the dashboard clock, Skye saw that it was nearly twelve forty-five. She didn't have time to think about her conversation with Bernadette right now or her mysterious statement. Skye had a meeting at the junior high at one, and the principal had requested that she come ten minutes before the appointment so that they could talk before the parent arrived.

Skye hurriedly started up the Bel Air and drove over to the middle school. She parked in the first available spot, grabbed her tote bag, and ran for the front walk. After signing in at the counter, she flew past Ursula, the school secretary, and dashed into the principal's office.

Neva Llewellyn narrowed her eyes as Skye rushed through the door. Crossing her arms, she demanded, "Did Homer have another emergency? It's extremely unfair the way he monopolizes your services. He almost always gets your extra half day, and he often steals time from the rest of us."

The principal was a tall, lean woman in her early fifties. She and Skye were on friendly terms, but Neva was a perfectionist who expected every-one to live up to her strict standards of behavior. Tardiness was one of her major pet peeves.

"Unfortunately, I can't blame Homer," Skye said. "A telephone call delayed me." She was

210

careful not to reveal that the call had been police and not school business. She didn't feel guilty—after all, she had used her lunch break to talk to Bernadette—but it was still better not to mention it. "I'm sorry I kept you waiting."

When Neva had taken over from the previous principal—a guy whose taste ran to neon sports signs, milk-crate bookcases, and athletic memorabilia—she had completely redecorated. The office had gone from college-dorm utilitarian to refined elegance. Skye seated herself in a Queen Anne chair and faced Neva across a gleaming wooden desk. She put her tote bag on the floor, grabbed a pen and legal pad from its depths, and breathed in the pleasant odor of vanilla that wafted through the air from a small bowl of potpourri tucked away on a butterfly table next to the ivory wall.

Neva waited until Skye was settled; then she straightened the sleeve of her lavender suit and leaned forward. "It's still wrong."

"What?" Skye's heart skipped a beat, but her expression remained composed. Was the principal referring to Skye's lateness?

"Homer's abuse of your schedule." Neva pulled a tiny leather memo pad from the middle drawer, plucked a sterling-silver pen from the crystal stand on her desktop, and jotted down a note.

"You mean because of the recent crisis?" Skye hazarded a guess.

"Yes." Neva lifted her chin. "I know the previous

social worker didn't work out, but the district needs to get you some assistance."

"I've asked, but the superintendent claims that no one has applied," Skye said, averting her gaze. She wasn't actually pushing the board to find someone for the position any longer. Her experience with the last social worker had dampened her zeal on the idea of filling that role. Although now that she was pregnant, circumstances had changed, and she'd have to line up some help pretty darn soon.

"I'll discreetly check into Dr. Wraige's assertion. His secretary is my cousin's wife, and she can pull the file and see if he's telling the truth." Neva tapped a perfectly manicured nail on her chin and wrote another note. "But right now we have another problem."

"Yes?" Skye poised her Bic over her legal pad, ready to take notes.

"The parent we're meeting with this afternoon attempted to enroll her son in school on Monday," Neva said slowly. "But she didn't have the child's birth certificate or legal proof of residency."

"And since I'm here, I take it the boy is in special education?" Skye asked. Unlike Homer, Neva didn't often involve Skye in issues that weren't related to children with special needs.

"He has a partially completed referral." Neva got up, took a folder from her file cabinet, and handed it to Skye. "Most of the components are finished, but the psychological assessment isn't."

"Of course it's not," Skye murmured, flipping through the file.

"Mom claims the birth certificate got lost in the move." Neva resumed her seat. "But looking at the boy's records, I have my doubts."

"Why is that?" Skye continued to scan the student's paperwork.

"He's a sixth grader, and the family has changed schools eight times. Plus, there is no record he attended school before second grade." Neva put on her glasses and read from the page in front of her. "On the day his mother attempted to enroll him, I noted that his speech was unintelligible, he was unclean, and he smelled of urine."

"According to this, he's twelve." Skye nibbled the end of her pen.

"Right." Neva wrinkled her brow. "But he looks at least fourteen. I swear he had a five-o'clock shadow. And he couldn't give me simple personal information, like his year of birth, home address, or phone number."

"With all the moves, his lack of knowledge of the latter two might be explainable." Skye tilted her head. "The former could be a result of his mother lying about his age, or it may indicate a low IQ."

"My fear is that this child might be a kidnap victim." Neva grimaced. "I know that sounds a little dramatic. But with all you see in the news, I can't help but wonder if he was abducted between second and third grade." She shrugged. "It would explain the missing birth certificate and perhaps his confused demeanor."

"That's a possibility." Skye nodded. "But more likely, his mother doesn't want him diagnosed as mentally challenged, and she moves him whenever the school comes close to completing an evaluation."

"That makes sense," Neva agreed. "Still, if she doesn't provide some proof that he is her child, I'm contacting the authorities."

"The problem with the scenario that I suggested," Skye said, running her fingers through her hair as she considered the information Neva had reported, "is why would the mother allow us to see the partially completed referral if she was trying to hide a disability? That's the part that doesn't make any sense to me."

"Well . . ." Neva's expression was sheepish. "I may have somewhat manipulated the mother into signing a release form. The referral wasn't with the stuff she brought in, but after meeting the student, I figured there *had* to be some special ed records somewhere."

"If she didn't give informed consent, we can't use the records you obtained with that signature." Skye stared at the principal, daring her to object. It was beyond unethical to deceive a parent into signing a permission form she didn't understand, and Skye was surprised at Neva. "Either she agrees, or we start the whole referral process over once the child is enrolled."

"You're right." Neva's shoulders drooped, and she exhaled noisily. "If she objects, we can't use those records. I swear Homer and the rest of the boys' club that runs this district are beginning to rub off on me."

Before Skye could say anything, the school secretary buzzed and announced that Mrs. Puissant had arrived. Neva quickly put away her notes and instructed Ursula to show the woman into the office.

Once Mrs. Puissant was seated and introduced to Skye, Neva asked, "Were you able to find Bundy's birth certificate?"

"Not yet." Mrs. Puissant shook her head. Her limp brown hair was fastened with a rubber band and lay like a droopy squirrel tail on her shoulder. She wore baggy jeans and an oversize sweatshirt with NO PANTS SATURDAY printed on the front. "But I have my rental agreement, and I found Bundy's baptismal certificate and his social security card." She gave Neva the documents.

Neva looked them over and handed them to Skye. The year on the baptismal certificate was smeared. She couldn't tell if it was 2005 or 2003.

"Well, we don't want to keep Bundy out of

school any longer, so we'll provisionally accept the baptismal certificate, but please bring in the birth certificate as soon as you locate it," Neva instructed the woman. "In the meantime, we'd like to speak to you about the referral begun by Bundy's previous school."

"How did you know about that?" Mrs. Puissant asked, glaring.

"You signed permission for us to request any special education records," Neva explained. "And Bundy's school sent them over."

"I did not give my consent for you to see those papers." Mrs. Puissant jumped to her feet. "There's nothing wrong with my boy. If you all are going to be as sneaky as those other schools, I'll just teach him at home until my lease is up and we can move to a better district." With that, she snatched the documents from Skye's hands and marched out of the office.

Skye closed her eyes. It would have been so much better if Neva hadn't tricked Mrs. Puissant into signing consent for the special ed records. After building some rapport with the woman, maybe Skye could have persuaded her to trust the district, allow them to evaluate her son, and get him the help he needed.

"There goes a future guest of Jerry Springer," Neva said after the door slammed behind Mrs. Puissant. Then the principal shook her head and added, "That went badly. I should have just

216

enrolled the boy and approached the mother once he was settled in."

"Probably." Skye nodded. "But even if you'd done that, it's hard to know how it would have turned out. Mrs. Puissant may have some intellectual challenges of her own. And it's clear her experiences with school authorities haven't been positive ones."

"I guess the baptismal certificate and social security card prove the boy wasn't kidnapped." Neva fingered the tasteful diamond stud in her earlobe.

"With everything so public nowadays, it must be a lot tougher to hide an abducted child than it used to be," Skye murmured, thinking about Emmy and all the information posted every second on Open Book.

"If that's true, I suppose that's a positive of social media." Neva smiled wanly. "There aren't as many places for criminals to hide anymore."

"Yeah!" Skye made a mark in the air with her index finger. "One point for the good guys. On the other hand, there goes our privacy."

"Now the whole world is like a small town and gossip is posted instantly," Neva commented, then added, "But even if that woman is Bundy's legal guardian, his future isn't looking too bright."

"Homeschooling is great for a lot of kids." Skye twitched her shoulders. "Although I don't think it works as well for children with certain special needs as it might for other students."

"Let's hope the next school district she moves into has more luck." Neva straightened her spine. "But after spring break, I'd like you to get in touch with Mrs. Puissant and try to convince her to give us another chance. I think she sees me as the bad guy, so perhaps you can establish a better relation-ship with her and sway her."

"I'll be happy to give it a try." Skye flipped open her schedule and penciled in a call to Mrs. Puissant on the Monday they returned from vacation. "But if you feel that he's being neglected, and by your description of his physical appearance, it sure sounds that way, you really need to report your concerns to DCFS."

"I plan to," Neva said. "But we both know that the Department of Children and Family Services is overworked and understaffed. If Bundy isn't in any physical danger, they won't do too much."

Skye nodded her agreement, then said good-bye to Neva and left the principal staring out her window with a frown marring her smooth forehead. Dealing with kids and their problems was a complicated business and educators often found it difficult to make the best decision when neither option was ideal.

As Skye walked past Ursula's desk, the secretary handed her a pink slip of paper. It was a message from Homer, and at first Skye was afraid that either a student or a teacher was having a delayed emotional reaction to Blair's death.

When she read the note, she was relieved the message wasn't regarding that type of crisis, but she cringed when she saw that Mrs. Northrup was demanding another meeting. Before leaving school on Monday, Skye had arranged for Ashley Northrup's file to be sent to Thorntree, so the fact that she wanted to meet with them again so soon was probably not a good sign.

Either the school had rejected Ashley's application, or more likely, it had teamed up with Mrs. Northrup and encouraged her to begin due-process proceedings against Scumble River High, hoping to get the home district to pay the cost of the tuition. *Holy crap!* Skye had never been through a due-process hearing, and she really didn't want to start now.

Skye hurried to her office and called Homer. She told him she was available for a conference anytime the next day. She also recommended inviting the special education director and the school district's attorney, but Homer laughed off her suggestions and hung up.

She sat for a second, staring at the receiver. Tapping her fingernails on the phone's plastic base, she contemplated contacting the lawyer and coordinator herself but reluctantly rejected the idea. Neither man would show up without the principal's approval. The only thing calling them would accomplish would be to infuriate Homer.

Skye shuddered. Being in a meeting with an enraged Homer was like being trapped in a hamster wheel with a rabid gerbil—a lot more dangerous than it seemed.

The rest of the afternoon went smoothly, and Skye felt a sense of accomplishment when she left at three forty-five. As she pulled out of the school parking lot, heading toward the police station, she thought about checking her cell for messages, then decided against it. At this point, it was quicker to drive to the PD than to pull over, power up the device, and jump through the various hoops necessary to listen to any waiting voice mails or view her texts.

While she made her way into the station, she wondered which volleyball team members Wally had decided to reinterview. Her money was on Keely and the team captain. But something about Juliette hiding her intelligence made Skye suspicious of the girl. There was more to that young woman than she allowed the world to see.

Had Blair confronted Juliette? A teenager's motives for their actions were far different from an adult's. A fact to keep in mind when they talked to the volleyball players.

CHAPTER 18

F2T—Free to Talk

W hat's up?" Skye greeted her mother, who was once again on duty behind the dispatcher's desk. "Is Wally with a suspect?"

May was on the telephone, but she covered the receiver with her palm and said, "He's waiting for you in his office."

"Thanks." Skye waved, and May went back to her conversation. *Phew!* As Skye walked away, she wiped imaginary sweat from her brow. So far so good. Her mother hadn't made any further reference to babies or Skye needing to lose weight.

Making her way down the narrow corridor, Skye paused in front of the coffee/interrogation room. She could hear several voices, but they were speaking too softly for her to pick out any words. The blinds were closed, indicating the space was occupied by persons of interest rather than an officer on an afternoon break. Which girl had been summoned, and was that her parents in there with her?

Wally met Skye as she started up the stairs. Giving her a quick hug and kiss, he said, "I asked Mr. and Mrs. Alvarez to bring their daughter in after school. They arrived a few minutes ago."

"I figured you'd want to talk to the volleyball team captain." Skye smiled at her correct guess. "Also, remember her father is the guy I chatted with at the dry cleaner's. Even though he appeared to be a fan of Blair, I imagine you have a few questions for him, too."

"Yep. About which volleyball parents didn't admire the vic." Wally put his hand on the small of Skye's back, guiding her down the hallway. He stopped to open the door, then stepped back and allowed her to enter first.

The coffee/interrogation room was a no-frills space not unlike the teachers' lounge at the high school. A counter with a sink ran the length of the sidewall, a long table took up most of the center area, and a couple of vending machines occupied the rear.

Having skipped lunch in order to call Blair's sister, Skye heard her stomach growl as she passed by a plate of cookies near the coffee urn, reminding her that she was starving.

Wishing she were back on her honeymoon, enjoying a thick steak in the cruise ship's dining room, Skye forced herself to smile warmly. She held out her hand to Roxy's father and said, "I don't know if you recall, but we met the other day at the dry cleaner's. I'm Skye Denison-Boyd. In addition to my job with the school, I also work as a psychological consultant to the police department."

"I remember." Mr. Alvarez shook her hand and said, "Call me Rock." He gestured to the petite blonde sitting by his side. "This is my wife, Vanna."

"Nice to meet you." Skye shook the woman's hand and then said to the couple, "And, of course, I know your daughter." She turned to the girl. "Hi, Roxy. Just to be clear, in this setting I'm not acting as your school psychologist. What you say here is no longer private, but nothing that you told me in our session at school will be shared with Chief Boyd or the police. Do you understand what I just told you?"

Roxy rolled her eyes, but after a sharp look from her father, she said in a polite tone, "Yes, ma'am. Am I in trouble?"

Before Skye could answer the girl, Wally introduced himself. Then he and Skye took seats facing the family. Once they were settled, he clicked on the old-fashioned portable tape recorder sitting on the table. The city attorney had recently decreed that the police had to make an audio recording of all official interviews. Announcing the date and time, Wally asked, "Rock, Vanna, and Roxy Alvarez, are you aware you're being recorded?"

After a nervous exchange of glances, all three answered yes.

"Please state your full names and addresses." After the trio complied, Wally said to Roxy's parents, "We have a few questions regarding Blair Hucksford's murder that we'd like to ask your daughter, and in order to make her more comfortable, we are allowing you both to remain with her during this conversation."

"Is she a suspect?" Mr. Alvarez asked. "Maybe she should have a lawyer."

"We are talking to several of the volleyball team members, and as captain, Roxy has a unique perspective," Wally said smoothly.

Skye noticed Wally avoided answering Mr. Alvarez's questions.

"Well, I guess it's okay, then." Mr. Alvarez looked at his wife, whose expression was wary, then asked, "What do you want to know?"

"How would you describe Ms. Hucksford's style of coaching?" Wally asked.

"She wanted to win and expected all of us to give a hundred and fifty percent in order to make that happen." Roxy twined her fingers together, then cracked her knuckles. "It was real important to her that we work together. And she always said the only way for us to shine was to do exactly what our coach told us to do."

"Did she ever ask you to do something you didn't want to do?" Wally asked.

"Sure. Who *wants* to do fifty laps?" Roxy sneered. "But I knew I had to follow her leadership in order to be a better athlete."

"Admirable." Wally's tone was mild, but the girl

stiffened. He raised a brow. "Did everyone on your team feel that way?"

"Everyone who wanted to stay on the team," Roxy snapped. "You agreed with her methods, sucked it up if you didn't agree with her methods, or quit the team. That's the rule."

"So you didn't resent Ms. Hucksford for making you do stuff you were opposed to doing?" Skye asked. "Because someone mentioned hearing you and Ms. Hucksford having a pretty loud argument a while ago."

"No. I definitely did not resent following the coach's guidelines." Roxy crossed her arms. "I have a goal, and Ms. Hucksford was helping me achieve it. I may not have always liked what it took to attain my objective, but I was willing to sacrifice to get what I wanted." Roxy curled her lip. "And yes, occasionally Ms. H and I disagreed on something concerning the team, but in the end it was all about the win. Besides, after we discussed the situation, Ms. H saw my point and agreed to ask Keely to rejoin the squad."

"Keely Peterson quit the team?" Wally asked. "When was that?"

"Sometime last month, or maybe it was the month before." Roxy sucked in her cheeks. "But as I said, Ms. H got her to come back."

"Why did Keely leave?" Skye wasn't as concerned about the timing as the motivation. "When I was chatting with your father at the dry cleaner's, he mentioned that you and she were the best players."

"She had a problem with Ms. H's methods, but they worked something out." Roxy flipped her braid over her shoulder. "As usual, Keely got her way, while the rest of us had to toe the line."

"I see," Skye murmured, hiding her surprise. Considering both Blair's reputation and Skye's own experience with the woman, the coach hadn't seemed like the type to capitulate to one of her player's demands.

"What did Keely get her way about?" Wally asked.

"She refused to do some of the team-building stuff, and Ms. H agreed to waive the requirement for her." Roxy's mouth formed a pinched-looking pout.

"What kind of activities did Keely refuse to do?" Skye asked.

"The usual." Roxy refused to meet Skye's gaze. "I don't remember the specific ones."

Skye asked several more questions about Keely quitting the team, but Roxy maintained she couldn't recall exactly which exercises her teammate turned down. Roxy was getting agitated, and Skye had run out of ways to phrase the same inquiry, so she gave up.

After a few seconds of silence, Wally said, "Tell me about Monday evening."

"Like I told you yesterday at school when you asked me, Ms. Hucksford scheduled a team practice for six o'clock." Roxy's voice was sullen. "We finished up at nine. I showered, dressed, swung by my friend Brit Jeffries's house to pick her up, and went home. She was spending the night with me so we could study for a math test the next day."

"You had two volleyball activities on Monday? One in the morning *and* one in the evening?" Skye asked. *Wow!* It was no wonder so many people thought Blair was preoccupied with the team. Her obsession with her job made Skye seem like a free spirit.

"Yep. In the morning we swam to strengthen our shoulder and leg muscles, and in the evening we practiced our serving, passing, net saves, and repetition drills."

"And all that took place in the gym?" Skye asked, wishing she'd had a chance to read Wally's and Quirk's reports before this interview.

"Yes." Roxy examined her fingernails. "Ms. H always reserved the gym, lockers, and pool. She didn't want any civilians around. And a few of the girls like to take a dip after practice."

"So no one besides the team members and Ms. Hucksford were present," Wally said.

"Right." Roxy nodded. "Sometimes the football players and Mr. Goodson join us, but not that night. It was just the girls."

"Was there anyone with Ms. Hucksford when you left?" Wally asked.

"There were a couple of kids who were waiting for their rides, but I saw their parents pull into the lot when I was driving away. We all had tests the next day, so no one wanted to stay for a swim." Roxy blew out an exasperated sigh. "I told you all this yesterday."

"You didn't mention Brit Jeffries. Why is that?" Wally asked.

"She's not on the volleyball team, so I didn't think you were interested in her." Roxy heaved another exaggerated sigh.

"Did you and Brit make any detours between her place and yours?" Wally asked, clearly unconcerned with the girl's annoyance.

"Nope. We went straight to my house," Roxy said. "Brit and I were both starving, and I had a phone interview with the SWIU coach set up for ten and I sure didn't want to be late for that."

"Roxy and Brit had something to eat." Vanna Alvarez joined the conversation. "Then Roxy talked to that SWIU woman for over an hour. Afterward the girls did their homework, watched TV, and went to bed around midnight."

"You didn't mention speaking to the SWIU coach yesterday either," Wally said sharply.

"I forgot." Roxy shrugged. "You made me nervous."

Skye exchanged glances with Wally. The time

of death had been set between eleven and twelve, so if they believed Roxy's parents, she had an alibi. They'd have to check with the SWIU coach and Brit Jeffries, but it looked as if Roxy was in the clear.

Wally continued to ask questions, rewording them to see if Roxy's story changed.

Finally, Rock Alvarez pushed back his chair and said, "My daughter has answered all your questions several times over. If you don't have anything new to ask her, we need to get home so she can get started on her homework and my wife can cook supper."

"Of course," Wally agreed, but he squeezed Skye's knee, indicating this was the time if she had anything to add. "We surely don't want to keep you from dinner. Thanks for your patience."

"We're happy to cooperate with the police," Rock said, standing.

"Mr. Alvarez," Skye said, getting to her feet and facing him. "Before you all get going, I just wanted to ask *you* a question."

"Okay." Rock twisted his baseball cap in his hands.

"You mentioned at the dry cleaner's that not all the volleyball parents felt the same way you did about Ms. Hucksford."

"Right." Rock's tone was neutral. "Some of them couldn't accept the time and commitment that playing on a winning team required."

"I imagine it is tough with the other extra-curricular activities and homework and all the rest of the teenage stuff," Skye said sympathetically. "Some people think winning isn't worth the sacrifice."

"Sure." Rock's ears reddened, and his nails dug into the ball cap's fabric. "But their daughters don't have a scholarship on the line. It's important for her to be on a winning team."

"When we chatted, you seemed like a big supporter of Ms. Hucksford."

"I was." Rock straightened his shoulders. "Ms. H saw how talented Roxy was and was making sure she was in line for one of the few spots on a college team."

"Which parents weren't on board with Ms. Hucksford's methods?" Skye asked, then glanced at Roxy. The girl's expression didn't mirror the hero worship on her father's face. Had Blair let her down some way? Although, if her alibi checked out, her feelings about her coach didn't really matter.

"The Inslees and Mac Peterson were the most vocal," Rock answered reluctantly. "The rest settled down once the team started winning."

After Rock stated that he had nothing more to add, the family left and Skye and Wally retreated to his office.

As Wally put the tape recording of the Alvarez interview into a manila evidence envelope, wrote the necessary information on the front, and made a few notes, Skye mulled over what Rock had revealed.

Finally, she murmured, "Parents can be funny about their kids' participation in sports. I think there was more drama than Mr. Alvarez was willing to reveal."

"Uh-huh." Wally didn't look up. "First thing in the morning, I'll be talking to the Inslees and Mac Peterson. Maybe Peterson can shed some light on why his daughter quit the team and then rejoined it."

"Juliette Inslee is on the school paper." Skye rummaged in her tote bag for her own pen and paper and jotted down a couple of reminders. "There's something more than meets the eye with that girl. It might be a good idea to arrange for her and Keely to come into the station after school tomorrow so we can question them."

"You read my mind, darlin'." Wally placed the completed evidence envelope into a drawer, then locked it and pocketed the key.

"Did Thor Goodson ever contact you?" Skye asked. She couldn't believe she'd almost forgotten about Blair's missing boyfriend.

"The ranger found him a couple of hours ago camped out in an unauthorized spot." Wally stood up. "Goodson's car had a flat tire and no spare. Evidently, he just *happened* to have outdoor equipment in his trunk, so he decided to just

231

stay there a few days to recover from his grief."

"Why didn't he answer the messages you left on his cell phone?"

"Dead battery." Wally opened the office door for Skye.

"How convenient." Skye started down the stairs. "Wasn't he afraid of losing his job? I mean, you can't just not show up for work."

"He used his three personal days to take Tuesday through Thursday off. I'm not sure why Opal didn't mention that, but I guess we didn't specifically ask her how much time he was taking off. She did confirm that his leave had been preapproved."

Wally led Skye into the garage attached to the police station. All the official vehicles were kept there, and Skye could exit through the space to get to her car in the parking lot.

"Again, very convenient," Skye muttered. "So where is Thor now?"

"The state police arranged to have his car towed and are escorting him to Laurel." Wally opened the squad car's door. "He'll spend the night there in the county jail, and tomorrow I'll have one of my officers go pick him up and bring him back here."

"You're arresting him?" Skye asked. "Can you do that without any evidence?"

"He's being held for questioning. I think it will do him a world of good to sit in a cell and contemplate the error of his ways. It'll put him in a more cooperative mood." Wally winked. "I have forty-eight hours before I have to arrest him or turn him loose."

"Right." Skye nodded. "I knew that. What's wrong with my brain lately?"

"Nothing, sugar." Wally smiled. "You just have a lot on your mind."

Wally started to slide into the cruiser, but Skye said, "Oh, speaking of that. I almost forgot. I finally talked to Bernadette. I didn't get anything about Blair's will, but her sister did say that she was ostracized from the family due to her exhibitionistic and perverted behavior."

"What did she mean by that?" Wally scratched his head. "Was she a stripper?"

"Bernadette wouldn't tell me, but I don't think it was that." Skye settled her tote bag more comfortably on her shoulder. "She said that Blair had sold her soul because of a stupid game, so I have to think it had something to do with volleyball."

"That sport did seem to be her whole life."

"And sadly," Skye said almost to herself as she waved good-bye to Wally and headed toward the parking lot, "maybe also the cause of her death."

CHAPTER 19

THX40—Thanks for Nothing!

Yawning, Skye unlocked her office door. It was 6:37 Friday morning and she was dog-tired. If anyone wanted to see bright-eyed and bushy-tailed today, they'd better go watch a squirrel.

She hadn't slept well the night before. Her dreams were a scrambled mess of telephones ringing and strobing flashbulbs. It was as if some subliminal courier were trying to send her a message about Blair's murder.

With one more gigantic, jaw-cracking yawn, Skye stepped across the threshold, came to an abrupt stop, and stared. *What in the heck!* Rows and rows of boxes were stacked so high she couldn't see over them. *Shoot!* How many rubber ducks had she ordered?

Pushing her way among the cardboard cartons, Skye frantically searched the cases until she found the bill of lading. *Oh. My. Gosh!* She'd added an extra zero and accidentally bought ten thousand rubber duckies instead of one thousand of the plastic fowl. Her bill was for more than fifteen hundred dollars. She hoped they were returnable, or her maternity clothing fund had just taken a hit.

Shit on a shingle! Some days the only good

thing about her job was that her chair spun around. Seated behind her desk, Skye dropped her purse to the floor as she read through all the fine print on the invoice. Finally, she found the section on how to send merchandise back to the manufacturer. Her heart rate slowed down and she drew in a shaky breath. *Phew!* That had been a close one. Thank goodness the company she'd selected offered free shipping on returns.

After stowing her belongings in a drawer, Skye called the custodian to bring his dolly to her office. Cameron arrived a few minutes later, and she requested that two of the crates be moved to the multimedia center. When he was finished with that, she asked him to call the freight company to pick up the rest of the cases.

Giving Cameron the return address label, Skye thanked him for his help and handed over her emergency stash of Archway Cashew Nougat cookies as a reward for his assistance.

With the first step in rectifying her error set in motion, her feelings of panic subsided and she grabbed the box of black permanent markers from her tote bag. As she headed down the hallway, she congratulated herself on having remembered to stop at the store to pick up the Sharpies on her way home the night before.

Skye's step quickened. The school newspaper staff was meeting in the library at seven, and the kids had only fifty minutes to number a thousand rubber duckies before the first bell summoned them to class. With less than a day and a half until the race, Trixie was busy motivating her cheerleaders to sell more ducks, so Skye was supervising the waterfowl numbering by herself.

There were generally a dozen students involved in putting out the *Scoop*, and all of them had shown up to help with the ducks. Skye assigned each teenager a specific range of numbers—such as one to a hundred or a hundred and one to two hundred—then passed out the markers. Once everyone was busy working, she strolled down the aisles, watching for problems.

Skye was a little surprised that Blair's death hadn't caused any major ripples in the school. As far as she could tell from lingering in the hallway during passing periods and hanging out in the faculty lounge, no one seemed very upset about the volleyball coach's demise.

In fact, after the initial reaction when Blair's death was announced on Wednesday, it was almost as if everyone had forgotten about her. A substitute science teacher had been hired for the remainder of the year, and everyone had moved on with their lives.

The school newspaper's editor, Paige Vitale, shared a table with Juliette Inslee. Paige had just turned seventeen, but she seemed more mature than most other kids her age. Maybe it was because she appeared comfortable in her own skin. Her shoulder-length brown hair was fastened in a low ponytail, and she wore a pair of cropped skinny jeans with a blue-and-white-striped scooped-neck T-shirt. Her makeup was minimal—just lip gloss and mascara—and a pair of silver hoop earrings were her only jewelry.

Juliette's style was the complete opposite of the older girl's look. She gave the impression that she spent a lot of time deciding what to wear and selecting accessories for that outfit.

Skye noticed that the Peter Pan collar on Juliette's shirt exactly matched the fabric of her short black skirt, and her jewelry picked up the floral pattern of the top. Her hair was a perfect blond curtain sweeping down her back and stopping just inches above her tiny waist. Her nails were flawless, as if freshly polished that morning. And her shoes looked brand-new.

As Skye noted the differences between the two young women, she saw that Paige was listening intently as Juliette poured out her heart. Skye was a little uncomfortable with eavesdropping on the girls, but she had a feeling this was her best chance to understand Juliette's puzzling behavior. Shushing her guilty conscience, Skye ducked behind a bookshelf.

Leaning against the smooth wooden shelves, she realized she'd come in on the middle of the intense conversation. Skye frowned. What had instigated the solemn discussion?

"Well, the thing is, people still think of you the way you were." Juliette drew a perfect twenty-seven on her duck.

Skye watched as the girl critically assessed her own work, then added a tiny bit more to the seven's vertical line. Juliette's penmanship was so precise the Olympic judges would have awarded her a score of ten—unless the Russian judge refused to cooperate.

Satisfied with her duck, Juliette continued. "Even though I lost a ton of weight the summer between eighth grade and my freshman year, some kids still look at me like I'm that same disgusting fat girl that they despised back in junior high."

"Really?" Paige asked. "I haven't heard anyone say anything mean about you."

"They may not say it out loud, but I know they're thinking it."

"How can you tell?" Paige selected a bright pink duck from her pile.

"I just can." Juliette anchored her tongue between her teeth and concentrated on producing an impeccable thirty-two on the side of a bright green duck. When she was finally content with her efforts, she said softly, "Which is why I love being on the volleyball team so much. I'm the only sophomore, and none of the other girls act as if they remember me from middle school."

"They probably don't." Paige continued to

work steadily. "Unless kids are your neighbors, relatives, friends of your siblings, or were in an activity with you, they usually only know their own classmates."

"Fortunately, I live in the country, my relatives are all older, and I'm an only child." Juliette smiled. "And I never thought I'd say this, but thank goodness I didn't have a social life back when I was a chubster."

"I'm glad high school has been a better place for you than middle school." Paige fingered her earring. "That sure isn't the case for everyone."

"It's amazing. The popular kids like me." Juliette beamed. "I'm finally somebody."

"You were always somebody." Paige wrinkled her brow.

"Yeah." Juliette sneered. "Right. All of me is beautiful, even the hideous, flabby, revolting parts."

"It's really a mistake to let other people influence how you see yourself."

Skye was awed at Paige's wisdom. Few adults understood the truth of what she was saying to Juliette, let alone seventeen-year-olds.

"Maybe for girls like you." Juliette's mouth formed a stubborn line. "But before I lost weight, I wasn't just a plain Jane. I was plain Jane's brother. For me being accepted by the popular crowd is the reason that I worked so hard to shed the pounds. It's the reason I eat nothing but plain lettuce and baked chicken and run miles and miles every day."

"It must have been very important to you." Paige skimmed an uneasy glance over Juliette. "And now that you've achieved that goal—"

"Now that I'm friends with the popular girls, I can't give it up." Juliette cut Paige off. "It's all I ever wanted, and I'll do whatever it takes to keep it."

"Oh." Paige put down the duck she'd been numbering and asked, a note of concern in her voice, "Like, what do you have to do?"

Juliette ignored Paige's question. It almost seemed that now she was talking to herself as she muttered, "Some people refused to do what Coach wanted, but not me." Juliette jerked her chin up. "The thing that made me mad was that one of the players, just because she was a star, got a free pass. Ms. H let her back on the team even though she walked out of team-building night."

"What kind of stuff did the 'star' balk at doing?" Paige asked.

Before Juliette responded, a loud voice from across the room rang out, "Ms. D, we need more ducks over here." Skye ground her teeth in frustration, then waited a beat to see if Juliette would continue, but she was silent. Finally, Skye left her listening post and brought the boy another set of ducks.

Making a mental note to investigate the objectionable bonding activities that both Juliette and Roxy had mentioned, Skye focused on making sure her newspaper staff completed the task. And when the bell rang at 7:50, one thousand rubber duckies had been numbered. She spent the next half hour repacking the ducks into their original boxes, carefully arranging each of the various colored waterfowl in numerical order to make sure no numbers had been skipped or duplicated.

Satisfied with her efforts, Skye left the cartons on Trixie's worktable and returned to her office. It was a good thing that all evidence of her ordering blunder was gone, because when she walked in the door, Homer was sitting behind her desk, glaring.

Uh-oh! This couldn't be good. The principal always summoned her to his lair, rarely venturing into the rest of the building. He'd often stated that the fewer students he had to see, the better.

"Mrs. Northrup is waiting in my office, and she's driving me crazy." Homer lumbered to his feet and shambled to where Skye stood poised to run away. "Where in the freaking hell have you been?"

"I had a before-school meeting with the newspaper kids." Skye grabbed her schedule book from the desktop, flipped it open, and checked the pink slip of paper clipped inside. "The message in my box says that the conference with Ashley's mom is at eight thirty." She glanced at her watch. "I still have ten minutes."

"She came early," Homer snarled. "And that idiot Opal wasn't at her post. That Northrup woman walked right past the front counter, barged into my office, and has been glued to my visitor's chair for half an hour," he growled. "She refuses to budge and just stares at me."

"Sorry." Skye kept her expression bland, but she was giggling inside. It was beyond amusing that for once Homer was the one trapped and uncomfortable. "So you left her sitting there?"

"Not alone." Homer grabbed Skye's elbow. "As soon as Opal got her butt back from wherever in the holy hell she'd been hiding, I ordered her to babysit the woman and came to find you."

He started to pull Skye into the corridor, and she dug in her heels. "I need Ashley's records." Skye jerked her arm from Homer's grasp. "And I'd like to grab a cup of tea from the faculty lounge."

"Get the folder, but you don't have time to make yourself tea and cookies." He watched Skye closely as she unlocked a cabinet and retrieved the file. "If you're good, after you get rid of that woman, you can use my new Keurig." He muttered to himself, "I can't believe they stuck a crappy tea K-Cup in my sampler pack. Real men drink coffee."

Skye grinned as she trailed Homer down the hall and into his office. Evidently, he didn't consider the prince of England a real man.

Once Homer dismissed Opal and the door closed behind her, Skye turned to the waiting parent and said, "Since you requested the meeting, Mrs. Northrup, why don't you start?"

"Thorntree Academy went over the records you sent them, and they tell me that Ashley needs another test before they'll consider her application." Mrs. Northrup thrust a piece of paper with an official letterhead at Skye. "They want you to give her the Autism Diagnostic Observation Schedule."

"I see." Skye frowned. "Ashley was originally diagnosed by a pediatric neurologist. Does Thorntree doubt the doctor's diagnosis?"

"I don't think so." Mrs. Northrup chewed her thumbnail, then shook her head. "They didn't say anything about her classification. Just that the test was required before their admissions committee could make a decision."

"Okay." Skye jotted down a note. She was more than willing to give Ashley the additional assessment; the problem was that she couldn't.

"So when can you get this Autism Diagnostic Observation Schedule thingy done?" Mrs. Northrup was clutching the strap of her purse so tightly her knuckles were white. "I know this is the last day before spring break, but can you do it this afternoon? Or I could bring Ashley in anytime you're available next week."

"Actually"—Skye chose her words carefully—"we don't have the ADOS."

"How much would this Adios test cost us to order?" Homer demanded.

"I really have no idea." Skye wrinkled her nose. "But my guess would be somewhere between five hundred and a thousand."

"That's ridiculous." Homer snorted. "Maybe you could borrow it from the co-op."

"That's a possibility," Skye agreed, then added, "But the real difficulty is that I'm not familiar with the ADOS. And without proper training, it isn't ethical for me to administer the instrument."

"Then the district needs to find someone to do it." Mrs. Northrup twisted a large masculine-looking gold nugget ring on her right hand.

"Can't you read the manual or something?" Homer snapped at Skye, lacing his fingers over his stomach. "Heck, every time the state changes its tests, I have to figure out the new instructions."

"No." Skye gripped the armrest of her chair. "That would not be best practices, and I won't do it." She closed her eyes, then suggested, "I know that speech pathologists are qualified to give the ADOS. Maybe Ms. Whitney has been trained on the instrument."

"Ask her," Mrs. Northrup demanded. "I'm tired

of everything taking so long. I want to know right now if she can do it or not."

While Homer dialed the phone, Skye tried to make small talk with Ashley's mother. "I was sorry to hear about the fire at your Laundromat."

"Thank you." Mrs. Northrup sighed and ran her hand through her hair. "It was just another awful thing in my already sucky life. First Ashley's problems, then Gideon dies"—she touched the ring on her right hand—"and now the fire." She bit back a strangled laugh. "Strike three and you're out."

"Will you be able to reopen soon?" Skye asked, patting the woman's arm.

"No." Mrs. Northrup shook her head. "I'm putting the land up for sale and I'm looking for a job."

"You know, the police department has a dispatcher position opening up soon," Skye offered. Char had announced her retirement as of the end of April. "You could put in an application."

"Thanks." Mrs. Northrup's expression softened. "I'll look into it."

"Belle doesn't know how to give that Adios either," Homer proclaimed, hanging up the receiver. Then, scowling at Skye, he said, "Next bright idea?"

"The co-op might have someone qualified," Skye said. "If you had invited the special ed coordinator, as I suggested, he'd know."

"No need to get him out here for a question that can be answered over the phone." Homer glared at Skye and picked up the handset. "We're better off without the co-op sticking their nose in our business."

"Right." Skye barely kept from rolling her eyes. Homer's paranoia was showing again. "Mrs. Northrup, since there are only two months of school left, maybe instead of rushing to send Ashley to Thorntree this year, it would be best to investigate ways to accommodate her here, and then allow her to start there as a sophomore."

"No!" Mrs. Northrup shouted. "I've waited long enough. She's going to Thorntree one way or another. Unlike this school, they have a summer program, and I don't want her to miss out on that."

"The co-op does have the test and someone can administer it, but not until the end of next month," Homer announced. "They'll get back to us with an appointment date and time." He raised a brow and said, "I'm afraid that's the best we can do, Mrs. Northrup. And we are within the legal time line with that solution."

"Sure." Mrs. Northrup jumped to her feet. "Hide behind the law. You all make me jump through hoop after hoop to get help for my daughter." She marched to the door. "But I'll get Ashley what she needs if it's the last thing I do."

As the door slammed behind the enraged woman, Skye and Homer exchanged glances.

Skye knew the special education process was frustrating to parents. Heck, it was frustrating to her. She'd do her best to expedite matters for Mrs. Northrup, but for the most part, her hands were tied.

CHAPTER 20

OBO—Open Book Official

That afternoon, as soon as Skye got to the PD, she told Wally about the conversation she'd overheard between Juliette and Paige. Before he could respond, she added, "We really need to find out about Blair's team-building activities."

"When I spoke to the Inslees today, they said that their issue with Coach Hucksford was the hours she required of her players." Wally leaned a hip against the wall opposite the coffee/ interrogation room door. "They said that their daughter didn't have time for much else, including her chores around the farm."

"Did they mention the bonding exercises at all?" Skye asked.

"Not specifically." Wally jiggled the keys in his pocket. "Just that Juliette felt the coach showed too much favoritism."

"Juliette wrote a fairly insightful article about

that topic for the *Scoop*," Skye commented, then added, "From what Roxy had to say yesterday, I'm guessing Keely is the player Juliette felt got preferential treatment." Skye tipped her head toward the interrogation room. "I can't wait to hear what Keely has to say about that, although I'm surprised her father isn't here with her."

"You can never tell how people will react to being asked to come to the police station for a chat." Wally chuckled ruefully. "Peterson said that Keely didn't need him to hold her hand, but the Inslees absolutely refused to bring Juliette to the PD. They told me that if we wanted to talk to her, we could make an appointment to meet with them in Laurel at their attorney's office."

"Then I'm glad I listened to Paige and Juliette's conversation this morning." Skye's guilt at eavesdropping lessened. "From what she said, it seemed that although Juliette wasn't happy about Blair's partisan behavior toward the star players, she was willing to put up with it. Apparently, being on the team made her a member of the popular clique, and she'd do anything to remain a part of that group."

"I still want to talk to Juliette." Wally levered himself from the wall. "But after what you overheard, her name's moved much farther down my list."

"What happened with Thor?" Skye asked. "Is he here?"

"Yep. I had Quirk pick him up." Wally put his hand on the interrogation-room doorknob, clearly impatient to start the interview with Keely. "He got here the same time that Keely arrived, so he's cooling his heels in the basement holding cell. He's been bawling for the past twenty minutes. He should be just about ready to spill his guts by the time we're done with Keely."

"Are you sure he's okay?" Skye didn't like the idea of Thor crying down there all alone. "What if he's sick or hurt or something?"

"He's fine. His tears are bogus." Wally smirked. "I've got Martinez babysitting him, or as it is officially called, on suicide watch, and he keeps hitting on her. He even asked her to help him chaperone the prom, claiming with Blair gone, he can't do it alone."

"Alone?" Skye scoffed. "Heck, we have a chaperone for every ten kids."

"Exactly." Wally paused before opening the door. "Okay with good cop, bad cop?"

"I guess." Skye sighed, not having to ask which role she was assigned.

"Are you all right with me acting angry at you for being on her side?"

"Sure. If you're all right with me seeming scared of you," Skye teased.

"No problem." Wally winked. "Although it does boggle the imagination."

"Very funny." Skye snickered softly, then

pasted a serious expression on her face and tilted her head toward the door. "Let's do this."

Wally and Skye entered the interrogation room. Wally adjusted the tape recorder, made Keely aware she was being recorded, and announced the date and time. Skye then immediately informed Keely that she was not there as her school psychologist. Once the girl had stated her name and address for the record, Skye added that she was the police psych consultant, so confidentiality no longer applied, then asked if she understood. Keely nodded, a flicker of apprehension in her hazel eyes.

Skye was surprised when a tear slid down Keely's cheek. The brash teenager she'd met on Wednesday now looked more like a frightened little girl. Evidently, the bravado she'd exhibited during that grief-counseling session had been a facade.

Snagging a box of Kleenex from the counter, Skye took a seat next to Keely and said, "I know this whole situation is probably scary, but if you answer our questions honestly, everything will be fine. Is that okay, or do you want to call your father or a lawyer?"

"Sure. Go ahead and call for help," Wally said as he sat down across from the women and sneered. "If you need your daddy or some other adult to protect you."

"I can take care of myself." Keely straightened,

wiped her eyes, and turned to Skye. "Ask your questions. I don't have anything to hide."

Skye smiled reassuringly, then said, "That's very good, Keely. Being forthcoming and telling the truth is the smart way to go."

"Unless she's the murderer," Wally jeered. "Then all your touchy-feely, positive-reinforcement crap is bad advice, isn't it?"

"Sorry, Chief." Skye exchanged a frightened glance with Keely.

"Watch it, or you can leave," Wally growled at Skye, then lasered Keely with a look that conveyed his distrust. "Did you kill Ms. Hucksford?"

"No!" Keely squealed, her mouth dropping open. "Why would I kill Coach?"

"We're asking the questions, little girl—not you," Wally snapped. "Where were you between eleven and twelve Monday night?"

"Home." Keely's shoulders drooped. "The other girls are still mad that I quit the team, so after practice I just went back to my house by myself. I told you that when you talked to me Wednesday at school."

"You said you were alone that evening," Wally said. "And your father's boss confirms that he worked the afternoon shift at the nuclear plant in Brooklyn. So you don't have an alibi for the time of Ms. Hucksford's murder."

Skye did a quick calculation and realized that Keely's father couldn't vouch for her whereabouts.

Including his commute, Mac Peterson would have been away from home from three thirty Monday afternoon to twelve thirty a.m. Tuesday.

"Well." Keely studied her hands as if they didn't belong to her. "I . . . uh . . . I can explain where I was and what I was doing that night, but you can't tell my dad this." She looked at Skye beseechingly.

"If it doesn't have anything to do with Ms. Hucksford's murder, we won't inform your father," Skye assured her, then quickly added, "Unless it involves hurting yourself or someone else."

"Dad doesn't want me online when he's not there." Keely squirmed. "But my friend Bryce lives in Las Vegas. With the time difference, he can only Skype with me after Dad goes to work."

"And you were Skyping with this Bryce Monday night?" Skye asked.

"Yeah." Keely fingered the trio of skulls adorning her left ear.

"We'll need his phone number." Wally's pen was poised over his notepad.

Keely recited the digits from memory, then demanded, "Can I go now?"

"You can leave when I say you can leave," Wally said, continuing his bad-cop routine.

"If Bryce confirms what you've told us, I'm sure the chief will let you leave," Skye said to comfort the girl. "But I do have a couple of

252

questions before we check with your friend. Is that okay?"

"Sure." Keely tore off small pieces of tissue, constructing a snow fort in front of her. "I mean, I guess so. What do you want to know?"

"We need to get a better idea of Ms. Hucksford's coaching style." Skye snuck a peek at Wally, who dipped his head in agreement at her line of questioning. "For instance, we've been hearing a lot about her bonding activities. Specifically, that you quit over them. What exercise made you decide to leave the team?"

"You won't believe me." Keely's lips trembled. "When I told Dad and he talked to Ms. H, she convinced him that I was exaggerating."

"That was before someone killed her." Skye's expression was grave.

"Fine." Keely flipped her ponytail, the red-dipped end disappearing over her shoulder like a foxtail. "But you won't like it."

"Whether we like it or not"—Skye scooted closer to the girl—"we need to know what was going on."

"At first, Ms. H just had us do some stupid feel-good stuff like sit in a circle and write our name at the top of a piece of paper. Then we passed it to the left and each player wrote something positive on top of the paper."

"That sounds pretty harmless." Skye had used that type of exercise in some of her own group counseling sessions with kids who lacked self-confidence.

"Yeah, but then things got weirder." Keely toyed with the stack of multicolor bangles on her wrist. "Coach turned off the lights and told us that she had taken apart a flashlight and hidden the pieces around the gym. Then she picked someone to be the monster and told her to go hide.

"The monster was supposed to tag everyone else, and once you were tagged you had to freeze. We had to find the flashlight and put it back together, then shine it at the monster, which would kill it. So if the monster froze everyone, she won, but if we got the flashlight together first, then the team won."

"I can see how that might help with building trust," Skye said.

"For little kids, but it was just a bizarre game for teenage girls."

"Maybe," Skye conceded. "Is that what made you quit the team?"

"No. That was bizarre but not creepy." Keely hugged herself, shivering as if she were cold. "Once we got the championship trophy, Ms. H got even more OCD about winning. If we had a less-than-perfect practice, she'd have a total meltdown. And when some of the girls wanted to get involved in other extracurricular activities, she blew her stack. She went on and on about how we were *her* girls and she had all the power over us."

"That does sound over-the-top," Skye said, a bead of sweat trickling down her temple. Whatever was coming was going to be bad.

"After a couple of the girls chose cheerleading over playing volleyball, Coach made us attend another bonding experience," Keely continued. "But this time, when we got to the gym, the guys from the varsity football team were in the girls' locker room."

"Was Mr. Goodson present, too?" Wally asked, leaning forward.

"Yes." Keely poked at a tiny hole at the neckline of her T-shirt. "He was there. He didn't seem too happy about it. But he was there."

"What happened?" Skye's imagination was running wild, and she hoped it wasn't what she thought it might be. She'd just read an article on hazing and bullying in a school psych journal, and this sounded as if it was headed into a very dark area.

"All the girls had to pick slips of paper from a bowl." Keely's voice cracked, and she cleared her throat. "Whatever number you pulled, you had to find the boy whose jersey number matched your paper."

Skye let out a soft gasp. This was going to be bad.

"The boys had five index cards, and you had to draw one and then do what was written on it." Keely closed her eyes and blew out a long breath.

"Like the good little robot she is, Roxy went first."

"And?" Skye asked, hoping against hope the tasks were something silly like hop on one foot or paint your face red and black.

"She had to kiss whichever girl the football player pointed to."

"And she did it?" Skye asked, now praying that all the girls walked out.

"Yes." Keely nodded. "The guy chose Juliette, and Roxy and she kissed."

"Who was next?" Skye asked, wondering just how much therapy these girls were going to need, knowing she wasn't equipped to provide it.

"Me." Keely rubbed the goose bumps on her arms. "My card was for . . . ah . . ." Her voice dropped and she whispered, "To have oral sex with the football player."

"Son of a b—" Wally exploded.

Skye cut him off. "Which is when you resigned from the team."

"Yes." Keely nodded vigorously. "I told the coach that I quit the squad, left the locker room, and went home and told my dad. But by the time he got to the school, the boys were gone and the girls were doing another stupid but harmless bonding exercise. Ms. H told him she and I'd had a fight and I was trying to get her into trouble." Keely's cheeks turned pink. "She reminded him that I'd been caught lying before

256

when I didn't want to do something. He bought her story hook, line, and sinker."

"Because as a father, he'd rather think you were fibbing than think an adult he trusted would do what you described," Skye explained.

"Maybe." Keely slumped in her chair. "But Dad wasn't thrilled when I agreed to play on the team again, so I think, deep in his heart, that he believed me. He just didn't want to admit it or deal with the problem. Since Mom left, he's been pretty depressed and barely functions most days."

"Why did you go back?" Wally asked. "Weren't you afraid of the coach?"

"Ms. H promised never, ever to do anything like that hazing with the boys again and said that I was exempt from all future team-building activities." Keely bit her lip, then twitched her shoulders. "And everyone begged me to play this upcoming season. Especially Roxy. She thinks she needs the team to win to get her scholarship."

"Did the other girls go through with what was written on those cards?" Skye asked, dreading the answer but needing to know.

"I doubt it. Coach Goodson freaked out after I read my card, and he stopped the game."

Skye turned to Wally and said, "What they did is illegal, right?"

"Hazing for sure. We'll have to see if anything else happened after Keely left that night before adding other charges like child abuse."

Skye nodded to herself. Sadly, a lot would depend on the other players telling the truth, and that was highly unlikely. In instances like this, everyone wanted to ignore the problem. And with Blair dead, it would be even more difficult to substantiate anything. Even if they couldn't get proof, she had to convince Homer he needed to fire Thor Goodson.

Wally asked, "Are you friendly with any of the guys on the football team?"

"I tutor a couple of them in math and science," Keely said. "Why?"

"Just wondering if Mr. Goodson ever had any inappropriate team-building activities with them before Ms. Hucksford's little party," Wally explained.

"I don't think so." Keely shook her head. "He and the guys seemed pretty shocked when Roxy and I read from our cards. I don't think he had any idea what was written on those index cards. Or what Ms. H had planned for that night. He was already ordering the guys to grab their stuff and get out of there before I even left the room."

After a few more questions, Wally asked Skye to step into the hallway. They asked Keely if she was all right, and when she assured them that she was fine, they told her they'd be right back.

Once they were in the hallway, Wally said, "We need to keep Keely here until we talk to Goodson."

"Want me to sit with her in your office?"

"No. Martinez can watch her. I want you with me when we interview the coach." Wally's expression was grim. "I was happy when Peterson didn't want to come in with his daughter because I figured she'd talk more freely if her father wasn't present, but now I wish we had a relative with her. Too bad her mother's out of state. We'll need to call Peterson to come get her. I'm not having her go home alone."

"I agree. Although Keely seems fine, she needs her father." Skye frowned. "But right now I'm more worried about the other girls."

"Especially since one of them might have killed the vic." Wally crossed his arms. "They all have a lot more motive than we thought."

CHAPTER 21

RDV—Rendezvous

While Wally went to get Thor, Skye escorted Keely to his office. Before taking the girl upstairs, Skye snagged a couple of brownies from the treat platter near the coffee urn, wrapped them in a napkin, and handed them to the teenager. After buying her a soda from the machine, Skye accompanied her to the second floor.

Once Keely was settled in Wally's visitor chair

with her snack, Skye said, "I'm really sorry Ms. Hucksford put you in such an appalling situation, and I'm even sorrier that your father wasn't there for you." Skye waited until Keely looked at her. "I also want you to know that the chief and I are going to make sure the school is aware of the incident and of Mr. Goodson's part in the hazing."

"I feel sorry for him, but he should have stepped up to the plate and stopped Ms. H sooner." Keely popped the soda can's top. "I was really worried about the younger girls." She broke off a corner of the brownie. "With Coach losing it like she was, I wasn't sure what she'd do next."

"And that's the real reason you rejoined the team," Skye said slowly. She'd known that there was more to it than helping Roxy with her scholarship. "You wanted to be there to protect the others if Ms. Hucksford tried anything like that sex game again."

"Maybe," Keely mumbled around a mouthful of brownie. "But don't tell anyone." She winked. "You'll ruin my tough-chick rep."

"It'll be our little secret." Skye crossed her heart. "But you need to promise to come to me if anything like that ever happens again, and please encourage the other girls to do the same."

"Sure." Keely didn't meet Skye's gaze. Instead, she used her finger to get every crumb of the brownie from the napkin and then she changed the subject. "This is really good. Do you know where they bought these?"

"Bite your tongue," Skye teased. "My mom's the dispatcher here, and she baked them. She'd have a fit if anyone even implied they were anything less than homemade. She brings food every shift and never anything from a store or even a packaged mix. You should taste the awesome chocolate chip cookies she brought the other day."

"All of her snacks are amazing," Zelda Martinez said as she entered the office. "I just wish Miss May would add a little Mexican cooking to her menu, but she says she doesn't do hot and spicy."

"Except her personality," Skye joked.

"There is that," Zelda agreed. Her long dark brown hair was drawn tightly back and fastened in a bun at the nape of her neck. Her face was bare of makeup, and the only jewelry she wore were tiny crosses dangling from her earlobes.

When Skye had first met her, she'd wondered if Zelda was trying to be one of the guys. But as they'd gotten to know each other, Skye had noticed that the young officer's short fingernails were always professionally manicured and painted with a bright red polish. Skye had realized that the woman was holding on to her feminine side while attempting to maintain a professional demeanor.

Leaving Zelda to keep Keely company, Skye

hurried back to the interrogation room. While she was almost certain that Keely would come out of this situation without too much emotional trauma, she just hoped the other girls had also escaped Blair's horrendous hazing experiment without permanent psychological damage. What had the volleyball coach been thinking to do something so disgusting?

As soon as Skye came into view, Wally stopped his pacing outside the coffee room's closed door and said, "Keely's alibi checks out. I just got off the phone with her friend Bryce *and* his mother. Both of them corroborate that he and Keely Skyped Monday night from about quarter to ten until a little past midnight our time."

"Good." Skye felt the tightness in her chest ease, glad the girl was off the hook. "How do you want to handle the interview with Thor?"

"Since you two are colleagues, you take the lead and I'll jump in."

"Okay." Skye put her hand on the doorknob. "But from what Keely said about Thor and Blair's relationship, I think he may respond more to a dominant woman, so I get to be bad cop this time."

"Not that I doubt you, darlin' "—Wally tenderly tucked a curl behind Skye's ear—"but I've never seen you be unkind to anyone."

"After what he and his girlfriend attempted to do to those children," Skye said, her lip curling,

262

"I won't have any problem whatsoever being mean to him."

"Go get 'em, tiger!" Wally chuckled softly, following Skye into the interrogation room.

Skye studied Thor. He sat slumped in a chair with his right hand cuffed to the leg of the bolted-down table. Wearing dirty canvas cargo pants, a ragged long-sleeved Henley waffle-knit shirt, and scuffed boots, his usual All-American blond good looks were hidden beneath a layer of grime and several days' worth of facial stubble.

Thor glanced up as Skye took a seat opposite him. Evidently frightened by her ominous expression, he whined, "I didn't want to do it."

"Hard to Taser someone by accident," Skye snapped. "Or unintentionally hold their head under the water until they drown."

"What? No!" Thor yelped. "I'd never kill Blair. I meant the hazing, not the murder. I saw Keely Peterson was here, and I figured she told you about that little incident in the locker room."

"Little incident!" Skye barely stopped herself from lunging across the table. "Sexual abuse is not a little incident, ever. You had no—"

"Keely told us that you were a less-than-enthusiastic participant," Wally interrupted.

He took the seat next to Skye, turned on the tape recorder, announced the date and time, and told Thor he was being recorded, then asked Thor to state his name and address.

After the preliminaries were complete, clearly trying on his good-cop role for size, Wally said, "So why don't you give us your side of what happened that night?"

"There was no sexual abuse." Thor gazed at Wally as if the chief were the last Band-Aid in the box and Thor was bleeding to death. "All that happened was two girls kissed each other—just lips, no tongue," he assured them earnestly. "Then I put a stop to it. I was totally shocked. I had no idea what Blair had written on those cards."

"Keely's departure and the possibility that she was about to expose your sick little games weren't the reason you broke up the party?" Skye demanded.

"Yes. I mean, no. I mean, I was mixed up." Thor shook his head. "I sort of thought that first kissing card was a joke. Then, when Keely read her card, I was so dumbfounded, it took me a minute to act, but I was never letting that go on." A tear slipped down his chiseled cheek. "I have sisters those girls' ages, and I'd kill anyone who forced them into a sexual situation."

"Which is why you murdered Blair," Skye pounced. "Because that's exactly what your wonderful girlfriend tried to do to her players."

"No. I loved Blair. I would never hurt her." Thor looked confused. "Besides, she promised never to do anything like that again, and she deleted all the photos. I watched her erase them to make sure."

"What in the world made Blair attempt that kind of vile hazing in the first place?" Skye demanded, unable to grasp why someone would do something so heinous to a child. Intellectually, she knew it happened all the time, but she had never been able to wrap her mind around the motivation behind the exploitation. And maybe she was sexist, but it was especially hard to understand why a woman would abuse and humiliate her own gender.

"Blair said that the girls needed to be toughened up. Needed to remember who was boss and who had the power in the relationship. She told me that when she was growing up, her father had been hard on her, and that's why she was a winner, because she never threw in the towel," Thor explained. "Apparently Mr. Hucksford was a lot easier on his older daughter, and Blair considered her sister a failure."

"Hmm." Skye wondered what exactly Blair's dad did to her. Abuse often begat abuse. Or to paraphrase the Bible, the sins of the father frequently influenced how their children behaved as adults.

"Blair said she needed my boys to scare the girls a little. You know, act all mean and dominant. She said that even though her players ended up taking the championship at the tournament, they had lost too many matches during the season." Thor shoved a lock of hair off his forehead. "When I told her that it was only a game, she smacked me and said that no one says it's only a game when *their* team is winning."

"So . . ." Wally encouraged.

"So I went along with her and brought my boys to the gym that night, but I never dreamed that she planned to have them involved in any of that sex stuff." Thor looked back and forth between Skye and Wally, then asked, "You believe me, right?"

Skye was unwilling to nod to indicate that she trusted him because she didn't, so instead she waved her hand for him to continue. Thor was on a roll, and she didn't want to interrupt him by speaking. If he had time to consider what he was saying, he might clam up and demand an attorney. So far, although he'd been read his rights, he hadn't asked for a lawyer. But he could always change his mind and stop talking.

"Blair and I had a big fight after what she did," Thor continued. "But the next day she realized she'd gotten a little crazy, and she said she was sorry." Thor seemed unaware of the tears dripping off his chin. "I believed her when she apologized."

"So you and Blair made up?" Wally said, leaning toward the younger man. "And at the time of her murder you were still a couple?"

"Yes," Thor sobbed. "The evening Blair died, we went to dinner at the Feed Bag. Then I dropped her off at the school for her volleyball practice. I came back around nine, and we decided to go swimming."

"Go on." Wally looked up from his notebook. "You took a swim and . . ."

"And then we messed around a little." Thor spoke into his chest. "But I didn't like doing it out in the open like that at the school."

"So then what?" Skye raised a brow. "Did Blair go home with you?"

"No." Thor ran his fingers along the scarred tabletop. "She thought I was being a prude and started teasing me and taking pictures."

"That had to be irritating. Having your girl-friend treat you like that." Wally's tone was sympathetic. "What did you do then?"

"I was getting pissed at her behavior, so I grabbed the phone from her, got dressed, and left her there alone." He sniffed back a tear. "If I hadn't done that, she'd probably still be alive today."

"You said she was taking pictures of you messing around," Skye said, slowly processing the information. "Were you . . . uh . . . unclothed?"

"Yeah." Thor bowed his head, as if reliving the embarrassment.

"And you took her phone because that was what she was using to take the photos?" Skye's own cell was so old it didn't have a camera, but everyone else seemed to have a device with that capability.

"Exactly." Thor's hands were clenched. "I didn't want to have her put up a picture of me with my pecker waving in the wind."

"By put up, you mean on the social networking site Open Book?" Skye asked, recalling Emmy's demonstration at the Feed Bag.

"Right. Putting up stuff on Open Book and getting the most 'enjoys,' 'visits,' and 'people fascinated' was like an addiction to her." Thor's expression was grim. "Blair exposed her whole life, and the life of everyone else around her, on that damn site for anyone and everyone to read about."

"Would they permit nudity?" Skye asked.

"I stay away from that site, so I have no idea what's allowed and what's not." Thor's rigid posture sagged. "But I think as long as it wasn't the full monty, no one complained." He growled into his chest. "I told Blair that there's this little thing called a diary and that I would buy her one so she didn't have to Open Book our every little problem or intimate moment."

"Do you still have her phone?" Wally asked. "It wasn't listed in the inventory of your property that I received from the county jail."

"It's probably at home somewhere," Thor said. "I might have stuck it in the pocket of the jacket that I was wearing Monday night."

"Do we have your permission to look for it at your residence?" Wally asked.

"Sure," Thor agreed. "The jacket's on the chair in my room."

"Thanks." Wally nodded at Thor, then turned to Skye and explained, "Quirk and Martinez didn't find the vic's cell when they searched her house, but we did see bills indicating that she had one. We've been looking all over for it but were afraid the killer took it."

"Maybe he did." Skye glared at Thor. He seemed pathetic now, but she couldn't forget that he'd participated in the hazing, even if he claimed to have stopped it before it got too out of hand.

"I didn't," Thor protested, trying to throw up his hands but unable to move them that far with his wrist shackled to the table leg. Clanking against the metal, he said, "These are starting to hurt."

"Aw. You poor thing." Skye wrinkled her nose in mock sympathy. "Just relax. The handcuffs are tight because they're new. But don't worry. Once you wear them for a little while, they'll stretch out."

Thor stared at Skye, seemingly stunned at her callous words, then turned to Wally and asked, "When did Blair die?"

"Between eleven and twelve," Wally answered. "Do you have an alibi?"

"Yes." Thor sagged back in his chair. "I left Blair about ten thirty and went to the Brown Bag. I meant to buy a six-pack at the liquor store, but I saw a friend sitting in the bar area and decided drinking with him was better than getting blotto alone. The bartender tossed us out when he closed at two a.m. He called my friend's wife to come and drive us home."

"That must have strengthened your friend's marriage to no end," Skye murmured, thankful she wasn't speaking from experience. She'd never seen Wally have more than two or three drinks. And never more than one in public.

"I'll need your friend's name and number," Wally said. "And his wife's name, too."

"Sure." Thor reeled off the information. "If they confirm, am I in the clear?"

"For the murder." Wally's expression was stern. "But not for the hazing incident. I'm going to have to charge you for that."

"And I'll need to report the episode to DCFS and inform Homer," Skye stated.

"I figured." Thor took a deep breath and buried his head in his free hand. "This is the end of my teaching and coaching career, isn't it?"

"Probably." Skye nodded, feeling a tiny tinge of sympathy. "The best you can hope for is not to be labeled a sexual predator."

Thor groaned. "I'm not like that." He implored Wally, "Please, please, please don't let them do that to me. I couldn't live with that."

"We're going to talk to every girl and boy who was there that night," Wally warned. "If they support your story, that you ended things right after the girls kissed, I won't pursue sexual-abuse charges."

"Thank you." Thor sobbed. "Thank you." He cried for several minutes. Finally, he wiped his eyes and said, "I blame Blair's father for all of this."

"Why?" Skye asked. Had her guess been right about him abusing his daughter?

"Because I think almost everything Blair did was to drive her dad out of his mind. He was already upset that her maternal grandmother had left her a trust fund that she'd be able to access when she turned thirty. He was able to control Bernadette with his purse strings, but Blair didn't work for him and she knew that she had a tidy sum coming to her in a few years." Thor grinned. "I bet he's ticked off that Blair left her sister the trust fund, especially since Bernadette is old enough to claim it immediately."

"So that's why the Hucksfords needed the attorney present during the Skype session with Simon," Skye said to Wally. "With a large estate, there was probably something in her will about her burial wishes."

"I'll check with Reid, but you're probably right," Wally said.

"The guy was an old-school Bible-thumper, and he raised her so strictly she ended up rebelling." Thor continued as if Skye and Wally hadn't spoken.

"There's nothing wrong with bringing up your children according to Scripture." Skye put her hand on her stomach. Her baby would be raised in the Catholic Church.

"Maybe it was his interpretation that was wrong." Thor shrugged. "But whatever it was, Blair knew her father read every word she put on Open Book. The whole placing scandalous stuff on that site was a jab at her father's beliefs."

"Well, that explains why her dad disowned Blair and what Bernadette meant by exhibitionistic pervert." Skye shook her head. "Unless Blair's parents physically or emotionally abused her, I'm not going to judge their religious views."

"I think they were strict, but nothing she said suggested abuse," Thor admitted.

"Then Blair's actions were her own responsibility," Skye said. "But that doesn't mean anyone had a right to kill her, and the police aren't going to allow the murderer to get away with it."

CHAPTER 22

EOD—End of Discussion

Thor's alibi checked out. The bartender and Thor's friend confirmed he'd been with them from eleven to well past midnight. After establishing that Thor was in the clear for the murder charge, Wally ordered him transported to the county jail to be held on the hazing charge.

While Wally and the city attorney discussed the evidence against Thor, Skye contacted DCFS and Homer and informed them of his and Blair's behavior. Homer whined about having to find another substitute, and DCFS promised to send an investigator as soon as one was available. Skye wasn't holding her breath on either the school district or the state agency's actions.

Having done her duty for her students, Skye focused on her responsibility to the police department. She and Wally spent the rest of the evening talking to the football and volleyball players and their parents.

It was an arduous ordeal, and while Skye was thrilled that the kids substantiated Thor's version of events and that none of them appeared to bear any long-term emotional scars, by the end of the evening, she was exhausted. As she and Wally trudged up the steps toward their front door, she could barely put one foot in front of the other.

Skye had passed hunger several hours ago and was now almost too tired to eat, but Wally insisted they grab a bite before going to bed. Thank goodness they had leftovers from the dinner Dorothy had prepared for them the night before. All they had to do was to heat up the remaining pulled pork and homemade rolls in the microwave and spoon the potato salad onto their dishes.

Skye fed Bingo while Wally got their drinks and filled their plates. Finally, they sat down at the kitchen table and dug into their meal.

Once she had taken a few bites of her supper, Skye said, "How in the world could Thor have allowed Blair to lead him so far astray? How could he have been that stupid?"

"Well"—Wally grinned—"you know why jocks play on artificial turf, don't you?"

"No." Skye was confused at the change of subject. "Why?"

"To keep them from grazing."

Skye giggled. Then she asked, "Did you send someone over to Thor's apartment to find Blair's cell phone?"

"I called Anthony in to conduct the search." Wally took a swig of beer. "He's doing a good job, and I'm hoping that I can hire him full-time as soon as I get the new budget approved by the city council."

"That would be great." Skye liked the young part-time officer, and as a native Scumble Riverite, he had the hometown advantage.

"The vic's phone was right where Goodson said it would be." Wally picked up his sandwich. "Unfortunately, it's password protected."

"Rats!" Skye ate a forkful of potato salad, then said, "Maybe Thor knows Blair's password."

"No such luck." Wally wiped his mouth with a paper napkin. "We phoned the jail and they asked

274

him. He claims she was really guarded about stuff like that, which is odd, considering her penchant for putting stuff on Open Book."

"Actually, that might be the reason behind her password secrecy." Skye frowned, thinking. "Maybe there was stuff she had on her phone that was even more scandalous than what she put on that site."

"I left orders for Martinez to go through the vic's possessions again tomorrow. Let's hope that she has the password written down somewhere." Wally took another drink of his Sam Adams. "Otherwise we'll have to wait for the county crime lab to find some way to get into the phone's contents."

"Too bad Justin is visiting Frannie at U of I." Skye licked barbecue sauce from her fingers. "I bet he'd hack into that cell in two minutes flat. He's always able to get into mine when I forget my password or somehow lock myself out of the darn thing."

Justin Boward was a twenty-year-old computer wizard who had been in counseling with Skye from eighth grade partway through high school. Once he'd overcome his depression and lack of self-confidence, he'd ended up coediting the school newspaper with his girlfriend, Frannie. After graduating from Scumble River High School a couple of years ago, he'd attended Joliet Junior College and was finishing up his final year there. In September he'd join Frannie in the University of Illinois journalism program.

"Yeah. Justin did a great job getting into that laptop's files from our December case." Wally finished his sandwich and turned his attention to devouring the rest of his potato salad. "Tomorrow, if you have time, maybe you could get on the Open Book site. You could nose around a little and see what Blair posted."

"I can do that in the morning. We don't have to be at the baby shower until four." Skye yawned and stretched. "Emmy showed me how to sign up for the site. She said some people have tight privacy controls so you have to be their 'pal' to see what they post, but others leave it wide-open. Let's hope Blair's settings aren't too restrictive."

"From what Goodson said, I'd bet Blair's page is available for everyone to see."

"Speaking of Thor, what's going to happen to him?" Skye pushed away her empty dish. "I feel a little bad for the guy. He seems to have gotten caught up in Blair's obsessions and made some poor choices."

"Since there was no gross bodily harm or death, the city attorney plans to charge him with a Class A misdemeanor." Wally polished off the rest of his beer and threw the bottle in the recycle bin. "That could result in a sentence of up to three hundred and sixty-four days of imprisonment plus as much as a five-thousand-dollar fine. But my guess is that Goodson will get supervision and community service."

"So after everything, he'll only spend a couple of nights in jail?" Skye wasn't sure how she felt about Thor getting off so lightly. She did feel a tiny bit sorry for him, but he still should have consequences for his actions.

"If Goodson hadn't decided to leave town and go hiking, he probably wouldn't have spent any time whatsoever behind bars." Wally put their dishes in the sink, took Skye's hand, and led her upstairs. "If we'd been able to locate him and talk to him Tuesday, we'd have cleared him on the suspicion of murder and his lawyer could have gotten him bail that afternoon on the hazing. But with him being arrested on a Friday night, he's stuck until the arraignment on Monday."

"The more I think about it," Skye said as she undressed, "the more I'm convinced that he decided to go to Starved Rock not because he was overcome with grief, but because he knew that what he and Blair had done to their teams was going to come out."

"Me too," Wally agreed.

Skye walked into the master bathroom. Before she turned her back on the shower, she cautiously eased open the glass door, glanced inside the stall, and closed it.

"You know, darlin', I understand that seeing the movie *Psycho* terrified you." Wally had

277

followed her and snickered as he observed her precautionary actions. "But what if one day when you check the shower for crazed killers, you find one? What's your plan then?"

"Run like heck while you shoot him." Skye snapped her towel at Wally. "You would protect me—right, sweetie?"

"With my life."

"Good." Skye brushed her teeth, and she and Wally climbed into bed. Before switching off the light, she said, "If Thor would have just faced up to his behavior and stuck around, things would have turned out a lot better for him." She paused. "But that's the real problem with him, isn't it? He isn't the kind of guy who is in control of his own destiny."

"Yep." Wally leaned over her and flicked off the lamp. "It surprises me that, for a coach, he isn't much of a leader."

"No, he isn't." Skye snuggled under the covers. Her eyelids drooping, she sighed. "And as an educator, he sure set a bad example for his students."

Wally must have gotten up and fed Bingo and then gone back to sleep, because when Skye opened her eyes, bright sunshine was streaming through the windows and he was snoring softly with his arm curved around her waist. Turning her head, still halfway expecting to feel nauseated but grateful when she didn't, she saw that it was almost nine o'clock.

The last time they'd slept that late was on their honeymoon and they'd been exhausted from a much pleasanter pursuit than investigating a murder. Which reminded her . . . Skye carefully rolled over and pressed a kiss to Wally's chest. The feeling of the warm, smooth skin on her lips encouraged her to reach lower. Either her new husband was having an extremely good dream, or he was awake.

"Good morning, sugar." Wally's husky baritone tickled her ear.

"It is now," she murmured, continuing her exploration. "Did you sleep well?"

"Like a big black cat." He chuckled at their private joke about Bingo's apparent habit of snoozing twenty-three out of twenty-four hours. "How about you? I think you were out the minute your head hit the pillow."

"I was bushed. The last few days have been grueling. Truth be told, I deserve a bonus for making it through the week at school without stabbing one of my bosses or colleagues in the eye with a ruler."

"I can just imagine." Wally stroked her hair. "Your job takes way too much patience and tact. It's a lot more fun to be the one issuing the orders than following them."

"I'll have to try that at home sometime." Skye

diverted her fingers from below his waist to the muscles of his arms, and Wally made a disappointed sound. "We haven't seemed to have much time alone lately." She looked up into her husband's dark chocolate eyes and arched a brow. "Are you up for a ride, cowboy?"

"Always." Wally flipped her onto her back and nuzzled her neck. "No morning sickness?"

"Nope." Skye tilted her head to the side to give him better access to the sensitive skin underneath her ear and purred, "Let's get this rodeo started."

It was past ten by the time Skye and Wally finally made it downstairs. On the weekends Wally usually made his famous blueberry pancakes and fried up some of the venison breakfast sausage his father regularly shipped him from Texas. But since the next meat delivery wasn't due until the following week and neither of them had made it to the grocery store, they had to settle for cold cereal.

Although Skye was still a little uneasy with the idea of a housekeeper, she had to admit that Dorothy's efforts were a godsend. With the house clean and the laundry done, the Saturday chores that had eaten up most of Skye's day were a thing of the past.

Lingering over a second cup of coffee, Wally said, "I'm going to run in to the PD for a few hours to help Martinez look through the vic's possessions for her password." He got up and washed out his mug, then dried his hands. "I wish I could call in a few more officers to assist with the search, but there's no money left in my budget to pay them, and I need to keep at least one squad car on patrol."

"Will you be back in time for the baby shower?" Skye asked. Vince had insisted on a coed party, something new to Scumble River.

"I'll make sure that I am." Wally kissed the top of Skye's head. "I can't afford to get on the bad side of my new mother-in-law."

"Smart move." Skye rose from the table and walked with Wally down the hallway. "We don't want to take away from Vince and Loretta's special day, so I'm thinking we'll wait and announce our impending bundle of joy tomorrow, after the duck races."

"How are we going to do that?" Wally asked, pausing in the foyer.

"Well, you know that Trixie's fund-raiser has blossomed into quite an affair." Skye put her arms around his waist. "The ducks are being released at the boat-launch area in the park at four, but a bunch of other events are scheduled earlier in the afternoon. How Trixie managed to pull it all together in less than a week is beyond me, but since I didn't want to be drafted to help out, I didn't ask her."

"Good plan."

"I thought so." Skye grinned. "Anyway, Mom decided to have us all over for dinner after the race, to help her eat up whatever food is left over from today's baby shower."

"What does dinner at your mom's house have to do with the race?"

"I have no idea." Skye shrugged. "Maybe because she figured we'll all be around for Trixie's fund-raiser. Mom's invited Grandma Denison, Vince and Loretta, Uncle Charlie, of course, and also Trixie and Owen, which should make telling everyone at one time a lot easier. That way no one's feelings get hurt because they weren't the first to know. We can even get your dad on speakerphone."

"Letting everyone know at once is definitely the way to go." Wally gave her a sweet kiss, then reluctantly released her. "I can't wait for the whole world to know that you're having my baby." He frowned. "I might be a little late for your mom's dinner, though. The reason I'm out of funds for the murder investigation is that I'm using the rest of my overtime reserves to pull in all the officers that I can to patrol the park on Sunday. But with a big crowd expected, I'll have to keep an eye on things, too."

"That's fine." Skye smiled. "Much to my father's displeasure, we aren't eating until six thirty, because Trixie's pizza party for the kids who were involved in the duck race doesn't end until six. You'll probably be free by then, and we'll make the announcement after everyone is finished with supper."

"Terrific." Wally grinned.

Once Wally was gone, Skye grabbed her grocery list and headed to the supermarket. Ninety minutes later, their food supplies were restocked and Skye settled in front of her laptop. Vince and Loretta's baby gift was wrapped, so she had two hours to read through Blair's Open Book postings before she had to get dressed for the shower.

It took a phone call to Emmy and a couple to Justin, but Skye finally managed to enroll in Open Book and access Blair's folio—which was what the site called the spot that held all of the members' messages. As Skye and Wally had suspected, the privacy controls were set to unrestricted, and she could see everything Blair had ever put up. From the sheer volume, it appeared the volleyball coach had recorded and shared her every waking moment.

There were photos of Blair's manicured toes, her cup of cappuccino, the view from her class-room window, and even the foil in her hair while she was getting highlights at the beauty parlor. Skye paused at that last one. It didn't look like Great Expectations, Vince's hair salon, but whoever had done Blair's color was very good. Skye would have never guessed the color variations in Blair's copper curls weren't natural.

The meaning of the pictures was mostly fairly obvious, but some of the messages Blair had written were more puzzling. Several seemed like warnings. There was one that read:

> Stop it, my Open Book pals! I understand that when the girls attend long practices, it's an inconvenience, but the last thing you should complain about is my winning method of coaching. I fixed a broken team. Thank me. Show your appreciation. And shut the hell up! Or there will be penalties.

Skye jotted down that message and a few others, before coming to another cryptic note.

> Hey, you all. My life must seem great, but it's not perfect. Someone knows how to make me happier, but they aren't cooperating. If that person doesn't come through pretty damn soon, there will be consequences!

Wally needed to see this, too. Skye wrote it down, then checked her watch. It was after two thirty. She'd give herself half an hour, but after that, she had to stop and change clothes.

Scrolling through the pages of the folio, Skye quickly glanced through more photographs. There were pictures of teachers and other people she recognized from around town, and nearly all of the snapshots seemed intent on capturing folks' most embarrassing moments.

Skye was *tsk*ing at Blair's meanness when she brought her cursor to a screeching halt. There in front of her were several photos of Skye climbing out of the pool, her bathing suit pasted against her body. It was not a flattering angle, and Skye cringed as she gazed at her sopping-wet appearance.

According to the time stamp, the pictures had been posted Monday morning at 6:21. Underneath the snapshots, Blair had typed, This is our chunky school psychologist, Skye Denison-Boyd. She needs to either lose weight or announce she's with child. I'm sure she won't be thrilled that I've put up these pix of her, but maybe next time she'll think twice before breaking my rules.

"Shit!" Skye screamed, her heart beating wildly. "Shit! Shit! Shit!"

"What in Sam Hill is wrong?" Wally ran into the kitchen, his hand on his gun.

"This." Skye pointed to the laptop's monitor. She had been so engrossed that she hadn't heard him come home. "Do you think that everyone already knows that I'm pregnant?"

"I'm sure our phone would be ringing off the hook if that were the case," Wally reassured her, then leaned in to inspect the picture more closely.

He let loose a string of curses, finally asking between gritted teeth, "Did you know she'd taken those pictures of you?"

"Of course not." Skye recalled the feeling of being watched that morning. "I would have never allowed her to photograph me."

"How could you have stopped her?" Wally asked as he scrolled up and down Blair's folio. "It looks as if she took pictures of whatever she damn well pleased, then put them all on Open Book. The more humiliating the snapshot, the better."

"And my guess is Blair finally put up a photo or a message that made someone mad enough to kill her. I didn't see anything, but maybe it's something that only the murderer recognizes."

"Or maybe the killer is a hacker who somehow managed to take it down from the site," Wally suggested. "I wonder if I can get a court order for Open Book to release its records."

"Right." Skye snickered. "By the time that happens, we'll be retired and living in Florida."

"Well, I'd definitely make the trip back here to prosecute the murderer."

"Me too!"

CHAPTER 23

BGWM—Be Gentle with Me

I've never been to a baby shower," Wally commented as he and Skye got into his Thunderbird. "What happens at these things?"

"They're usually pretty boring." She rolled down the window. The weather had finally warmed up, and the Ford was stifling inside. "We eat, play a couple of silly games, and then watch the guest of honor open gift after gift."

"That doesn't sound too bad." Wally started to back out of the driveway, but stopped and asked, "It's at your parents' place, right?"

"Uh-huh." Skye put the window up. Now she was cold. Pregnancy had thrown her internal thermostat all out of whack.

"Wasn't the shower originally going to be held in Laurel at Harry's restaurant?"

"That was never going to happen." Skye adjusted the seat belt. Why was it suddenly cutting into er neck? "Loretta's mother wanted the shower held at Harry's, because she said any other venue made it look like the hosts were too cheap to spring for a restaurant meal."

"Who exactly is putting on this shindig?"

"Technically, the cousins and I am." Skye

wrinkled her nose. "But Mom made all the plans. We just paid our share and shut up."

"What a surprise." Wally's lips quirked. "Imagine May taking over."

"Loretta's mother tried to grab control, and the location of the shower became a battle of wills between the soon-to-be grandmas, but Mom insisted that generations upon generations of Scumble Riverites had always held their celebrations in their homes, and she wasn't changing her family traditions for city folk."

"And May won."

"Of course." Skye flipped down the visor to check her hair. Good. The humidity hadn't turned the smooth style she'd achieved using hot rollers and massive quantities of hair spray into a mass of curls—at least not yet. "Mrs. Steiner decided to hold her own baby shower. Hers is next weekend at Everest in Chicago." Skye stuck out her bottom lip. "I wish we were going to that party. Everest is rated as one of the country's best restaurants. Chef Joho's food is world-famous, and the view is supposed to be out of this world."

"Darlin', if you want to eat at Everest, we can go anytime, or to any other restaurant your little heart desires." Wally reached over and took her hand. "We can celebrate being pregnant."

"I've heard reservations at Everest are hard to get, so it will probably take a while," Skye said. "But that would be amazing."

"Consider it done." Wally turned onto the road leading to the Denisons' farm.

"Keep your eyes peeled for deer," Skye warned. "Dad said the population is out of control, and there've been lots of cars running into them along this stretch."

"Yeah, I heard that, too." The corner of Wally's mouth turned up. "In fact, we had a deer–vehicle incident late last night."

"Was anyone hurt?"

"The driver of the pickup truck was fine, but the fiberglass whitetail buck in Mayor Leofanti's front yard is resting in pieces."

Skye laughed, then said, "Uncle Dante must be fuming."

"He wanted the guy arrested for deerslaughter, but the best we could do was reckless driving and DUI." Wally pulled into the Denisons' already packed driveway. "Hey, it looks like the party is being held in the garage."

"I figured as much." Skye twitched her shoulders. "With all the relatives and friends, and then Vince insisting it be a coed shower, there wouldn't be room in the house." She frowned. "I sure hope Loretta is okay with the arrangements. She's used to places like Spiaggia and Tru, not my parents' garage—even if it is cleaner and nicer than a lot of people's houses."

"By now Loretta knows the drill." Wally got out of the Ford, picked up the present from the backseat, and walked around to open Skye's door.

"Yeah. You're right." Skye took Wally's hand and allowed him to help her. Exiting the low-slung car in a skirt and heels was tricky. She'd chosen to wear a black-and-white dress with an A-line cut that hid her blossoming figure and black peep-toe pumps. "It's not as if Loretta doesn't have any idea of how we do things around here."

As they navigated the white pea-gravel drive-way, Skye admired the huge trees that surrounded her parents' redbrick ranch. Because of the cool March, the yard wasn't in its usual putting-green condition yet, but a few more weeks and her dad would have it up to his standards. Some folks speculated that Jed used manicure scissors instead of a mower to cut the lawn, but she knew he achieved the perfection through an obsessive devotion to every blade of grass, twig, and flower petal.

With the exception of May's concrete goose, which she had dressed in a diaper, baby bonnet, and pacifier, the scene looked like a picture from *Country Gardens* magazine. May tended to clothe the faux fowl according to her frame of mind, and Skye was relieved that this time the poultry's outfit suited the occasion rather than containing an underlying message aimed at her.

Unless, of course, her mother had figured out

Skye was pregnant. *Nope!* Not going there today.

Skye turned her attention to the open garage. She had talked May out of the Precious Moments theme and the Little Princess idea, but hadn't been able to sway her mother from the Baby Love concept, so everything was pink. The whole shebang, from the giant banner that read WELCOME TO THE FAMILY, BABY APRIL to the plates, napkins, cups, plasticware, and favor bags, were a pale pink. As were the crepe paper streamers, bunches of balloons, and centerpieces of carnations in milk-glass vases.

It looked as if the entire space had been turned into an enormous cotton-candy machine. It could have been worse; a brighter hue would have felt like they were inside a gigantic Pepto-Bismol bottle. Skye snickered softly, envisioning all the family's übermasculine men hunkered down in May's pale pink world.

She glanced at Wally, who was staring into the garage with his mouth hanging open and a bemused expression on his face. Finally, he sniggered and said, "Your mom really goes all out, doesn't she?"

"And then some." She had a scary flash of what May would do for Skye's baby shower. Images of a gigantic golden throne and life-size angels hanging from the ceiling zoomed through her head.

She must have whimpered, because Wally asked, "Are you okay?"

"Uh-huh." Skye took a deep breath. "I just spaced out for a sec."

"Well, you sure had a funny expression on your face." He tilted his head.

"I was just trying to decide what shade the tablecloths were." Skye pointed. "What do you think? Dusky rose or cameo?"

"Darlin', most men see only a dozen or so basic colors. For example, peach is a fruit not a color. Same goes for plum, and celery is a vegetable." He scratched his head. "And no red-blooded male knows what in the hell constitutes mauve."

"Your Texas is showing." Smiling, Skye poked him in the biceps.

"And that's a bad thing?" Wally wiggled his eyebrows. "I thought you enjoyed a little ride with a cowboy now and then."

"Anytime, sweetie. Anytime."

"I'll remind you of that when I get you alone." Wally kissed her, then asked, "Where is everyone?" He gestured behind them. "There's at least a half-dozen cars parked in the driveway, so we can't be the first ones to arrive."

He was right. The scene was set, but all the chairs were empty. She'd forgotten that he was unaware of the preparty protocol.

"The shower doesn't actually start until four thirty." Skye explained the empty garage. "But the aunts and cousins come early to help get everything ready for the 'real' guests."

Before Wally could respond, Skye heard the back door open and May yell, "What are you two standing around outside for? Come in and give us a hand. Vince and Loretta will be here any minute."

"Coming." Skye entwined her fingers with Wally's and led him inside. She felt sorry for him. The poor man had no idea what was in store for him.

As Skye put her purse on top of the dryer in the utility room and indicated that Wally should leave the gift there as well, she spotted a new decoration on the wall. It was a plaque bearing the image of a woman wearing a 1950s-style dress and apron with the words: LIFE IS MADE UP OF MANY CHOICES. YOURS IS TO REMOVE YOUR SHOES OR MOP THE FLOOR.

After she and Wally complied with the sign's instructions, they followed May through the swinging louvered doors. The green-and-white-striped walls of the large kitchen/dinette had recently been repainted dark beige, and the peninsula now sported a deep brown granite top. Usually stools edged the counter, but today a group of women ranging in age from midtwenties to late seventies was around it. They all looked up as Skye and Wally entered, waved their hellos, and then went back to their conversations.

"Come give Grandma a hug." Skye's grand-mother greeted them from the round glass and rattan table—another new addition from May's latest redecoration binge. When she had Skye enfolded in her arms, Cora said, "As usual, you look pretty as a picture. Marriage seems to be agreeing with you. You're absolutely glowing."

"Thank you." Skye kissed her grandmother's cheek. "Being married to Wally is totally amazing."

Wally hugged Cora, too, and then said, "Skye's made me the happiest man alive."

"When I watched you two making your vows, I could tell that this was a marriage that would last." Cora's voice cracked as she said, "I'm just glad that I was still here to see Skye find her soul mate."

Skye had leaned down to give Cora another kiss when May ordered, "Wally, go keep Jed company in the living room."

"Yes, ma'am." Wally saluted and whispered to Skye, "Call me if you need me."

"Get cracking, Skye. Food isn't going to get out on the table by itself." May glared at her daughter. "Don't make me put my hands on my hips."

Skye replicated her husband's salute and complied with her mother's order. Her assignment at these affairs was always the relish trays, so she automatically opened the refrigerator and started grabbing jars of gherkins and pickled beets, plastic bins of cherry tomatoes, and bags of cauliflower florets, sliced bell peppers, and cucumber rounds. Several compartmentalized crystal platters were stacked on the nearby countertop, and she filled each section with a different ingredient.

While Skye completed the trays, she saw one of her second cousins glance both ways and then pop a cookie into her mouth. Before she could swallow, May pounced on her and said, "What do you think you're doing, eating instead of working?"

"I thought this was a come-as-you-are party." The twentysomething woman giggled. "I came hungry."

"Well, stop it." May shook her finger and moved on to scrutinize the next person on her list.

Finishing up with the relishes, Skye stepped over to help Ilene Denison, who was married to Skye's cousin Kevin. Ilene was in charge of putting Saran Wrap on the trays of chicken-salad-, tuna-salad-, and ham-salad-filled cream puffs, which were another family party staple.

Ilene glanced up and said, "So how's Loretta enjoying parenthood?"

"Fine, I guess." Skye felt a twinge of guilt. She'd been so busy at school the past week, she hadn't had time to stop by or call her sister-in-law. "Why?"

"Well, with her being such a rich, fancy lawyer, I just wondered how she was handling the glamorous duties of being a mother." Ilene arched a brow. "I mean, once you've applauded a bowel movement, it's pretty much downhill from there."

"Well, I—"

"And I need to warn her," Ilene cut off Skye. "DVD players do not eject peanut butter and jelly sandwiches, despite what the TV commercials show."

"I take it Kevin Junior has been giving you a hard time," Skye guessed.

"That's one way of putting it." Ilene closed her eyes. "This morning he decided to invent a new form of baseball that he calls fanball. You throw a baseball into the ceiling fan. Apparently, whichever player gets it to go the farthest wins. Kevin hit a home run, and now the picture window in our living room has a huge crack."

"Yikes." Skye patted Ilene's arm sympathetically. "Does insurance cover that?"

"Not with our deductible. You know what they say about the shoemaker's son going barefoot? Same goes for the insurance agent's family." Ilene rolled her eyes, then said, "That reminds me. Has Wally said anything about the rash of fires we've been having around Scumble River?"

"Not too much," Skye said cautiously, surprised Ilene had brought up the arsons instead of Blair's murder. "I know Wally talked to some guy who he thought might be the pyromaniac, but I didn't hear the results of that interrogation."

"Well, Kevin says the insurance claims are

killing his company, and his boss is super ticked off at him." Ilene's teeth worried her bottom lip. "Kevin said it's starting to add up higher than the damage from the last tornado."

"Really?" Skye tore a piece of cellophane from the cardboard cylinder and struggled to get it onto the dish without turning it into a useless ball of plastic. "How many fires have there been?"

"Let's see. I think it was four— No, wait. I'm pretty sure it was five. I almost forgot the first one because there was a long time between it and the rest of them," Ilene answered. "But because they've all been businesses, the claims are for a lot more than when it's just a residence."

"Why's that?" Skye asked absently, concentrating on what she was doing.

"Not only are the buildings and contents more expensive, but the insurance company also has to pay for the owner's lost income."

Before Skye could comment, her mother interrupted. "Aren't you girls done with that yet? Vince, Loretta, and Baby April just pulled into the driveway, and everyone else is already in the garage."

Skye hid a smile, recalling when Vince and Loretta had announced their daughter's name. Vince had joked that they chose April because it came before May. His mother had not been amused.

"Sorry, Aunt May," Ilene said, hurrying out of

the kitchen juggling several wrapped trays. Over her shoulder, she added, "I was finished with mine a long time ago, but Skye was distracting me."

Skye gritted her teeth, finished her last platter, and after slipping her shoes back on, followed her cousin-in-law outside with the remaining plates of cream puffs. She'd have to remember to ask Wally if that guy he'd questioned had been the arsonist or not. The murder investigation had pushed the fires out of her mind.

Rushing into the garage, Skye noticed that it had been scrubbed cleaner than an operating room before surgery performed on the doctor himself. Jed's workbench and cabinets were covered in white sheets, and the concrete floor was pristine.

Skye put her tray on the buffet table, then greeted Trixie and Owen, who were admiring Jed's model tractor collection. The Farmall red, Caterpillar yellow, and John Deere green glowed like the lights of a traffic signal.

Owen gestured to the long narrow shelf circling three of the four walls and said, "It looks like your dad's been busy polishing up his toys."

Before Skye could respond, Loretta, Vince, and the baby entered the garage and were immediately surrounded by aunts and cousins fighting over who got to hold the newborn. The three of them made a striking family portrait. At six feet tall, with obsidian black hair and mahogany skin,

Loretta looked like royalty from some exotic African country, a queen wearing Ferragamo patent-leather sandals and carrying a Tory Burch clutch.

Vince was a few inches taller than his dazzling wife and handsome enough to be featured on the cover of *Cosmo* magazine's hot-men-of-the-year supplement. His finely carved features, perfectly styled butterscotch-blond hair, and the green Leofanti eyes made most women catch their breath and dampen their panties.

Not surprisingly, Vince and Loretta had produced a beautiful baby. April had a flawless caramel complexion, her mother's dark ringlets, and her father's emerald eyes surrounded by lush dark lashes. Skye heard the words *precious, extraordinary,* and *exquisite* being tossed around, and flashbulbs were going off as if the trio were modeling for the next issue of the *National Enquirer*.

For a moment Skye frowned. Wally was handsome, but she was at the most, pretty. No way would their baby be able to compete with his or her gorgeous cousin. Would their child feel inferior?

No! Definitely not! She shook her head. Appearance would not be how her son or daughter was judged. She would make sure of that.

While Skye had been daydreaming about her upcoming motherhood, May had entered the garage. Now she announced, "Will everyone please take their seats? The food is set up buffet style, and as the guests of honor, Loretta and Vince will be first. Grandma Denison will be next; then please go up according to your table number."

Skye had been assigned to pour the iced tea, milk, and coffee, so she was one of the last to fill her plate. By the time everyone had been served and Skye took her place next to Wally, she was starving. She'd been so engrossed in examining Blair's Open Book folio that she'd forgotten to eat lunch, and her breakfast cereal had been seven hours ago.

"You look a little pale." Wally wrinkled his brow. "Are you okay?"

"Just really hungry." Skye patted her stomach. "I keep forgetting I can't skip meals anymore without getting a little dizzy."

"I'll be glad when everyone knows you're pregnant," Wally whispered. "Then your mom will make sure that you're the first to eat."

"She'll make sure of a lot of things." Skye's smile was rueful.

"True." Wally popped a chunk of cheese into Skye's mouth. "But we'll cope."

"Right." Skye chewed and swallowed. "But my mother can be hard to deal with."

"Not for me." Wally fed her a bite of chicken-salad-stuffed cream puff. "I don't feel the need to please her like you do. And if she gets ticked off, too bad."

300

"Uh-huh," Skye murmured noncommittally. Wally would just have to experience the wrath of May for himself. As she polished off the food on her plate, she frowned. What was it she wanted to ask Wally? She couldn't recall. *Hmm.* Maybe a slice of cake—or two—would jog her memory.

CHAPTER 24

KISS—Keep It Simple, Stupid

Sunday afternoon, Skye hummed The Lovin' Spoonful's "Daydream" as she got into her car. Earlier, when she and Wally had come home from church, it had still been overcast, but now the weather was ideal—seventy-eight degrees, with low humidity and lots of sunshine. Father Burns had been right: Worry looks around. Sorry looks back. But faith looks up. He'd told them to trust God, and it was now a picture-perfect day for a gathering in the park and the rubber duck race.

Wally had gone into the police department right after Mass. He and Martinez hadn't had any luck locating Blair's password, and he wanted to inspect her possessions one more time before giving up and turning her cell phone over to the county crime techs on Monday. He'd reminded Skye that he'd be on duty for the festivities, but if he didn't see her there, he'd meet her later in the day at her folks' house to make their big baby announcement to the family.

It was quarter to three when Skye pulled her Bel Air into a slot near the Dumpster at the Up A Lazy River Motor Court. She cut diagonally across the asphalt to the southwest tip of Charlie's property and took the wooden footbridge over to the park.

Once the city council sanctioned food and beverage sales, Trixie's rubber duck race had morphed into an all-out event unofficially dubbed Party in the Park. The vendors' tents were set up shoulder to shoulder along the river's edge, and the area was swarming with people. Once again she marveled that Trixie had been able to arrange this affair so quickly.

Although the rubber duck race wasn't until four, there was plenty for people to do all afternoon. The odor from the Lions Club's pony ride added a tang to the air. And children's laughter rang out from the 4-H club's kiddy tractor pull, where boys and girls ages five through eleven were competing on pedal tractors.

Another crowd pleaser was the St. Francis bingo pavilion. The church was selling homemade desserts to folks while they played games like picture frame and postage stamp for cash prizes. As Skye walked by, she saw her mother bent intently over her card with her dauber at the ready and a look of fierce concentration emblazoned on her face.

Having promised to take the last shift selling rubber ducks for the race, Skye waved at her mom and continued to walk. She greeted family and friends almost continuously as she made her way down the length of the park peninsula toward the tip where Trixie had said the booth would be located.

It seemed that almost everyone in Scumble River was at the impromptu festival, and she hoped that meant lots of cash for the no-kill animal shelter.

The hand on Skye's watch had just ticked to the number three when she reached the boat docks. She could see Trixie sitting on a lawn chair behind a card table. A sign next to her, festooned with pictures of adorable animals available for adoption, read:

ALL PROCEEDS GO TO SAVE THE KITTIES AND PUPPIES!

ONE DUCK—$10

TWO DUCKS—$15

SIX DUCK QUACK PACK—$40

TWELVE DUCK FLOCK—$75

An impressive list of prizes donated by local stores and businesses was posted underneath.

Waving to Trixie, she climbed down the roughly hewn stairs cut into the soil. The rocky shore was hard to walk on in sandals, and she wished she'd worn her Keds instead of her flip-flops.

When she reached Trixie, she gestured to people

in line to buy ducks and said, "Looks like business is good."

"At this rate we'll be able to finance the shelter for a whole year!" Trixie bounced in her seat. "All the groups participating in Party in the Park are donating five percent of their profits." She pressed her lips together. "Except Earl Doozier. He claims that he already did his part when he got the permit. I sure wish I knew how he did that."

"No, you don't." Skye shook her head. "Where is the Doozier clan set up?"

"He claimed the prime spot next to the picnic tables."

"Crap!" Skye cringed. She didn't like the idea of the Dooziers right in the thick of things. She'd hoped that Trixie would have assigned him a place more on the fringes of the crowd. "Do you really need me here? I should probably check on Earl."

"Actually, I don't. We're nearly sold out." Trixie frowned. "I wish I had had you order more ducks, but I was afraid we'd be stuck with cases and cases of the little beasties and nowhere to store them."

"So I can go?" Skye edged backward, glad she'd never revealed her little computer error to Trixie. Her BFF would have teased her until the end of time.

"Sure." Trixie accepted a ten-dollar bill from a little old lady and allowed her to choose from the few remaining numbers. "Go make sure the Dooziers aren't blowing up anything."

"More likely, Earl is fleecing some unsuspecting tourist," Skye muttered as she hurried away.

The Dooziers were her friends, but it was always good to know what they were up to in case she needed to step in and rescue someone. Often their scams resulted in bruises or trips to the ER. Although, more often than not, it was the gullible folks from out of town who visited the hospital rather than the Dooziers.

At the entrance to Earl's game, a flattened carton box read:

CORNHOLE TURNAMINT
GAURANTEED FUN! FUN! FUN!
ENTREE FEE $25.00
1ST-PLACE WINER GETS 20%
2ND-PLACE WINER GETS 10%
3RD-PLACE WINER GETS 5%

Okay. That seemed like a fair prize system. Skye let out a breath of relief and walked past the misspelled signpost. Several feet back, a folding table with a pyramid of beanbags piled in the center teetered on crooked legs. Sitting with his cowboy boots propped up on the table was Earl. He had on a pair of shorts, and over his bare chest he wore a camouflage vest with an attached artillery belt holding beanbags. A bandanna tied around his head had slipped down over the upper third of his face.

Clearing her throat, Skye stepped closer and said, "Earl?"

He turned away from her, and a nanosecond later, a snore that sounded like a backfiring Weedwacker erupted from his open mouth. Business had obviously been slow. Most people in Scumble River knew to avoid the Dooziers' schemes, and the Party in the Park hadn't been planned far enough in advance to attract tourists.

Should she try to wake Earl or thank God for small favors and leave? Before Skye could decide, a group of kids loped into the game area, shrieking and hollering. One brave—or more accurately, foolish—boy lobbed a water balloon at Earl.

The liquid-filled projectile was an inch short of its target, but water still sprayed over the sleeping man. Earl leaped from his chair, wrestling off the bandanna that was blinding him, and whined, "I wuz jes restin' my eyes, honey pie."

The kids ran away giggling and Skye said quickly, "It's me, Earl, Skye." She had taken a step closer but hastily moved downwind. The excessive use of aftershave could only delay the need to bathe for so many days, and Earl had exceeded the cologne's expiration date. "I just stopped by to see how your tournament was going."

Earl scowled. "Ain't no one wants to play."

"That's a shame."

"It's okay." His wide smile revealed several stumps and missing teeth. He patted the plastic pistol tucked in his waistband. "If life gives you lemons, squeeze the juice into a water gun and shoot the suckers in their eyes."

"Uh." Skye shook her head. "That's not a good idea. Maybe if you're patient, people will come by to play later."

"Well, I'm ready to go round 'em up if they don't." Earl tapped the butt of his toy firearm.

"Where're Glenda and the kids?" Skye hoped his wife would keep Earl in line.

"Oh. Here and there." He scuttled toward Skye. "Glenda was lookin' finer than a new pair of snow tires on a Cadillac Escalade, so she wanted to show herself off."

Skye allowed herself to be hugged, trying not to make contact with any of his many tattoos. Tats usually felt smooth, but Earl's were as odd as he was, and they radiated a heat that she figured explained his predilection for going shirtless even in the coldest weather.

"Are you all having a good time?" she asked, extracting herself from his embrace.

"Sure." Earl let Skye go and scratched the bowling ball–size potbelly that hung over his waistband. "Beer and sunshine. A man cain't ask fur more than that."

"Definitely." Skye backed away.

"Hey, are you hot on the trail of that teacher's

murderer?" He tugged at his greasy brown ponytail. "It's been a couple or three days ago, right?"

"A little more."

"I miss her on Open Book," Earl said, the sunshine highlighting the bald spot on his head. "She sure had some funny stuff there."

Before Skye could speak, she spotted an elderly woman wearing a neon orange muumuu and hot pink high-top sneakers teetering across the grass toward them. She looked old enough to have had buffalo as pets and meaner than Custer at his last stand.

The infamous MeMa had arrived. She was the family matriarch and Earl's grandmother, or maybe great-grandmother; Skye had never quite figured out the Dooziers' twisted family tree.

MeMa walked up to Skye, squinted, and quavered, "Are you knocked up?"

"Uh." Skye paused to consider the best way to respond. "Why do you ask?"

"That picture Earl showed me on the computer." MeMa sniggered. "You sure as hell looked in the family way in that shot."

"Not my best angle," Skye said cautiously.

"Ain't that the truth?" MeMa's smile was like a rusty chain saw, and her faded brown eyes disappeared into her wrinkles, giving her the appearance of one of those dried-apple dolls.

"Nice chatting." Skye's heart was pounding.

She was not telling the Dooziers about the baby before her own family knew. It was time to skedaddle. "Good luck with your tournament."

"You sure you want to leave?" A crafty expression stole over MeMa's face. "You could play Earl's game first. Then we'd forget all about seein' that picture."

"Maybe later." Skye kept retreating.

"You know that dead lady sure did like putting embarrassing stuff up for the world to look at." Earl reached into a cooler, fished out a dripping Pabst Blue Ribbon, and popped the top. He gestured to the empty cans he'd arranged in a solid triangle and grinned. "My food pyramid is made outta beer cans."

"Cute." Skye hesitated, curious what Earl had to say about Blair.

"Sometimes that teacher woman put up pictures and then took 'em down so fast you almost thought you were imaginin' things."

"Interesting." Skye walked backward. She was almost out of earshot, and when Earl didn't add anything to his observations about Blair's Open Book practices, Skye hurriedly bade the Dooziers good-bye and ran for it.

Holy smokes! That had been close. Good thing they were making the baby announcement tonight.

Arriving back at the rubber duck booth, she helped Trixie put away the money. While she counted the cash, she thought about Earl's comments. Why would Blair put up pictures and comments, then take them right down? And did those actions have something to do with her murder?

CHAPTER 25

YBS—You'll Be Sorry

Trixie held a walkie-talkie to her lips and said, "Paige, start the race."

It was four o'clock, and Skye stood on the shore next to her friend, watching as the ducks went bobbing out of sight. From her vantage point, the rubber ducks looked like brightly colored M&M's quickly disappearing down the river.

Skye turned from the water and asked, "Who's collecting the ducks at the railroad bridge?"

"Owen's in charge of the group of students waiting at the finish line."

"How did you rope your poor husband into doing that?"

"He volunteered." Trixie's expression was innocent, but Skye didn't buy her act. "I figured some people are really competitive, so it would be best to have a guy there watching over the kids. Plus, he's got his shotgun in his truck if anyone gets too rough."

"Over a duck race?"

"When there's money involved, you can never tell." Trixie clipped her walkie-talkie to her belt. "Not to mention the people who want to win at all costs." She twitched her shoulders, then said, "Speaking of husbands, here comes yours."

Skye opened her mouth to greet Wally, but before she spoke, a thought hit her, and instead of saying hello, she demanded, "Did you ever figure out Blair's password?"

"No." He sighed. "I'll have to send the phone to the crime lab tomorrow."

"Something Trixie just said gave me an idea." Skye grabbed his hand. "Can you leave here?"

"I guess." He craned his neck and looked around. "Sure. The vendors are all packing up. Let me tell my officers to handle traffic control without me."

"Meet me at the police station." Skye gave him a quick kiss and hurried away.

As she drove herself to the PD, Skye considered her theory. Blair's whole self-concept was wrapped around being a winner, and Skye would bet her new Betsey Johnson sandals that the volleyball coach's password was some variation of that theme.

Using her key to let herself in through the PD's garage entrance, Skye walked down the narrow corridor. It had taken her quite a while to get out of the motel's parking lot, and when she turned the corner, Wally was already standing in the open doorway of the coffee/interrogation room.

Wally held up a bright red cell phone. "I take it that your idea has something to do with this."

"Uh-huh." Skye brushed past him. "Let's do this in your office."

As soon as they were seated and the door was shut, Wally asked, "Did you figure out Blair's password?"

Skye explained her thoughts about Blair's mental image of herself, then said, "So I wonder if she uses something like *winner*."

"Let's give it a try." Wally tapped the keys, then shook his head. "Any other guesses?"

"*Winner2006* or *2006Winner*." Skye leaned forward and watched Wally enter those suggestions and several variations like *06Winner* and *Winner06* and similar combinations.

"Nope." Wally slumped back in his chair. "Son of a buck! I thought you were onto something."

"How about *Champion, Championship, 2006Championship,* or *Championship2006?*"

Wally tapped away, and a moment later he turned the cell toward Skye. "We're in."

"Can you find the pictures on her phone?" Skye asked, then explained what Earl had said about the snapshots on Open Book appearing and then disappearing within a few seconds. "I think Blair might have been using her habit of taking snapshots and putting up photos to blackmail people. After all, Thor said that she didn't get her inheritance until she turned thirty. So she only had her teacher's salary to live on. Which, if she grew up in a wealthy environment, might not seem like much to her. I bet if she hadn't died that night after she took my picture, she would have tried to get something from me in order to take it down."

"Okay." Wally got up and pointed to his chair. "You sit here and get Open Book on my computer so we can compare what she has on her folio and what she only has on her cell."

They worked steadily through the photos until Wally thrust the phone at Skye and said, "Look here. This woman seems familiar, but I can't place her. And the series of snapshots of her on the vic's cell isn't on her folio."

"That's Oriana Northrup. Her daughter is a special needs student at Scumble River High." Skye squinted at the tiny screen. "Who is that she's handing a bundle of cash to?"

"That's Banjo Bender, the guy I suspected of setting all the fires the past few months," Wally answered. "I wish I could have arrested him when I had him, but we didn't have enough evidence to hold him."

"I guess we can't expect all the bad guys to confess," Skye sympathized.

"Northrup, as in Northrup's Clean and Bright?" Wally said, and when Skye nodded, he continued. "That's why she looks familiar. She owns the Laundromat, which if I recall correctly, was the first building to burn down in Scumble River's string of fires. It happened just before midnight the day we left on our honeymoon."

"That explains why I don't remember it more clearly. I read about it in the paper after we got back, but I wasn't around for the gossip."

Skye's mind raced as she viewed the rest of the pictures, which were time- and date-stamped.

As they went through the rest of the photos, they found one of Banjo Bender setting fire to the Clean and Bright, and Wally quickly scrolled back through the series. First was Oriana handing Bender the initial stack of cash, then Bender setting the fire, and finally, Oriana giving him another pile of money.

"Did you notice when that last picture was taken?" Wally asked.

"Two weeks ago." Skye did a quick calculation. "It was probably right after the insurance check arrived. From the previous photos, it looks as if Oriana gave Banjo a partial payment to set the fire. Then, in this final snapshot, he'd completed his assignment to burn down her business, she received the insurance money, and she's paying him the rest of his fee." She frowned. "How in the world did Blair get these pictures?"

"The vic's house is next to the Laundromat." Wally rubbed his chin. "Martinez mentioned that it was a good thing that the Clean and Bright wasn't open twenty-four hours because Blair's

bedroom balcony overlooks the parking area."
Wally pressed his fingers to his temples. "This
would explain the ten thousand dollars in cash
we found in the vic's safe."

"Money that Blair got from blackmailing
Oriana." Skye nodded. "Do you know how much
insurance Oriana collected on her business?"

Wally walked to a file cabinet and selected a
folder. He flipped it open and said, "She owned
the building, so she collected a cool quarter of a
million bucks, plus an additional amount for lost
income."

"That's certainly enough moola to make
blackmail worthwhile." Skye pursed her lips.
"Blair must have demanded hush money right
after she witnessed Oriana giving Banjo the final
fee for the arson. Then I bet Blair got greedy,
pressed for another payment, and that's when
Oriana decided to kill her."

"I agree." Wally reached for the phone on his
desk and dialed. A few seconds later he said,
"Quirk, I need you to go pick up Oriana Northrup
for questioning in connection with the murder
of Blair Hucksford." He read the woman's
address off the file. "If she's not at home, sit on
the house until she gets there."

"Wait," Skye said before Wally ended the call.
She had an idea.

He told the sergeant to hang on and motioned
for Skye to speak.

Skye took a deep breath and said, "Trixie mentioned that Oriana's daughter was a member of the community service club that put on the duck races. And remember, I told you that Trixie arranged a pizza party for those kids from four thirty to six."

Wally looked at his watch and said, "It's five thirty."

"The gathering is at the bowling alley, and considering what I've observed about Oriana as a parent, she'll be waiting in her car to pick up her daughter way before the celebration is due to end."

After determining the license plate number of Oriana's vehicle and running it to find out the make and model, Wally conveyed the information to Quirk and told him to check the bowling alley parking lot for the suspect.

Once he had replaced the receiver in the base, Skye asked, "Do you want me with you when you interrogate Oriana?"

"I think it would be best, since you have some relationship with her."

"Then I'd better let Mom know we're both going to be late for dinner and to go ahead and eat without us."

While Skye used her cell to phone her mother, Wally made another call. "Martinez, I saw Banjo Bender at your location. Is he still there? He is. Good. Arrest him and bring him to the PD."

When Skye got off the phone with her mother,

she asked Wally about his call. "What was that all about?"

"Martinez's assigned to keep an eye on the beer tent in the park, which is open until six. I noticed Bender bellied up to the bar there earlier, and he looked as if he was settled in for the long haul."

While they waited, Wally contacted the city attorney to request a search warrant for all of Oriana's and Banjo's properties. The lawyer complained about bothering a judge on a Sunday night but eventually promised to make the attempt.

Within half an hour, Banjo Bender was led into the PD, and a few minutes later, Quirk escorted Oriana Northrup through the door. They were read their rights and both declined representation. While Oriana was fingerprinted and Banjo was put into the basement holding cell, Skye went into the interrogation room to set things up.

Oriana was still protesting her innocence when Wally led her to her seat and continued through-out the whole tape-recorder ritual. But once the woman saw the first few pictures on Blair's phone, she snapped her mouth shut so hard Skye thought she heard a tooth crack.

After a few seconds, Oriana said, "It's not what it looks like."

"Oh?" Skye shot Wally a quick glance. Where had they heard that before?

"I was paying Banjo to watch the Laundromat. I don't know why he burned it down."

"Why didn't you call the police?" Wally asked. "And why did you give him additional cash a couple of weeks ago?" He showed her the second series of photos on Blair's phone.

"I was afraid Banjo would hurt me if I told on him or refused to give him more money." Oriana looked at Wally as if he were crazy. "That man's a criminal."

"Why didn't you report Blair when she tried to blackmail you?" Skye asked.

"She wasn't," Oriana said quickly, and then crossed her arms. "And you can't prove otherwise."

"Did you know that when you get a lot of cash from a bank, very often the serial numbers are sequential?" Wally asked conversationally.

"No." Oriana wrinkled her brow, then must have decided to tough it out. "What's that got to do with me?"

"Once we get a search warrant, which should be within the hour, we'll go through Banjo's place with a fine-tooth comb." Wally leaned back. "My guess is, along with arson materials, we'll find some of the money you paid him. At that point, Banjo's lawyer will advise him to take a plea bargain—a lighter sentence for the arson in return for giving evidence against you. Once he testifies that you gave him the cash, we'll connect the bills he has to the ones that Blair had in her safe, thus establishing that she was blackmailing you. And then we'll charge you with murder."

"I . . ." Oriana gulped, a look of panic on her face. "A jury will believe me over a career criminal."

"Maybe." Skye shrugged. "But how about the evidence? Why else would you have given Blair ten thousand dollars?"

"Uh." Oriana wrinkled her brow. "I . . . uh . . . She was tutoring Ashley."

"Right." Wally's voice was knife-edged. "And you paid her in cash."

"Yes." Oriana's voice cracked. "She wanted to avoid paying taxes."

"Blair taught junior and senior level science." Skye leaned forward. "She wouldn't have been qualified to tutor a student with special needs like your daughter."

"That doesn't prove anything!" Oriana screamed. "You're twisting everything."

"In fact, the reason you hired Banjo to torch the Clean and Bright was to get the money to send Ashley to Thorntree Academy. Even though during our initial meeting you tried one more time to get the public school district to foot the bill, it was pretty obvious that you knew the school board would never pay for a private placement." Skye's tone was sympathetic. "And you wanted your daughter to have the best education possible, not just what was deemed appropriate."

"She needs more than just what you all deem appropriate," Oriana snarled. "She needs to be able to take care of herself once I'm gone, and you're right, I knew the public school would never agree to pay for Thorntree."

"I understand," Skye said soothingly. "Often, when kids start high school, parents realize that time is running out for their children to get the education that they need to succeed later in life and the parents panic. But unlike most parents, you decided to take matters into your own hands. Your request that Ashley attend Thorntree was about a week after the check's arrival."

"I . . . I . . ." Oriana scrubbed her eyes with her fists.

A glint from the woman's finger caught Skye's attention, and she leaned over to Wally and whispered, "I bet that gold nugget ring she's wearing is what caused the gouges on Blair's scalp."

Wally rose, took an evidence bag from one of the cupboards, extended it, and said, "Please place your ring inside, Mrs. Northrup."

She hesitated but complied, then asked, "Why do you want my ring?"

"Because when the crime techs match it to the wounds on the victim's head and find traces of Blair's DNA in the grooves"—Wally dangled the bag in front of the woman's eyes—"it will be physical proof that you killed her."

"Maybe I do need a lawyer." Oriana slumped in her chair.

"Only if you want to escalate the proceedings." Wally hooked his thumbs in his belt loops. "And it'll take a lot more time. I hope you have someone to watch Ashley for the rest of the night. Quirk told me you called a neighbor to pick her up from the pizza party. Will your friend be able to keep Ashley all night?"

"No. She works the third shift." She looked at Skye. "What do you think I should do?"

"Well, you do have a right to counsel," Skye spoke carefully. "But then you won't be able to tell us your side of the story. We won't know the mitigating circumstances of the situation." She paused to let Oriana think about what she'd said, then asked, "Do you want to call your attorney?"

"I'm not sure." Oriana sniffed.

"Well, you can anytime." Skye didn't want the judge to throw out her confession because Oriana's rights hadn't been upheld. "But let me tell you what I think happened." She smiled reassuringly at her. "I think you were just trying to talk to Blair that night. Tell her you couldn't keep giving her money because you needed it for Ashley's tuition. I totally understand how you felt you had to get the best education for Ashley, but I bet Blair didn't. She probably attacked you. She's much bigger than you are, so you Tasered her in self-defense."

"That's right." Oriana nodded vigorously. "Blair called me about quarter to eleven that night. I only picked up the phone because the school's name came up on caller ID." Oriana's shoulders slumped. "I know since it was so late, it was stupid, but I was afraid to ignore a call from the school."

"I understand." Skye patted the woman's arm. "What happened next?"

"When I answered, Blair demanded that I meet her at the pool and bring her another ten thousand dollars or she was putting the pictures of me giving Banjo Bender money on Open Book. Then she hung up before I could say anything." Oriana's voice cracked. "So I drove over to the school, and she let me in that back door. She had a key to disable the alarm. I explained that I'd paid everything I could and my daughter had to have the rest."

"But Blair didn't care about that." Skye sucked in a lungful of air. The teacher's greed left her breathless.

"No. I should have known better. She wouldn't let Ashley on the volleyball team even as a manager, so why would she be reasonable about blackmail?" Oriana glared. "Blair laughed at me and said all she cared about was living the good life. It wasn't her concern if some kid couldn't go to a special school. The money would be wasted on a girl like Ashley."

"That must have made you really angry," Skye murmured encouragingly.

"It did." Oriana jerked up her chin. "I told her

that I didn't have the money with me and would have to get it from the bank the next day, but when I tried to leave, Blair lunged at me. I grabbed the Taser from my purse because I was scared she was going to hurt me."

"You just happened to have a stun gun with you?" Wally asked.

"I used to close the Laundromat and collect the money from the machines all by myself," Oriana explained. "I bought the Taser for protection and always carried it in my bag."

"And when you zapped Blair, she fell into the water," Skye guessed.

"Yes." Oriana nodded. "But I didn't mean to kill her."

"Buzz. Wrong answer," Wally pounced. "If you didn't mean to kill her, why did you hold her head under the water?"

"But, but . . ." Oriana stammered.

"The forensics can prove your ring caused the wounds in Blair's scalp." Wally raised a brow. "If, as you claim, you Tasered her in self-defense, you would have never touched her head."

"You're confusing me," Oriana whimpered.

"Let's talk about something else for a minute," Skye said. "Why did you turn off the electricity?"

"I read in some mystery novel that confusing the temperature would make it hard to determine time of death," Oriana blurted out, then added, "I knew you all wouldn't believe that I was just protecting myself, so I wanted to make it as hard as possible for the police to figure things out."

"And that was your second mistake," Wally said. "You left your fingerprints on the electrical panel in the boiler room. You might be able to convince a jury that your prints in the pool area were present because you'd been swimming there with your daughter, but nobody is allowed in the boiler room except the custodian."

"Mrs. Northrup." Skye made her voice soothing and her expression understanding. "If you tell us what happened and show remorse, I'm sure the prosecutor will take the death penalty off the table."

Oriana collapsed against the back of the chair. It was clear that she had run out of ideas on how to deny her guilt and realized that she was running out of options. "The death penalty? Oh, my God . . . What will happen to Ashley?"

"Is there anyone I can call for you?" Skye asked gently. "Family or a friend?"

"My sister lives in Chicago." Oriana buried her face in her hands. "She'll take care of Ashley." Oriana sobbed. "The insurance company will want their money back, won't they?"

"I'm afraid so." Skye felt sorry for the woman, who had been so desperate to secure the best education for her daughter.

"Then Ashley will end up in the Chicago Public School system." Oriana wiped her cheeks with the backs of her hands. "And I did it all for nothing."

Skye and Wally exchanged a look. Poor Ashley was the one who would suffer the most. Having to move to a new school and losing her mother to the prison system. It was sad. The girl had been doing well in the program Skye had designed for her. She could only hope that wherever she ended up being enrolled could manage a similar setup.

Wally wrapped up the questioning and had Oriana write out her confession. Three hours later, her case had been turned over to the city attorney, Ashley's aunt had arrived, the search warrants had been executed, the evidence secured, and Banjo Bender had leaped at the deal the lawyer had offered him to testify against Oriana.

It was nearly ten o'clock when Skye and Wally finally were able to leave the PD and head home—long past the time anyone would still be at May's dinner party. They'd have to make their big announcement another time.

As they walked up the steps of their house, Skye said, "Even though we've seen it before, I'm surprised Oriana confessed as fast as she did."

"She's obviously not a hardened criminal, and regular people find it difficult to maintain a lie."

"That's true." Skye nodded. "At school, the first-time wrongdoers usually cave in quickly. It's the habitual offenders who can look you right in the eye, and even if you have a video of their transgressions, deny everything."

"And don't forget"—Wally's smile was grim—"we had DNA, fingerprints, photos, and motive. With all that against her, she really had no choice."

"We all have a choice." Skye blew out a long breath. "Oriana Northrup made the wrong one when she put this entire sequence of events in motion and decided her need for money was reason enough to break the law."

"And she's going to pay the price." Wally kissed Skye's temple. "Which is why you and I do what we do."

"Too bad she's not the only one affected by her actions." Skye rested her hand on her stomach. "It's always the innocents who suffer the most."

EPILOGUE

E2EG—Ear-to-Ear Grin

The next day, Skye gazed at the curious faces gathered around her dining room table and said, "Sorry Wally and I couldn't make it to dinner last night."

She and Wally had decided to ask their family and friends for lunch. Grandma Denison, Loretta, and the baby were free most of the time, May's shift at the PD didn't start until four, and with spring break for Skye and Trixie, the wet fields for

Owen and Jed, Vince's salon closed on Mondays, and Wally and Charlie being their own bosses, everyone was available. It had been tough dodging the question as to why they were having a party on a weekday afternoon, and the day after the other parties, but Skye had promised all would be revealed after dessert.

Skye's parents, along with her grandmother, had been the first to show up, but before May could begin her interrogation, everyone else streamed through the front door. While the adults fussed over April, Skye put out the food and Wally filled drink orders.

Once they were seated, May asked, "So tell us all about catching the murderer."

Skye knew there was no avoiding the matter, so she passed the platter of roast beef and summarized how they had solved the crime.

Uncle Charlie tilted his seat back, unconcerned when the Victorian mahogany balloon-back chair groaned under his weight, and said, "But if this Northrup woman hired Banjo Bender to torch the Clean and Bright, why did he set all the other fires? We've had three or four more since the Laundromat burned down."

"That's a good question." Skye looked at Wally and asked, "I wasn't in on his interrogation. Did he explain that?"

"Bender's a pyromaniac," Wally said, helping himself to a spoonful of mashed potatoes. He handed the bowl to Loretta and explained, "When Oriana caught him putting a match to a pile of trash in the woods behind her house and suggested she'd pay him to burn down the Laundromat, he realized he could make money from his hobby."

Vince snickered. "What did he do, put an ad in the paper?"

"Not quite." Wally took a sip of his iced tea. "He studied the local businesses. Noted which ones didn't seem to be doing very well, then casually 'ran into' the owners and somehow managed to work the conversation over to insurance."

"And since he's pretty well-known in these parts as a firebug, I suspect the rest was pretty easy," Grandma Denison commented.

"Exactly." Wally nodded. "Everyone knew he liked to set fires, but with the photos we can finally prove it." Wally narrowed his eyes. "We'll be investigating the other mysterious fires. I'm expecting that we'll be making several more arrests before this whole matter is resolved."

"Didn't Bender approach anyone who turned him down?" Trixie asked. "And if so, why didn't they report him to the police?"

"I'm sure there were people who refused his offer," Wally answered slowly. "But from what he's told us, he phrased it in such a way that he never really came out and said that they could pay him to burn their businesses."

"And as to why no one reported him to the cops,"

Charlie added, his voice cynical, "I'm betting that the folks he approached weren't the most upright citizens. People like that have a policy of not getting involved with the authorities."

"No doubt." Wally tipped his head in Charlie's direction, acknowledging his agreement with the older man. "No doubt."

"It's hard to feel sorry for Blair," Owen said, putting a biscuit on his plate and ladling gravy over it. "Blackmailers feed on people's desperation. Everyone is entitled to their privacy."

"Some people got more to hide than others," Jed mumbled around a bite of green bean casserole.

"Those two should have shut up and asked for a lawyer," Loretta snapped.

"There's a lot of physical evidence," Skye pointed out.

"I could have gotten them both off." Loretta crossed her arms. "And a woman like Oriana doesn't deserve to spend years and years in prison. She only did it for her daughter to have a better life." Loretta glanced at her own baby daughter and added, "She may have broken the law, but if that teacher hadn't blackmailed her, no one but the insurance company would have gotten hurt."

"Which is why we're glad you're on maternity leave," Wally said with a wry grin.

"You need to start using your powers for good instead of evil," Skye teased.

Loretta snorted and said, "I think I'll look into

Oriana's case while I'm off." She returned her attention to her plate, muttering, "I bet I can get her a better deal than her court-appointed attorney."

"Did Blair blackmail other people, too?" Vince asked.

"Judging from the pictures we found on her phone and what we know about what she put up on Open Book, I'd say it's highly likely she's been indulging in some form of extortion for quite some time," Wally said. "I wonder if she would have continued once she turned thirty and received her inheritance."

"I somehow doubt she'd have stopped," Skye said. "This might have been the first time she asked for money, but I bet she's asked for little favors or gifts. She was the type to revel in the power." Skye took a bite of the beef and was relieved when it melted in her mouth. It would have been embarrassing to serve tough meat to her mother.

"I think you're onto something." Trixie snapped her fingers. "I remember noticing that Blair had a Coach purse that looked an awful lot like the one our new math teacher had just bought. And I thought it was odd that the social studies teacher volunteered to take Blair's detention duty for her."

"I suppose asking them is useless." Wally took a bite of his salad. "They sure wouldn't want to admit to whatever secret she was using to black-mail them."

"With Banjo's and Oriana's confessions, there really is no need to build a case, so why embarrass them?" Skye glanced at her husband. "What will happen to all the photos on her cell?"

"Once the case is settled, we'll return her phone to her estate, but I think those snapshots might be accidentally deleted before it gets mailed back to them." Wally used his napkin and then added, "Reid confirmed that Bernadette is Blair's heir. The attorney was a part of the Skype call arranging Blair's funeral because she left specific instructions that she did not want to be buried in California in the family plot."

"Wow." May shook her head. "I guess some family fights follow you to the grave."

"I just feel bad for Ashley Northrup." Skye sighed. "She's a sweet girl."

"She's done really well in the GIVE group," Trixie piped up. "She's made some friends and seems really comfortable and happy there."

"Her accommodations seem to be working in the classrooms, too." Skye pursed her lips, frustrated that Ashley would suffer from her mother's actions.

"Then you'll be happy to hear that Oriana's sister has decided to relocate to Scumble River and allow Ashley to finish school here. She's a medical transcriptionist and can work from anywhere," Wally announced. "She came by the station this morning to let us know she would be moving into the Northrup house later in the week."

"Yay!" Skye and Trixie both clapped their hands together.

While they finished their meal, the conversation turned to the weather and spring planting. When everyone had pushed their plates aside, Skye rose from her chair and said, "I'll go get dessert."

"I'll help." Wally leaped up from his chair, putting one hand on May's shoulder and the other on Trixie's to keep them in their seats. "You all relax."

After clearing the table and bringing out the dessert plates, Wally and Skye went into the kitchen. While he got his father on his cell phone and put him on speaker, Skye carried the cake to the dining room.

As Skye set it on the table, May read the icing message out loud. "What will Baby Boyd be? A he or a she?"

It took a moment for the words to sink in; then May screamed and jumped to her feet. Her gaze immediately shot to Skye's stomach and she said, "You're pregnant?"

"Yes." Wally put his arm around Skye. "We're having a baby."

After everyone had congratulated them, May cut to the chase and asked, "When?"

"The end of September."

Charlie took a swig of beer, allowed a soft burp to escape his lips, then said, "Good thing you guys got married when you did."

May hugged Skye and glared at Charlie. "She got pregnant on her honeymoon." May looked at her daughter. "Right?"

"Right." Skye winked at Wally and hugged her mom back.

"Did you hear all that, Dad?" Wally spoke into his cell phone.

"I did." Carson Boyd's voice was thick. "Congratulations, son. I couldn't be happier for you both. I'll clear my schedule and plan to spend the last week in September and the first week of October in Scumble River."

"Thanks, Dad." Wally's expression was stunned. "Can you really spare that much time from the business?"

"For my first grandchild?" Carson chuckled. "Hell, I may move company headquarters to Chicago or retire and let your cousin take over."

"The announcement went well," Wally said later that evening from his recliner.

"Yes, it did." Skye put a piece of cake on the table in front of him. "Though I was worried for a bit when Mom and your father got into a shouting match about family names."

"I had no idea my dad would be this excited."

Wally patted his knee, silently inviting her to sit down. "He's already talking about where the baby should go to college."

"I think you may have gotten a taste of what I go through with my family." Skye snuggled on his lap.

Wally chuckled and said, "I wonder how Bingo will react to the baby." He reached down and stroked the feline in question, who was sitting by the chair, staring at them.

"He'll have to adjust." Skye took a deep breath. "We're all going to have to get used to some big changes in our lives."

"Good ones." Wally hugged her.

"Definitely." Skye brushed a tear away. "It's just a lot to take in. And now that we've shared the news, it somehow seems more real than before."

"Don't worry." Wally took her chin in his hand. "I promise you that we can handle whatever having a family throws at us."

"I know." She looked into his warm brown eyes. "I can deal with anything as long as you're by my side."

"And it would take wild horses to drag me away." Wally pressed his lips gently to hers. "So I think we're safe."

As Skye deepened the kiss, a flicker of unease shot up her spine. She sure hoped her new husband hadn't just jinxed them.